off GUARD

GLEN ROBINS

Glen Robins Books
www.glenrobinsbooks.com

This is a work of fiction. As such, all characters, organizations, and events portrayed in this novel have either been created by the author or fictionalized. Any resemblance to real persons, either live or dead, or real events is purely coincidental. Creative liberties have been taken with the depiction of the roles and operations of certain governmental and law enforcement agencies.

chapter One

Collin trudged up the beach, away from the plane, through the soft, pale sand in the grayish predawn light. Each new step required more effort than the last as his feet sank into little craters of his own making. The effort to lift his knees and drag his weight forward was slowly depleting what little energy he had left. It had been a long, sleepless night, capping off a week full of long and sleepless nights. Things had not gone the way he had planned and he was ready to rest.

Given his lack of sleep over the past three days and the energy he had expended to save his own life and safeguard the security of the country, it was no wonder Collin struggled to traverse the 150 feet up the sloping shore to the tiny hut where he hoped the magical, sleep-inducing orange juice sat chilling in the refrigerator.

Collin's whole body hurt. Penh's men had seen to that. His face was bruised from the multiple beatings they had inflicted on him. After repeatedly being punched and kicked, his ribs and midsection ached as well. All the swimming and diving over the past twenty-four hours to save himself and retrieve his laptop from the bottom of the ocean had given his arms, legs, and lungs a fantastic, though exhausting, workout.

Yes, he wanted some food and some sleep, in that order.

His batteries were indeed running low and he needed to rest. Despite his weary body, Collin's mind was keyed up over recently transpired events. Sleep wouldn't come, not without help. The murder of one, and possibly a second, person weighed heavily on his soul, even though he realized it was self-defense. He looked ahead at the simple hut, a wedge of pale yellow light spilling through its doorway, and adjusted his course to be sure not to waste a single step.

When he reached the half-open bamboo door, he stumbled into the tiny beach house on the Caribbean coast of Honduras, looking for the orange juice, the magical orange juice laced with a powerful sleep aid—he didn't even know what it was—that had helped him just the day before to enjoy the best sleep he had gotten since his wife and children died in that thunderous wreck on Interstate 80, coming down the mountain from Lake Tahoe, eleven and a half months ago.

Yes, Collin Cook was ready for food and sleep. He was pretty sure he deserved it.

With his laptop onboard the plane, safely enveloped in the rubbery watertight sea bag, Collin felt he had accomplished his mission for the day. He had scuba dived deeper than he had ever dived before to rescue it. He had fought off another pair of Penh's hired thugs, who had also dived to the wreckage of the *Admiral Risty*, spearing one of them in the chest. He had had to swim through the plume of that man's blood to exit the boat, a harrowing experience for anyone.

His next mission, which he was ready to embark on immediately, would be a day-long siesta.

Lukas Mueller, Collin's friend since middle school and a deep-cover, high-ranking National Security Agency officer, had reminded him during the long plane ride back from the site of the wreck that if he wanted to live, Collin had to stay at least one step ahead of Penh.

All of Lukas's talk of executing a plan flawlessly rattled around Collin's weary brain. He knew what hung in the balance, or at least he had an idea. Lukas had been light on the details, giving Collin only what information he needed to take the next step. There was more going on in Lukas's complex and finely tuned brain than he shared with his simple civilian friend. But Collin was OK with that. He wanted to live and he wanted to protect his family and country. Those were his two primary motivations for getting this involved in something that he really shouldn't be involved in.

he can get and he's obviously dug deep enough into that computer to know there's something more than a guy like me would ever have on it."

"Right," said Lukas. "And if we make changes to it at this point, he'll know someone with more experience than you've got is tampering with it. Again, my concern is that he'll be wary and start covering his tracks. Our best hope is to try to catch him off guard if we can."

"Look, I'm not trying to run away from him at this point, my friend. This thing won't end until he gets what he wants or gets thrown in prison."

"Or is dead. I wouldn't mind seeing him dead, truth be told."

"Right, you sinister bastard," chuckled Collin. "You don't mind as long as someone else does the dirty work."

"I didn't say that. I'd be happy to pull the trigger."

"What are you saying there, my friend?"

Lukas paused, sucking in a breath. "You know we were at MIT at the same time. But there's history between me and him. Bad blood, you know. I've seen what he's capable of. That's why I've kept him on my radar all these years. At some point, a ruthless juggernaut like him was going to rear his ugly head and I vowed I'd be there to cut it off if I possibly could."

"Dude," Collin said, careful not to use Lukas's name out loud, as he'd been instructed, "I'm getting the chills right now. You're sounding pretty scary."

"Yeah, I know. But that bastard killed a friend of mine out of revenge ..." Lukas's voice trailed off as if the memory had clamped his throat shut. "Then he tried to frame me for it."

"Why didn't he go to jail then?"

"No one could prove it. It looked like an alcohol-fueled overdose, but we're talking about a mature, studious MIT grad student with the career track she'd always wanted buttoned down, not some sorority-rushing freshman. She was not the party type."

"Sounds like she was more than a friend."

"She was. We had plans …"

"Then how do you know it was Penh?"

"I just know. Things like that don't stay secret forever, but everyone who knew him knew he'd find a way to shut them up for good if they ever confronted him."

Collin waited, expecting Lukas to continue. When he didn't, he prompted his friend. "So how did it end?"

"We all graduated two weeks later and went our separate ways. I was questioned extensively and put under a shadow of suspicion, thanks to some bogus information Penh gave the investigators. That's when I accepted the offer from the NSA, even though I could have made much more money somewhere else. I told them the story, and they helped clear me of all charges and accusations. With their resources, I knew I could track him and perhaps prevent him from doing what he's about to do now, carrying out his threat to cripple the West and punish them for their greed and abuse."

"So you knew about his plans since graduate school?"

"Yeah. I probably had more interaction with him than any other classmate. For some reason, I befriended him and he trusted me. He opened up to me and my friend Theresa. When she threatened to expose him to the authorities, he killed her. Made it look innocuous. But I knew her well, knew she'd never drink like that."

"Do you think he knew that you suspected him of giving the bogus information?"

"Maybe, maybe not. I played dumb, but also steered clear of him."

"And Penh knows you work for the NSA?"

Lukas snorted. "No. Because it was all very clandestine, the offer I signed and accepted came from what appeared to be a legitimate IT company in Manhattan. That's what I told everyone and that's what was posted on the school's website. Now, disconnect the laptop and get going. When you get to Mexico, I'll have a security detail set up to guard you and the computer. We'll run a ruse to lead front of him until the same spokesman arose and cleared his throat and bowed again in deference to their leader. "Sir, if I may, it appears there was a sea plane in the area of the wreckage. The shots that were fired at the boat that carried our brave divers came from the vicinity of that plane. It also appears Mr. Cook boarded that plane and that it departed to the north moments after the shots were fired."

Penh cocked his head and squinted his eyes. "So Mr. Cook is indeed receiving assistance from some external source. But who?"

The spokesman for the group sat quickly and began to peck at the keys of his computer. He looked up at Penh, who was pacing at the far end of the room, and added, "I have something here."

Penh grunted and lifted his head.

"It's a signal coming from Mr. Cook's computer. It appears he is on the move."

Penh stepped quickly to the man's side. The man pointed at a pulsating blip on the screen in southeastern Honduras.

"Very well. Send a message to our team in Mexico City informing them that I will move up my arrival date. Now that we know where Cook is, we can execute ahead of schedule. Let's bring the moth to the flame and scorch him." Penh turned on his heels and stormed out the door. His footsteps could be heard as they pounded along the concrete hallway outside and down the metal stairs.

All seven men let out a collective sigh and the tension in the room dissipated with Penh's departure. Nervous glances were exchanged. The foreman surveyed the other six men with a steely glare, then sat down. The tapping and clicking of keyboards and mice resumed, timidly at first, then more vigorously as the spokesman reminded them of the task ahead of them and the amount of work they needed to do to accomplish it.

* * * *

Dejection wasn't quite the right word. Nor was irritation. No. The best way to describe Nic Lancaster's mood alternated between utter frustration and absolute humiliation. Or maybe futility. Every time he thought about Collin Cook, one of those emotions took control. Collin Cook, the everyday American who was supposed to be so easy to find and track and apprehend had proven to be anything but. It should have been an easy assignment. Nic, the brightest and hardest-working young detective in Interpol London's Cybercrime Task Force, felt he was destined for a meteoric rise through the department's ranks. All he needed was to break one big case and his lane on the fast track would be assured. His name in headlines and front page photos would surely follow.

Finding this Collin Cook fellow appeared on the surface to be just the kind of case he was looking for. Cook was supposed to lead Nic to the "big fish," Pho Nam Penh, the cyberterrorist responsible for shutting down the Royal Bank of Scotland for a full day back in April and pilfering millions of dollars from dozens of international banks over the past several months. He and his group were the primary suspects in these and several other embarrassing attacks, but they were, for all intents and purposes, invisible. At least until a photo surfaced online showing Penh sitting with Cook in a London pub. That's when Nic got his big break, the assignment that would propel his career into the next realm.

This Collin Cook was nothing more than a former electrical supply salesman from California who had experienced a great tragedy and was wandering around Europe apparently trying to find himself. The photos that came to light on the Internet showed otherwise. Cook, perhaps because he had become disaffected with life, had turned to crime. His new cozy relationship with Penh, as evidenced by the London photos as well as a second set of photos

chapter Three

Rob Howell, Collin's best friend and neighbor since kindergarten, had practically grown up in the Cooks' home. He knew the code to open the garage door and the code to silence the house alarm, the one Collin's dad, Henry, usually didn't bother to set. He had been checking in at the house since Emily and Sarah were rescued from their kidnapping ordeal. Henry and Collin's brother, Richard, and sister, Megan, were all staying in Emily's La Jolla condo at Emily's insistence. It was five minutes from the hospital to make it easy for the family to visit Sarah. Since Emily was in the hospital, she wanted someone to be there to take care of her plants, she said. Perhaps that was the reason, but Rob suspected the real reason was to have people in and out of her condo so as to ward off invaders. Being abducted played tricks on people's perceptions, he knew.

Likewise, Henry seemed happy to have Rob drop by their house daily. He, too, wanted there to be at least some activity at the house. After all, it was in that very garage that Henry was knocked down and Sarah dragged away by those evil men. Who knew if they were still lurking around?

Making his way to the Cook home after picking up his morning coffee prior to his 6:00 a.m. conference call with a client in New York, which he would handle from the comfort of the Cooks' den downstairs, Rob scanned his surroundings as he approached the security entrance to the gated community. He punched in the numbers and waited as the gate made it arduous elliptical trek across the cobblestoned drive. Nothing seemed unusual. At least, not at first. He inched his rented Ford Fusion through the entrance and came to a stop in front of the large panel of locked mailboxes situated just inside the gate to the right. In his rearview mirror, he saw the gate shudder and jerk as it started to close. He parked in the widened pull-out space in front of the mailbox shelter, complete with a red-tiled roof. As he pushed the door open and swung his legs out, something grabbed his attention. He listened to a distant sound drawing closer. The roar of a powerful motorcycle engine approaching grew louder, reaching ear-piercing levels as it turned the corner and barreled through the slowly closing gate. Both the driver and his passenger were clad in black leather biking gear and black helmets. A dark face shield obscured the driver's features, but the passenger had her shield up and smiled at Rob as the motorcycle gracefully glided past him and angled to make a right turn at the end of the short entry road. Her smile caught Rob's attention. The exotic young Asian girl locked eyes with Rob long enough to flash a seductive smile and wink at him. As they rolled past him, her head swiveled to maintain eye contact, even as her macho boyfriend revved the potent engine and banked hard into the right-hand turn. They were out of sight a split second later.

He smiled as he stood up and congratulated himself on the fact that he still had it. Nothing like being admired by a beautiful girl at the beginning of a beautiful summer day. With an extra spring in his step, Rob rounded the hood of the car and fumbled in his pocket for the key to the Cooks' mailbox, still thinking about those eyes. It was like that girl was trying to cast a spell on him or something. And that smile. There was something behind it, almost like recognition. As he opened the mailbox and dug out a small stack of catalogs, an assortment of special-offer letters and postcards, and a few bills, something caught in his mind, like a pebble in his shoe. Why did that girl look at him like that? Was she scoping him out for some reason?

The fact that she had an exotic Asian face should have given him pause, taking into account recent events. He chastised himself for profiling. Just because she was Asian should not make him think that she had anything to do with Emily and Sarah's kidnappers. There

* * * *

Scripps Cancer Research Patient Clinic, La Jolla, California
June 17, 5:28 a.m. Local Time

A nurse fussed about, checking the readouts from both Emily's and Sarah's monitors. Dr. Emily Burns, an emerging research scientist at the Scripps Cancer Research Center next door, working in the field of enhanced enzyme therapy for cancer, woke with a start and let out an anxious gasp. The hairs on the back of Emily's neck had raised. Even while sleeping, her heightened awareness of her surroundings caused every synapse to fire through her agitated nervous system, protecting her from people who lurked nearby. The startled nurse realized what she had done and apologized profusely for sneaking up on her. "I'm so, so sorry. I didn't mean to wake you. I know you need your rest."

Emily gulped in a lungful of air and tried to hold it, hoping to steady herself. But it escaped in a frantic burst. That was followed by another gulp and another burst, which resembled sobbing, but without the tears. These nerves—it seemed like they would never return to normal. Finally, she managed to hold her breath for a hurried three count, then exhale on a five count. "I know. It's not you, it's just …" Emily's voice trailed off because she didn't really want to go into it. Not now.

"I understand how guarded and anxious you must feel. I think I would be the same way," said the nurse. She tried her best to carry on as usual. "I'll just take down your vitals and let you get your rest." With an extended index finger that shook slightly, she poked the screen of the tablet computer nestled in the crook of her arm. She was one of three nurses who had been attending Emily and Sarah since they arrived almost two days earlier. She was the youngest and nicest of the three. Her kindness and attention to the emotional, as well as physical, pains of her two patients had been as soothing as any medications the doctors prescribed.

"No, it's OK. You don't have to rush out of here." Emily bore the scars, both internal and external, from the kidnapping at the hands of Pho Nam Penh's men. An arcing gash on her cheek and another on her chest bore witness to the savagery of her abductors. The plastic surgeon had done an amazing job to minimize the scarring. But the emotional wounds ran much deeper and would not heal as well or as quickly as the knife's trail.

Emily had never been assaulted. Violence and terror were things that happened on TV and in the movies, not in La Jolla, California, and not to a research scientist with a PhD from Harvard who spent the majority of her waking hours in a laboratory or hunched over her computer keyboard in her cozy temperature-controlled office.

Particularly devastating and humiliating and horrifying was how close she came to being raped, on camera even, while tied to a table by those brutish demons. Their faces, their voices, and their smells lingered behind every thought, in every movement of every person she saw, and in the very ether around her. Emily tried but couldn't seem to escape the scenes she had been part of. The young guy with the pierced eyebrow and spiky hair holding the knife against her face, then slicing downward, the cold sensation of the blade followed by the warmth of her own blood trickling down her cheek. Her stomach twisted as images ran through her head yet again: of the older man with the tattoos on his neck tying her to the table and filming and video conferencing his boss and Collin while the younger one strutted like a peacock and flicked his tongue.

She shuddered as she recalled the younger man's sweaty palms against the skin of her legs as he held her and cut away her silk dress slacks and his hot, smelly breath against her neck as he did his best to seduce her with his animalistic rituals. The shame. The dehumanizing. The denigration.

For someone used to being in control of her situation—at least as much as anyone can be—being constricted, confined, degraded, narcotic pulled him into a dream-like state.

He felt his body being dragged and pulled and stuffed into the backseat, but felt no pain, no discomfort. His eyelids were too heavy to pry open, so he gave up. Instead, he dreamed of the pretty Asian girl and her smile, sensing they were near. The car doors slammed shut one at a time. Then he was gone, completely oblivious to the outside world, not knowing who she was or where she was taking him. All concerns got swallowed up as a tranquil fog enveloped his consciousness.

* * * *

Los Angeles, California
June 17, 6:12 a.m. Pacific Time

"How are we going to follow this hunch of yours, Reggie?" asked his partner, Spinner McCoy. Spinner's Texan drawl and boyish optimism usually softened Reggie's hard-edged skepticism. Not this time. This time he was taking the hard-edged approach. "We got nothing to go on except a couple of people on a boat that was fired upon saying they saw a small plane heading north. That's not much."

"I know," admitted Reggie Crabtree as he studied the computer screen. "I know." Reggie wasn't being his usual unflappable self. Normally, Reggie operated on facts and logic. Sure, he had his gut instincts, like every good detective. But he always made sure to check his gut against reality. This time, however, was an exception. This was all gut.

Spinner cocked his head, studying his partner. "So, what's our game plan? I mean, where do we even start?" He walked around the desk and stood behind Reggie, leaning toward Reggie's screen.

Agitated and jumpy, Reggie tapped repeatedly at a spot on his screen. "Well, I figured we should start looking at all possible points north of Providencia Island. Why don't you try to figure out what the range is of a small aircraft? That should help us narrow it down."

"You're kidding, right? You do realize, don't you, there's no feasible way to narrow it down without something more to go on."

"You have any better suggestions?"

"Does the term 'needle in a haystack' hold any meaning for you, Reggie?"

"All I know is that sitting here doing nothing won't help us one bit. Waiting for a lead or an eyewitness account to fall in our lap doesn't seem too productive, either, so I'm trying to do some detective work, you know, like we're paid to do."

"Ah, I see, doing *something*, no matter how futile, is better than doing nothing, eh?" Spinner walked back to the opposite side of Reggie's desk, his cowboy boots thudding heavily on the low-pile carpeting, and stared at his partner for a long moment.

"Yeah. You have any better ideas?" Reggie tapped the computer screen again with his index finger.

"How about a ballistics report on the bullet from the wounded guy's shoulder? Do we know if anyone on that boat took a video or pictures? Have we asked for any of that?"

"Be my guest, partner. Good luck getting any cooperation out of the Colombians. But, as you say, doing something is better than nothing."

Spinner's eyes narrowed, but he never broke his gaze until he abruptly exited the room without a word. Only the echo of his boots against the linoleum floor could be heard as they trailed off down the hallway.

Five minutes later, he was back in the room. Reggie looked up at him, brow furrowed in curiosity. "I thought you were going to get information out of the Colombians."

"Not me. Lancaster's on it."

"Lancaster?"

"Yeah, he's the one with the connections to the Colombian Navy—or his boss is. Let's not waste our time. Let's waste his."

through his thoughts. But the ones that kept him awake were the ones of Stinky struggling for his life as Collin squeezed his victim's midsection between his knees. The feeling of Stinky's mass slumping, heavy and lifeless, knowing he'd snuffed out a man's life, made every muscle in his own body tense up. Even the pilot noticed Collin go rigid and shot him a quizzical look. Collin waved him off and tried to think of something more pleasant.

Collin forced his eyes shut, trying hard to escape into some other world. He relaxed and thought about playing Frisbee with his dad on the beach. He thought about the dog he had as a little boy. He thought about surfing. Each of these peaceful and happy memories was interrupted by a ghastly, more recent experience like bumping into Stinky's grayish, bloated corpse as he was attempting to escape the sinking sailboat. Or the spurt of blood and bubbles when he speared the diver that was looking for his laptop. Or the sound of his mother's voice, all frail and weak, when she told him to "do what Ronnie would do."

These memories parted like a curtain, making way for the most visceral of all of his nightmares: the shriek he heard over the phone as his wife, Amy, watched an out-of-control semitruck careen into the hillside and roll over onto the minivan carrying her and their three small children. That panicked, helpless cry haunted him still, nearly a year later, every time he tried to sleep.

Finally, he gave up on sleep and just stared out the window some more.

The pilot gave him another long look, then keyed on his mic and spoke for the first time since takeoff. "You all right? You seem pretty fidgety over there."

"Yeah, I'll be fine. Just can't seem to get comfortable."

"You sure there's not something eating at you?"

"Yeah, no. I guess I'm just too tired to sleep. You know how that is."

"Happens to the best of us sometimes. But we're going to be flying for quite a while today and I know you didn't sleep at all last night, so find a way to get some shut-eye if you can."

"How much longer to Belize?" said Collin, trying to shift the attention away from himself and onto something less probing.

"I reckon another half hour or so."

"How're we doing on gas?"

The pilot was silent as he studied his gauges. "We're all right."

"That wasn't too convincing. What does that mean?"

"It means one way or another, we're going to be fine."

"That means you're not sure we're going to make it, are you?"

"No, no. We'll make it. The question is, will it be Plan A or Plan B?" said the pilot with a manufactured air of confidence. His eyes scanned the landscape below, then the gauges in front of him, then the ground again.

Sleep was now out of the question for Collin. The attempted nonchalance by the pilot didn't work and Collin found himself leaning toward the pilot's instrument panel, trying to decipher the gauges and indicators. Not knowing where they were going to land this airplane created a new set of worries. At least the haunting images of the past few days were gone. While Collin didn't quite rejoice at the prospect of shifting to Plan B, which he knew nothing about, he was glad to have something else occupy his mind for a while.

cool under pressure. The reassurance in his voice gave Collin hope.

Turning to the pilot, Collin said, "The only question now is if we can make it to the airport."

"Luckily, the alarms go off when there is still about five gallons of fuel left. We'll make it. We just need him to handle the logistics so we can leave again as soon as we refuel." Seeing Collin's face, he grinned and added, "Welcome to the exciting world of covert bush piloting in Central America."

* * * *

Kuala Lumpur, Malaysia
June 17, 10:40 p.m. Local Time; 7:40 a.m. Pacific Time

Pho Nam Penh leaned one shoulder against the wall next to the window, one leg crossed over the other at the ankles, and stared out over the darkened and empty marketplace. It was silent outside except for the occasional barking dog or honking horn in the distance. He blew smoke upward toward the ceiling and watched it spiral as it climbed. His face was a mask of cool indifference. Every movement was calculated to display the image of a general in total control. The men in the room needed to see that, needed to believe in him as their leader. One battle had been lost, but the war was still on, and the next battle would be theirs. Of this he was supremely confident. The nonchalance of his body language conveyed that.

"Sir," said the foreman from across the room. "The CCTV feed just went blank." His fingers danced across his keyboard as he spoke.

"What? How?" said Penh, as he pushed off the wall with an elbow to stand straight.

"My contact at the fueling station said that surely we at the Ministry of National Security should know since it was at our command. He also said that only select personnel are allowed on the airfield at this time and he is not one of them, as I should well know."

"Ask him who gave the orders," Penh demanded.

A whir of key tapping in a message window. "Sir, he says it was General Duarte."

"Good. Then find this General Duarte and ask for more information about the situation," instructed Penh. "I assume the name and email account you're using is an authentic one and of high enough rank."

"Yes, sir," said the foreman as he opened another chat window and typed furiously.

Both the foreman and Penh stared at the screen, silently awaiting the general's reply.

When the message popped up on the screen, there was a simple answer. No queries, no probing, no verification of identity. "The American NSA," it said.

Penh straightened up. He scratched his chin as he began a slow pace toward the window. His jaw muscles quivered and his nostrils flared. Sharp, audible intakes of breath punctuated every other click of his loafers on the concrete floor. "Belize is a member of the Commonwealth of Nations. So, being under British control, they are allies of the United States. It makes sense that they would cooperate so readily." A pause as he turned on his heels and headed back to the wall opposite the window. "Now we know that Mr. Cook has help from someone in the NSA."

Another pause, another sharp breath. "That explains a lot." Penh curled his upper lip as his head nodded. "Mr. Chao," he snapped his finger shot and shot a look across the table to an older man with a few wrinkles around his eyes and a few gray hairs in his facial stubble. The older gentleman stood. "What have we learned from Mr. Cook's cloned hard drive?"

"Well, sir, we know that there are unusual security protocols and verification scripts that run upon start up. We know there is biometric ID verification and a register that indicates past access to the United States government's national secured database. We have

Scripps Cancer Research Patient Clinic, La Jolla, California
June 17, 9:09 a.m. Pacific Time

Emily turned toward the rustling sound to her right where Sarah was stirring in her bed, struggling to open her eyes. When she finally did, Emily greeted her with as cheery a "Good morning" as she could muster.

"I guess you could call it that," said Sarah. Her tone did not carry its customary upbeat tenor.

"You don't sound like your usual self over there, Sarah. What's the matter?"

"I would much rather be in my own bed at home. I'm not a big fan of hospitals, you know. They're too noisy; it's too hard to sleep here," said Sarah, rubbing her eyes. "What time is it, anyway?"

Emily chuckled. "Well, it's after nine o'clock. You seem to have slept pretty well, all things considered."

Sarah looked embarrassed. "Is it really? Aren't I a lazy mutt?"

This made Emily smile. For such an elegant and classy lady, Emily found Sarah to be refreshingly candid and self-deprecating when they were one-on-one. She held no pretenses nor false images. She was what she was and cared little what others thought of her. Sarah Cook was her own woman and was comfortable being who she was.

"I thought Rob said he was bringing coffee this morning. Shouldn't he here by now?" asked Emily.

"Robert has never been terribly punctual, so I wouldn't worry too much about him just yet. But if he said he's bringing coffee this morning, maybe he could bring me one of those croissants or coffee cakes they sell at the coffee shops. I'm starving."

Emily smiled even wider. "I'll check your diet chart first to make sure it's approved," she said, with an exaggerated teacher-like wag of the finger. She scrolled to his number quickly and placed the phone to her ear. She turned to Sarah, pulling her brows together and twisting her lips in disappointment. "Rob, this is Emily. Hey, on your way in, assuming you're on your way to visit us, could you also get some croissants and coffee cakes for me and Sarah? Thanks, amigo. See you soon."

As Emily hung up, a puzzled look still on her face, the door burst open and a jolly "Good morning, ladies" boomed forth. It was Henry. He held a bouquet of flowers in each hand and an ear-to-ear grin on his face. Megan and Richard, Collin's sister and brother, followed closely behind. Megan carried a bag with the logo of a popular bagel shop on it while Richard carried a drink holder with four cups of coffee. The fifth cup he held out for his mother. Everyone wore smiles and giggled, doing their best to chase out the fears and worries and pain of the last several days.

Megan announced the assorted bagel flavors as Richard passed out the piping hot cups to the others in the room. Once everyone had their coffee and bagel in hand, Henry launched into a story about the odd woman down the hall from Emily's condo and her peculiar puppy. He described the woman's mismatching outfit, her droopy stockings, her misaligned wig, and the unused cane which hung over her arm. He'd bumped into her in the elevator as she was heading out to walk the dog. Despite the warm weather, the tiny Chihuahua was dressed in a thick sweater and woolen booties. Henry roared with laughter as he described the sight, but added that she was a very affable and talkative lady and he had enjoyed their conversation.

"That's Mrs. Greenbauch," said Emily. "She is the kindest, sweetest lady, even though she may have lost her fashion sense years ago."

When the laughter subsided, Emily looked around and asked, "Has anyone seen or heard from Rob this morning? I thought he was the one bringing coffee."

Richard looked at Megan. Megan looked at Henry. Henry looked at Richard. Each in turn shrugged and shook their head. "Should we call him?" inquired Henry.

"I already tried," said Emily. "It went to voicemail. He usually

chapter Seven

For the first time since he started working the Collin Cook case, Nic Lancaster was preparing to leave work at a normal time and join his friends at the pub like a normal person. The fire inside that Crabtree and McCoy had reignited earlier in the day had cooled off, thanks to a stunning lack of progress obtaining any viable new leads on the whereabouts of one Collin Cook, American escape artist. Because there was nothing urgent happening with the Cook case at the moment, there was nothing preventing him from being a normal person for one night.

Even his boss, Alastair Montgomery, had encouraged him to go home and take his mind off it for a while. "I'm sure a bit of rejuvenation is in order," Alastair had said at the end of their routine late-afternoon meeting.

Not only had he been working eighteen-hour days since late April trying to locate and apprehend Collin Cook, hoping it would give him the information he needed to arrest Pho Nam Penh for his many crimes against Britain, but Nic also hadn't had a vacation in almost two years. After all the setbacks he had experienced during this case, Nic knew his temper and disposition had inflicted damage to nearly every one of his relationships. He'd already lost a girlfriend in the pursuit of his ambitions. It appeared that his friendships were also in jeopardy. Today that would change. Tonight, he would enjoy a pint or two with the lads and engage in conversation about something besides detective work and fighting terrorism.

A night at the pub with Manchester United playing on every television set in the place and the accompanying crazed atmosphere seemed the perfect antidote for his self-inflicted alienation. Football, beer, and a chance to forget the stress for a while. A perfect, well-deserved evening was taking shape.

After logging off, Nic spun out of his chair and grabbed his coat off the hook near the opening of his cubicle, a smile on his face and a bounce in his step. He wasn't more than six paces down the corridor when his cell phone began to play "God Save the Queen"—his standard ringtone for work mates. Pushing away the instinct to ignore it and go on his jolly way, Nic answered it on the fifth ring.

"Lancaster, you're going to want to see this," said Peter, the dungeon-dwelling techie with the earrings and dyed black hair that poked up at odd angles.

"You messing with me, Pete? Right now? I'm heading out to watch the Man U match at the pub with some mates."

"Messing with you? Why would I do that? You promised me a promotion when I help you find this guy, remember?" said Peter in mock protest.

Nic exhaled through his nose. "What've you got? It better be good."

"Wait, did you say you were going to the pub? I don't believe I've ever heard those words pass from your lips," said Peter, exaggerating his shock.

"Shut up, you bloody tosser."

"This shouldn't take too long, but I do think it rather important to your case. Get down here and check it out for yourself."

"Right. Why did I ever think I could get away for an evening with my mates?"

Nic took a right at the bottom of the steps instead of a left. Had he gone left, he would have been at the front doors, then the sidewalk, just a few paces from the entrance to the tube. The tube would have taken him to the pub and a nice evening out. Taking the right turn instead led him to another set of stairs that ended in the basement where Interpol's IT department was temporarily housed while their floor underwent major renovations. His pause marked promises."

Henry gave it one more try. "You know Rob, Emily. Always making a deal or setting up a meeting." Henry chuckled to himself, then added, "Or a tee time."

"Yeah, but he would at least return my calls, wouldn't he? Even if he were busy, he wouldn't be that rude. I just know he wouldn't."

"My guess is he's in the middle of something important. Why don't we all go for a little walk outside? I think you ladies need some fresh air," said Henry.

"Yeah," added Megan. "The fog's burned off and the sun is out. Let's get out of here and enjoy some sunshine."

Just then the young nurse knocked and entered. After taking vitals and checking with the attending physician, she gave the family the OK to stroll around outside so long as Sarah had a walker.

Outside, the last remnants of "June Gloom" lingered along the ridges to the west, across Interstate 5. It was common place for fog to envelope the coastal cities this time of year. Typically, the sun would burn it off by noon. All that remained of the fog bank was a very thin, wispy layer of gray clouds that looked like strands of silk pulled apart and laid across the hilltops.

Emily took a deep breath as she surveyed her surroundings. Two buildings to the south and across the eastern parking lot was where she had been abducted just three days earlier. Megan and Richard each held an elbow as they helped their mother walk along ahead of Emily and Henry. Sarah was obviously unfamiliar and uncomfortable with using a walker. Eyeing Emily from the side, Henry fell into step with her as they sauntered behind the trio.

"You holding up OK there young lady?" he asked.

"Sure. I'm doing fine," she said after a slight hesitation.

"You don't seem too convinced."

"I'm still worried about Rob. I can't shake the feeling that something has gone wrong just because it's so unlike him to not show up when he said he would. And for him to not even call me back … It's just completely out of character for him. Don't you agree?"

"I'm sure he's fine. Rob's a big boy. He can take care of himself," Henry said with confidence and a hint of pride.

"I was just really hoping he would show up. He promised we'd talk."

Henry nodded slowly but didn't say anything for a few steps. "In the meantime, maybe the fresh air and sunshine will do you some good."

"Well, this is the first time I've been outside since …"

"That's what I figured." Henry took two more strides before continuing his thought. "Your office is near here, isn't it?"

"Yeah. The next building over." Emily gestured ahead of them and to her left.

"Tell me what you like most about your work."

A smile spread across her face and she pulled in a deep breath. "Where should I start? I love everything about it. The science. The research. The people. The pace. The idea of curing cancer and saving lives. The whole thing is exciting and invigorating."

"What is it that makes your work invigorating?" Henry asked, keying in on the last word in her description.

"The challenge, I guess. There's always something new to learn or some new angle to apply to my research. You know, the idea of trying to solve a complex problem one piece at a time is a huge challenge and I find that invigorating."

"I'll bet it is. It must take a great deal of patience, too. I'd imagine the breakthroughs you've had lately didn't just happen overnight."

"You're right about that. They've been a long time coming."

They neared a grove of trees, bisected by an access road. Across the road, Henry could see benches lining another walking path and recognized it from the description he'd heard.

"Is this where it happened? Is this where those animals grabbed you?"

"Sounds like the grown-up version of 'Are we there yet?'" the pilot said with a snort.

"I suppose so. It's just that I'm missing my Game Boy and DVD player to keep me entertained."

The pilot, who was probably in his sixties, laughed. "You grew up in a different era than I did. We had to endure the family car rides without any of that stuff. Talk about long trips. Geez."

"Yeah, kids these days have it way better than I did, even," Collin laughed, then stopped short as he thought about his family.

"What's wrong?"

"Nothing," Collin lied. "Just a random thought hit me. I should call to check in and get an update," said Collin, looking at his watch.

"Why not? You got nothing better to do."

Collin pulled his phone out and powered it up. He noticed the time and realized they had crossed over into Mexico and changed time zones. When Lukas answered, he reeled off a list of questions he had been pondering the past couple of hours. "How's my mom doing? And Emily? Are they home yet? When will they be released? When can I talk to them?"

"Whoa, hold on there, cowboy. That's a lot of questions in one breath. Let me answer as best I can. First, your mom and Emily were still in the hospital, receiving treatments for dehydration, cuts, and possible infections, last I heard. They're both traumatized, so a counselor has gotten involved, but I don't have an update on a possible discharge date. As far as talking to them, I don't think that would be a good idea at this point. The less they know, the better."

"I would feel so much better if I could just talk with them and hear their voices. It would help me and I'm sure it would help them, especially my mother."

"For now, we need to stick to our plan and get you to a safe place where we can get you ready for the next phase of our plan. OK? I don't know who might be monitoring their calls and I'd rather keep things quiet for the time being."

"What did you mean you didn't have an update? Hasn't Rob kept you informed?"

Lukas hesitated momentarily, just long enough for Collin to catch it. "Yes, he has. That information is all from his latest report."

"Which was when?"

"Just hours ago," said Lukas.

"How many hours ago?"

Lukas sighed. "I haven't heard from him yet today. Our last conversation was after he left the hospital last night."

"Why haven't you heard from him today? It's what, ten forty-five in California?"

"I'm sure there's a reasonable explanation. I'm sure he'll check in very soon."

"That makes no sense coming from you. You always know what's happening. Have you tracked his phone? Do you know where he is and what he's doing?"

"I have. He's at your parents' house. He's been there quite a while with no activity on his phone. I know he went to pick up their mail and check on the house earlier this morning. Maybe he's taking a nap."

"It's not like you to not know every detail."

"When he doesn't answer his phone for hours, it's very difficult to know every detail," Lukas said, the exasperation leaking into his tone of voice. "All I can tell you at this point is that I'm working on reestablishing communication with him. I'll let you know more when I find out what's going on. OK?"

"Yeah, I guess," said Collin, pinching the bridge of his nose and closing his eyes. "I was hoping for some good news to take my mind off the heat and dehydration here."

"Hang in there, pal. You'll be landing on a remote airstrip our people control out in the countryside. They'll supply you with whatever you need, OK?"

"Good, we need water, lots of ice-cold water. We need Diet Coke.

He glanced over at the pilot, whose face had turned pale and clammy. Collin noticed that the perspiration that had been beading up on his forehead and brow was no longer there. It had dried up and his eyes were glazed over. He was conscious and breathing, but not focused. His headed lolled from side to side and his body twitched involuntarily. "Hey, man, you all right?" Collin shouted. "Pull out of it, man. I need you. I can't fly this thing on my own."

Collin checked the controls again. Altitude was 815 feet. Heading was 303.5 degrees, meaning they were going north by northwest. He had no idea if that was the right direction, but he would figure that out later. For now, he had to keep the plane in the air until the pilot came back around.

From what he could see and based on the first aid training he had once received, Collin surmised the pilot was suffering from dehydration and possibly heat exhaustion. The lack of sweat was a huge concern. That meant his body had locked down all fluids to keep the vital organs functioning. He also knew the first and best thing to do was to give him water, but they had none left in the plane. Their water bottles had been finished off an hour ago, before the air conditioning went caput. Without water or medical attention, the pilot's core body temperature would rise. In these conditions, that rise could be precipitous and dangerous. Trapped in a metal box flying over the jungle with no air conditioning, he had no way to stop the increasing body temperatures for either of them and nowhere to land to find help. His brief tutorial on landing a plane would most likely not be sufficient to bring them to the ground safely. This was a bad predicament. Both of their lives were now in jeopardy.

Collin began to wonder why he was not in as bad a shape as the pilot. Then he remembered: the pilot had been drinking Red Bulls all day. Collin had stuck to drinking just water, other than the one swig of Red Bull the pilot had shared. There were at least four empty cans of the stuff, maybe five, rolling around behind the seats, all of which had been drunk within the past two hours or so. To boot, the pilot hadn't eaten anything. Perhaps those drinks had done more harm than good. On an empty stomach, who knew how one's body would react to that much artificial stimulation. No matter. He had a crisis on his hands and no real way to deal with it.

"I'm not very good at making nice when people insult my kids, you know," said Reggie, exasperated.

"I can only imagine. Good luck with it, though. That ought to be an interesting conversation to start."

Another slow-down as they approached the El Toro Y where Interstate 5 and Interstate 405, two of the busiest thoroughfares in Orange County, merged. It was almost always a nightmare, no matter the time of day, and this day, nearing lunchtime, was no exception.

Reggie smirked at Spinner as they nearly came to a stop behind a long line of cars. "Might have more luck with your friend. No bad blood there, I hope."

"Nah, nothing like that. I'll reach out to him and see if he can dig around for us," said Spinner as he pulled his phone from his jacket pocket. "But you know how all those clandestine guys are, they never share information. No one really knows what anyone else is doing."

"Maybe that's true, but it's worth a shot. If you play it right, you might be able to work the interagency rivalry to your advantage. Just a thought."

* * * *

In the air above Southeastern Mexico
June 17, 1:25 p.m. Local Time; 11:25 a.m. Pacific Time

The pilot's whole body shook. He mumbled something incoherently and tried to take control of the plane again. Collin pushed him back and told him to just relax. The pilot's condition was worsening, as were Collin's chances of survival. Not only was the pilot not flying the plane, his mental and physical state were deteriorating. Collin realized there was no way the pilot was going to snap back to normal before it was time to land.

For now, things were fine. Collin had the plane flying level and in the general direction of their destination, but there was still the landing to deal with.

Before panic set in, Collin thought clearly enough to call Lukas. He'd know what to do. He always did.

But there was a problem. Lukas was not answering the phone. Panic welled up inside, but Collin fought through it with logic. He focused his thoughts on his assets first: *We're still fifty miles from our destination. I've got half a tank of fuel, so I can stay in the air a good long time. What did he say? Total range with full tanks was three and a half hours. I've got an hour of leeway. Worst case, I have to land this thing. How hard can it be? He walked me through it already. I'm a fast learner. As long as there's a place to land and someone to guide me through it, I'll be fine. Stay strong.*

When the gentle Germanic voice of his good friend greeted him and asked him to leave a message, he did: "I'm in trouble here, Lukas. I need your help. The pilot is out of commission, too sick to fly this plane. Please call me back as soon as possible."

Collin studied the instrument panel in front of the pilot and the display screen in front of his seat as he repeated positive mantras to himself, willing himself to keep his mind engaged and his fears at bay. *Fuel level: good. Altitude: 865 feet. No obstacles on the horizon. But where are we supposed to land? It should be coming up here soon. Half an hour at the most.*

The screen in front of him was an interactive map that showed him where he was in relation to things on the ground. Working quickly, Collin was able to locate the flag on the map that marked their destination in Villahermosa. The little white plane icon indicated his current location. A line pointed out from the front of the plane icon showed his direction. When he turned the wheel slightly each way, he noticed the line move. He also noticed his altitude changing each time he turned. Keeping the wings centered in the little altimeter gauge was tougher than he expected. When he steered, if he wasn't careful, he would lose a hundred feet or more in

chapter Ten

"Hello, Miriam. I'm really glad you're here," said Collin in response to Miriam Hastings's no-nonsense greeting. Collin had mustered his poise and projected his confidence as best he could. "I'm not a hundred percent sure how to land this thing, although the pilot here talked me through our last landing. So at least I've seen it done a few times. I'm hoping you can help me."

"Tell me, Collin, how much experience do you have flying in small aircraft?"

"None, until a few weeks ago. Since I've spent most of the last two or three days in this plane with this pilot, so it's not completely foreign to me anymore. But, I have to admit, I wasn't always paying attention to what he was doing."

"That's all right. We'll get you through this, Collin," said Miriam in a smooth and even tone. "First things first, then. Do you know what the yoke is?"

"Yep. I'm holding it right now. I know it controls the attitude of the plane, including changing direction and pitch."

"Very good. How about the throttle? Do you know where it is?"

"Yes, I do. It's the knob to my left with the red handle."

"Correct. How about the knob next to it? What color is it?"

"It's blue and it's for the flaps."

"You've picked up quite a bit during your time on board. I'm impressed." Miriam continued in similar fashion through the mission-critical indicators, gauges, knobs, and switches. Most of which were on the pilot's side of the cockpit. However, Collin demonstrated that he knew where they were and that he was able to reach them when needed.

Collin added, "I also figured out a few things about the navigation system while I was waiting for this call, so I think I'm heading in the right direction according to the GPS screen in front of me."

"That's good," said Miriam. "Can you tell me your heading."

Collin squinted at the screen and wiped the sweat from his brow. "Yeah, I'm heading north, bearing 356.7 degrees."

"Can you tell me your exact location right now? Read me the latitude and longitude. Should be at the bottom of your screen."

Collin rattled off the numbers, with the degrees north and west and confirmed his airspeed, altitude, and fuel levels. He could hear typing in the background and was sure she was plugging in the coordinates on a mapping program to get a visual. Miriam assured him that he was doing a fine job and that if he listened closely he would be on the ground safely in less than twenty minutes.

Miriam's calm, steady voice added to Collin's confidence. She made flying a plane feel like doing yoga for the first time. It wasn't exactly comfortable, but with some guidance and encouragement, it wasn't all that bad. They practiced descending, ascending, banking from side to side, as well as reducing power on the throttle and increasing it. Miriam talked him through the various steps of the approach and landing until Collin could repeat them back to her and indicated he knew where each of the controls was and how to use them. After a few repetitions, Miriam announced, "I think you've got it. You're ready to land this thing."

"You sound a lot more sure than I feel," Collin said, shaking his head as he searched the dotted land spread out before him. "So far, keeping this thing in the air seems a lot easier than putting it on the ground."

Collin looked over at the pilot slumped against the door. His eyes were closed, mouth open. Collin placed a finger on the carotid artery in his neck to make sure he still had a pulse. He did and it was racing. *That can't be good*, he thought.

"What can't be good?" Miriam repeated.

Collin became aware that his thought had exited his mouth.

Area and had dealt with some of the most congested roads in the state, pounded on the steering wheel and exclaimed, "Why must we go so slow, people? Just move it. Come on."

Spinner McCoy smirked and tapped the screen of his phone. He had just finished leaving another voice message, bringing his total for the drive to thirteen. He was getting nowhere fast, just like their late model Taurus stuck behind the Camry ahead of them and boxed in on both sides by lines of cars moving along somewhere between zero and ten miles per hour. "Frustrating, isn't it? I think our timing just sucks."

Reggie scowled as he looked at his partner. "That's not helping."

"I know, but we have to realize what we're up against. We just need a little help from someone in the know."

"I'm going to try my friend in Naval Intelligence and see what he might know about any of this," said Reggie.

"Is this the guy that pissed you off?"

"Yeah. I haven't talked to him since that incident, but it's not like we talked that often before it, either. I don't know what to expect, but I guess I have to be ready to swallow my pride, if that's what it takes," said Reggie, wagging this head.

"There are worse things, you know."

"Like what?"

"I don't know, maybe like not having a friend that could possibly provide valuable information to help our investigation, for starters."

"You're no help." Reggie pulled his phone from the holder on his belt and unlocked the screen with his thumbprint. Another press of the button and a polite computer voice asked how she could help. "Look up Tom Sanders."

The voice said, "I found the number for Tom Sanders. Do you want to call Tom Sanders?"

"Yes. Call Tom Sanders."

The phone began to ring. On the fourth ring a deep, gravelly voice answered, "This had better be good, Reggie."

Reggie stared at the phone, twisting his face. He decided to push through the ambiguous greeting. "I'm fine, Tom. How are you?"

There was a throaty chuckle, then a throat being cleared, then a happy-sounding, "How the hell are you, man? It's been too long since I've heard from you."

Reggie, his eyes wide open and eyebrows drawn together, shot a look of confusion and surprise toward Spinner, who shrugged back.

"I'm doing great, Tom," said Reggie, trying to match the enthusiasm in Tom's voice. "It *has* been a while. I apologize for not doing a better job of staying in touch, but you know how it is sometimes? Work gets crazy and the family keeps you busy. Throw a vacation or two in there, next thing you know, it's been a couple years since we've talked."

"I hear you, brother. I get the sense, though, that this isn't a social call. You're not just calling to shoot the bull, are you?"

"I'm afraid not. I need some help on a tough case that has had us baffled for a month and a half now."

"Oh, another one of those, huh?" Tom's husky laugh seemed to echo in the car. He cleared his throat again. "What've you got?"

"I've got a guy on the run. Been on the run for seven months. This started as a missing persons case, then escalated into a criminal investigation. Turns out our boy has been hanging with some enemies of the United States and is now implicated in a number of cyberattacks on a handful of banks and major corporations. Tens of millions of dollars are missing and we think he might have some answers for us."

"I'm with you, Reggie. Just not sure how I can help. That's not really my field, you know."

"I know. I'm getting to that. Our guy has eluded us for the past six weeks. Every time we get close, he disappears again. We could never figure out how he was doing it until just now. Through some contacts at Interpol, we discovered that our man has been getting help from someone in the NSA."

"You seem to be out of harm's way now," said Miriam. "We need to reduce your speed, Collin."

There was silence for a moment. When Collin spoke, his voice was still shaky. "Right. Reduce speed. Roger that."

"Push in the throttle and bring your speed down to one hundred knots."

Collin did as instructed and let her know when he had accomplished this task. Slowly, his confidence returned.

"Can you see the air strip yet? It should be about two miles ahead of you. From this altitude, you should see it."

Collin squinted ahead through the damaged windshield. He saw what looked like a grass field with a long dirt driveway next to a tin-roofed barn, somewhat distorted through the wiggly lines running every which way through the glass. After he described it for Miriam, Lukas butted in and said, "That's your runway, buddy. The tin roof should have some white markings on it saying, 'Morales Aperos y Semillas.'"

Collin snorted. "You're pretending to be a tool and seed shop?"

Indignant, Lukas retorted, "Why not? It works. And no one else was using it."

"Can we discuss this later, boys? We need to stay focused here. Collin, you need to adjust your heading so that you're coming at that air strip at a ninety-degree angle. Can you do that?"

Collin turned sharply to his left, then adjusted to the right, lining up the nose of the plane with the long side of the barn and the runway in the distance. "Roger that. I'm coming in perpendicular."

"Good. What's your altitude and airspeed now?"

"Looks like I dropped to about nine hundred seventy-five feet and my speed is down to about one hundred five knots."

"That's just about perfect. Stay at that altitude and speed for the time being."

"Roger that," said Collin, unsure how to respond.

"OK, you'll want to turn ninety-degrees to your right until you are running parallel to the runway with it out your left-hand window. The runway should be just off the tip of your wing as you do this."

Collin banked to his right and made the necessary adjustments to straighten out. "Done."

"Good. Now you're going to go out about two miles or so, then you're going to make a ninety degree turn so that the end of the runway is now just beyond the tip of your left wing."

The steady purr of the Cessna's engine filled the headphones. "I think I'm about there."

After a minute of silence, Miriam continued. "OK. The runway should be about two miles behind you now. Turn ninety degrees so that you're running perpendicular to the direction of the runway again."

"OK. Got it," Collin said, his throat feeling tight with the building tension. His voice was not only strained, it was dry. Extremely dry. Dangerously dry. Collin realized that the strain was making him light-headed, which reminded him of his need for water. Shaking his head, he told himself it would be all over, and he and the pilot would both be dead in three minutes or less, if he didn't hold things together. He said a silent prayer.

"Good," said Miriam, maintaining her reassuring tone. "Now, another ninety-degree turn so that your nose is pointing at the end of the runway and reduce your speed to about eighty knots. Got it?"

"Roger." Again, Collin did as he was told. "OK. I'm pointing at the end of the runway now. Airspeed is ninety-two knots."

"That's too fast. Push in your throttle a little bit, then straighten it out and get yourself lined up for approach. Pick a spot on your windscreen and point it at an object at the far end of the runway."

"OK. There's a boulder out there to focus on, but these damn cracks are making it hard to stay focused. Things keep jumping up and down a little bit."

Miriam audibly sucked in a breath. "Just do the best you can to keep that boulder lined up with a spot on the windscreen. Now

chapter Twelve

"Sir," said the foreman as he stood and bowed. "Your driver has returned. He will take you to the airport now."

Pho Nam Penh checked his watch again. "Very well. It appears we've done all we can with the cloned drive from Mr. Cook's computer, have we not?"

"Yes, sir. We have run every test and used every method at our disposal to obtain the missing data, but have not been successful. It is not on this drive. Of that, we are certain."

Penh stood and straightened his coat and tie, then asked for an update on the location of the team who had abducted Rob Howell.

"They are at the hotel in El Centro, sir. Mr. Howell is being prepared, as are all the necessary documents."

"Very well," Penh said. "What is their timeline?"

"Final preparations have been made. They will be leaving the hotel shortly."

As he turned the handle on the door, Penh paused. "They need to expedite their departure. Remind them that the NSA is involved. They can't be too careful."

"Yes, sir. They are aware and are taking extra measures."

"Also, be sure to give them the address in Mexico City," said Penh as he stepped toward the exit. "Have them bring the hostage to me there. I have special plans for him."

"I will inform them of your request, sir. Shall I instruct them to drive all the way there?"

"Absolutely. It is too risky to fly. Besides, it will take me twenty-four hours to get there, anyway. No need to take unnecessary chances."

"Yes, sir."

"You are tracking the movements of Collin Cook?"

"Yes, sir. Using the app we planted on his laptop."

"Good. I want to know where he is at all times." Penh pulled out his cell phone, tapped on it a few times, then turned to the man, showing him the screen. The man rattled off a series of numbers that Penh punched into the phone. A moment later, a beep sounded and a red dot appeared on his screen. "Very well. Carry on."

He swung the door open and marched down the hallway, the familiar cadence of his loafers striking the concrete fading as went.

* * * *

Econo Lodge Motel, El Centro, California
June 17, 11:36 a.m. Pacific Time

The beautiful Asian girl with the full lips, perfect teeth, and large coffee-colored eyes, leaned in close and touched his cheeks, chin, and nose with a triangular sponge pinched between her fingers and thumb. With only a slight accent she said, "So handsome. So dignified. You look perfect," as she smiled at him.

If she hadn't shot him with that tranquilizer dart, Rob thought he would be flirting with this girl right now and maybe getting somewhere. She seemed to enjoy working on his face and touching him. Under normal circumstances, that may have led to something more, like a passionate kiss or an invitation to a romantic dinner. He probably would have touched her face with equal amounts of tenderness and adoration and smiled at her and said, "Perfect."

But maybe he was just imagining things. It was hard to tell. Realizing that he had unknown chemicals in his system, maybe his reactions to her were a little too dramatic. How could he know what his response to her would have been under normal circumstances?

At the moment, Rob Howell found himself in circumstances that were far from normal. Held captive in a cheap motel in the middle of the desert with heavy doses of some sort of sedative running in to apprehend and extradite him. They'd have us do it because they don't do law enforcement kind of stuff." Spinner paused and stared at Reggie as the thoughts continued to take form.

"Go on."

"They've kept the Bureau out of this investigation for a reason."

Reggie furrowed his brow. "But they know we're working the case. They must."

"Yeah, probably. But instead of sending us to arrest Collin, they're rescuing him and flying him through Central America under the radar. Which begs the question: what are they planning and where?"

Reggie thought on that for a moment. "If they're doing all this—protecting and hiding Cook—what are *we* doing?"

Spinner raised his eyebrows and cocked his head to the side. "They're using us, too."

"How do you figure?"

"We're a decoy, a smokescreen."

"A smokescreen?" Reggie's voice pitched upward. "For what?"

"For whatever they're cooking up, pardon the pun."

"Wait, I see what you mean. We're being played to make Penh think that we're chasing Cook, which we are, so that Penh can then follow us and find Cook."

"And when he does, the NSA is right there to get their man."

"Cook is the bait." Reggie sighed.

"And we're the bird dogs."

"We must look like a couple of Keystone Cops bumping around in the dark," Reggie fumed.

"We're doing our job, Reggie, like the trained professionals we are. We're trying to solve a puzzle while someone else holds a handful of the pieces."

"That someone else is supposed to be on our side."

"They are on our side and they know exactly how we operate," Spinner continued, almost as if talking to himself. "Are we being played? It looks that way. But are we being mocked for it? I doubt it."

"There are a million questions at this point. But no answers. I'd rather not be somebody else's pawn, know what I mean?"

"I expect we'll be stonewalled if we try too hard—"

Reggie's phone began to play a musical tone from somewhere in the console area between the two seats. Reggie reached for the charge cord, plugged into the outlet under the radio, and followed it until he found the phone lying on the floor between the driver's seat and the console. "Crabtree here."

"Reggie. It's Tom Sanders. Listen, friend, I've been making some calls and asking questions about this Collin Cook and Pho Nam Penh, trying to get a few answers for you. Of course, I got nowhere."

"Thanks—"

"Until a few minutes ago, when I got a call from the deputy director of the NSA. Know what he told me?"

Reggie's eyes went wide and it took him a few seconds to shake off the shock of that revelation. "To back off?"

"Not quite in those words, but essentially he told me that the agency is involved in several active operations 'to protect American interests and lives in the region.' He explained that he couldn't go into details, but assured me that he had knowledge of those operations and had sanctioned them 'for the benefit of the individuals involved and the nation as a whole.'" Tom inflected his voice to show that he was quoting the deputy.

"That's interesting. You must've really stirred things up there, Tom," joked Reggie. "A call from the deputy director?"

"You're the one stirring things up, not me. The deputy did inform me that they 'do this kind of thing all the time,' I guess in an effort to appease me and lead me to believe that everything's just fine."

"You didn't buy it?"

"I do and I don't. I get the sense that there's a big picture that they're not sharing with us. He knows more than he can tell me, that much I'm certain of. And, with my position on the Intelligence Committee, that concerns me."

"Well, you've answered some questions and raised a few new ones. I appreciate your help."

Tom breathed in, then continued. "I didn't pick up on anything in his voice that leads me to believe he's bluffing or trying to cover something. I think having these questions raised by a member of the Intelligence Committee is at least partly to blame for the way it got sent up the flag pole. I'll keep you up to speed with what I learn. Sound good?"

"That's more than I thought I could ask for. I appreciate it, Tom."

"Well, at this point, I need to know for myself what is going on. That big picture that they are seeing has got to have some implications for my group here in Naval Intelligence as well as your group at the Bureau. I did a quick search of our database and brought up a report of a search that one of our navy vessels performed in the Caribbean a little over month ago. They were looking for your guy, Collin Cook. Eyewitnesses said he had boarded a sailboat named *Admiral Risty*. Our crew tracked that boat down, boarded it, searched it, but did not find your man. Then again, two weeks ago, our vessels, in cooperation with the Coast Guard, were searching for him again after Hurricane Abigail and came up with nothing. So my group has been called into the hunt, only to come up empty-handed—twice. Plenty of reason for me to snoop around and get a few answers."

"Please don't get yourself into any trouble over this."

"I find the lack of interagency communication stunning and perplexing. There's been some needless spinning of wheels in the hunt for this Cook guy. I think we deserve some answers based on the resources that have been wasted, don't you? Plus, doesn't the FBI deserve to be brought in to a situation like this where you're pursuing a case and they have information about that case?"

"Seems logical to me, but—"

"That's my point. If it's logical, why isn't it being done? That's the whole purpose of the committee. I'll contact you when I know something."

"Thanks, Tom."

After ending the call, Reggie shot Spinner a curious look. Spinner was drumming his knee with one hand, and rolled his cell phone around in the other. "I don't know what to make of that, chief. This case just got more convoluted when I thought that wasn't even possible. The deputy director? That's a long way up from where we started."

"That's what makes me nervous."

"Let's find out what the Cook family knows and see if we can fill in a few more puzzle pieces," said Spinner.

chapter Thirteen

Collin tried to pull the nose up, just like he'd seen the bush pilot do in Colombia a few weeks earlier, while the plane was in the air. Sweat continued to stream down Collin's face and forehead. He was light-headed and dizzy to begin with; the impact only made it worse.

Miriam was rattling off instructions that he could barely comprehend, but he heard her say to push the throttle all the way in and press on the foot controls to brake and steer. He did as he was told, but the plane was not slowing fast enough. The boulder at the end was fast approaching.

The plane bounced hard a second time, causing the comatose pilot's body to pitch forward into the yolk on his side. Collin felt the increased pressure on his controls and fought to limit the effect, but it was too late. The sudden movement caused the plane's nose to point downward and its wings to pitch at an angle. The right wing hit the ground first, causing the plane to flip and spin in the air before it sheared off with a horrendous, metallic screech. He felt another shuddering crash. The roof smacked against the earth with a loud clap. The impact violently jolted his upside-down body against his shoulder-and-lap restraints. With his head dangling in midair, he looked out his side window and realized the plane was sliding sideways on its wings and roof toward the large boulder at the end of the landing strip.

Collin squeezed his eyes shut and prepared for the final impact, sensing that this might be the end for him. The plane stopped sharply. The pilot's side lifted into the air a few feet. All momentum stopped and the left side of the plane slammed back down to the ground.

Opening his eyes, Collin realized the barbed wire fence had arrested their slide just before impact with the big rock. He closed his eyes again and said, "Thank you, God."

He could hear the urgent voice of Miriam Hastings in his ears, pleading with him to share information. Collin first leaned over to the pilot and checked his pulse. Then he pressed the button on his headset wires, which dangled in front of his face, and said, "I'm OK. We're upside down and tangled in the fence, but we're alive."

Miriam gasped, held her breath as he spoke, then blew a sigh of relief through his earphones when he said he was OK. A tense and awkward laugh escaped her before she gathered her composure and congratulated him on his first landing.

"Thank God you survived," she said.

"I already did," said Collin dryly. His voice was strained, make weaker by his inverted position.

Lukas chimed in, too. "You gave us quite a scare, buddy. Are you hurt?"

Collin struggled to suck in a deep breath. He blinked hard to try to focus, then kept his eyes closed to fight back the nausea. Though he felt like he'd been through the rinse cycle in a washing machine, his sense of irony was still intact. "You should've been here to film it, Lukas. I'm sure it was a spectacular sight to see. Worthy of a *Jackass* episode, no doubt."

Lukas let go of a stymied half laugh, half sob that expelled the tension in the air. Miriam made another, similarly nervous sound and Collin knew it was a miracle he was alive.

Just to further break the tension, Collin added, "I'd like to try it again. I'm sure I can do better in the style department next time."

"We'll have to work on your technique before we let you get your license," she quipped. "But any landing you survive, I guess, can be considered a good landing."

"I'd suggest your next flight be in a simulator, for everyone's safety and well-being," said Lukas.

Collin chuckled a nervous, pained chuckle. "Roger that. But, seriously, thank you for your help, both of you."

The relief in Miriam's voice was palpable. "Don't thank me too much. I don't know if I want this to go on my resume."

"Don't worry, Miriam, I'll take the blame for this one, being a rookie and all."

"I have to admit, that was one of the most frightening experiences any pilot could have. For a first-time flier, you handled it as well as could be expected. Things could have turned out much worse."

"And for that, I am truly grateful. I'd better work on getting the real pilot taken care of, though."

Collin tried to focus his attention on the pilot suspended by his harness next to him. He pushed his head back against his seat and felt his face. It was pasty white and clammy. His breathing was fast and shallow and his pulse was galloping.

Becoming aware of movement and activity outside the plane, Collin wiped sweat from his face and peered through the cracked glass, A late model Ford pickup truck moving toward him. There were four gunmen in the back, two standing in a ready-to-fire position, and two sitting or kneeling along the side, scanning the perimeter of the airfield. They, too, looked ready to shoot.

The truck pulled up alongside the inverted airplane. Collin's view was both distorted and limited by his position. He watched closely as a door on the far side of the truck opened and a set of shiny black boots hit the ground. Three other pair of boots—all desert camouflage in color—landed, one after the other, from the back and side of the truck and began to approach cautiously.

After letting the headphones drop to the ceiling, Collin worked on getting his door open. Before he could get the door open, the barrel of a black handgun filled his vision. It was held by a man crouched next to the plane, wearing a flak jacket, black gloves, and a camouflage T-shirt. His black hair stood up in a fresh crew cut neatly styled with hair gel to make it appear like a prickly carpet. Without a word, the man motioned for Collin to stay still. Reluctantly, he moved his hands above his head, letting gravity hold them there. "I thought you guys were expecting us," he said, not moving.

"We have to verify your identity," the man said in a very military-style voice. It was more of a command than a statement.

"What do you need? I'm afraid my driver's license is in my checked luggage." Collin was trying to blunt the rising frustration. He wanted to cooperate and be civil, but he was hanging upside down and had a man dying next to him. It was one hundred degrees and he felt like he was baking from the inside out in a pressure steamer. He was in no mood to play games.

"Show me some ID"

"You're serious? What is this, some sort of traffic stop? Did I run a light?"

"Shut up, smart ass, and show me what you've got."

"I've got nothing on me. It's all packed in my bags in the back. I'm Collin Cook. Certainly someone in Washington radioed ahead to tell you we were coming and we have a medical emergency."

The man glared at him warily, squinting his eyes. "I don't care if you're the pope. Until we're satisfied that you're not hostile and not carrying a plane full of explosives, we're going to take appropriate measures to protect our own safety. Got it?"

There were bumps and bangs coming from the rear of the plane as compartment doors were opened and their contents pulled out.

"Yeah, sure."

While Collin and Flat Top were arguing over proper identification, the other two had opened the pilot's door and were disentangling him from the seat belt and shoulder harness, pulling wires out of the way, and preparing to pull him out of the cockpit. One of the men looked through the plane at Flat Top and said, "It's him. It's Mamba."

"Mamba?" Collin said, screwing up his face.

"That's his handle. We don't use real names around here."

"OK, but Mamba?"

"He's a Lakers' fan. Loves Kobe."

"Right, I get it. But Kobe Bryant's nickname is the Black

far too much situational knowledge about Collin Cook and the circumstances surrounding him." Lukas sighed and ran his fingers through his blonde hair. "I shouldn't have …" His voice trailed off, but he quickly regained focus and continued. "Again, this is high priority, so let's get to it."

* * * *

Highway 111, US-Mexico border south of El Centro, California
June 17, 12:13 p.m. Pacific Time

A blockade at the border caused a backup that slowed the specially-equipped minivan to a crawl in a line of cars waiting to enter Mexico. A blue handicapped placard dangled from the rearview mirror. US Border Patrol agents, two per lane, stopped and inspected each car before waving it through the checkpoint. The sumptuous Asian girl and her perfect face sat in the driver's seat, sporting her perfect bow-shaped smile and straight white teeth. Motorcycle dude sat in a bucket seat next to Rob's wheelchair in the back. Just for good measure, he stabbed Rob in the arm with a syringe as they inched toward the front of the line.

Rob saw the movement and understood what the boyfriend was doing, but felt nothing. Inside, he was hollow and numb. His limbs, like dead weights, wouldn't move, no matter how much energy he exerted. He wanted to crash the edge of his hand into the guy's larynx as hard as he could, then jump out the side door, and run to the guard station. But his arms ignored his brain's requests and sat motionless in his lap while his feet remained stationary on the footplates of the wheelchair. There was no way he could speak, even before the additional dosage, because the drugs had already filled his mouth with a wad of cotton balls covered in peanut butter, or so it seemed. Only grunts emerged when he tried to yell, and preventing the grunts was probably the reason for another shot. The Asian pair didn't want him to draw any attention to himself.

The two spoke some words back and forth that Rob didn't understand. If he had to guess, he'd say the motorcycle dude was telling the pretty girl to stay calm and act like everything was OK. He was sure they had a script and were rehearsing it. Either way, they didn't seem particularly worked up or nervous. Her warm brown eyes exuded confidence and cool as she glanced back at him through the mirror and flashed that seductive smile. Motorcycle dude was cockier. He sneered at Rob as he made some unintelligible remark.

The driver's window rolled down and the pretty girl played her part beautifully. She spoke in respectful, gracious tones and smiled abundantly. Probably melted the guard's heart, like she had Rob's. She handed him a stack of passports and explained that they were on their way to inspect a factory her father was interested in purchasing. The guard stood up straight so Rob could only see his hands flip through the documents. He then put his face back into the frame of the window. "Ma'am, mind if I take a look in the back?"

"Not at all," she replied cheerfully.

The side window rolled down and the guard stuck his face in and peered at Rob in the wheelchair, then at the younger man in the seat next to him. His hands opened the passports again. He seemed to be studying something, probably the photos. Rob wanted so badly to get his attention, but he couldn't move. No sounds came out when he tried to scream. The only thing he managed was to rock his body to the side so that he slumped at an angle. The strap across his chest, hidden from view under his coat, prevented him from pitching himself forward in an effort to create a scene. The guard must have caught the movement, as did the motorcycle dude, who made a sickly sweet "uh-oh" sound as he gently straightened Rob in his chair.

The guard took a second look. Motorcycle dude waved him off like everything was fine now. The guard seemed to accept the gesture and slapped the passports shut and took a step back toward the driver's window, returning the passports to the pretty Asian lady. "Thank you, ma'am. That'll be all," he said as he waved her through the barricade.

As the minivan picked up speed, motorcycle dude unleashed a brutal cross to Rob's cheek. Rob barely felt it, but realized the inside of the car was spinning just before everything turned dark and fuzzy.

* * * *

Kuala Lumpur, Malaysia
June 18, 3:27 a.m. Local Time; June 17, 12:27 p.m. Pacific Time

From the back seat of his limousine, Pho Nam Penh barked at his driver to hurry up, despite the fact that they were traveling over 135 kilometers per hour down a stretch of open freeway. His Mercedes S-Class glided so gracefully and noiselessly that he had not noticed their speed until the driver informed him. Penh sat back and drew in a deep breath as he looked out the windows at the dark emptiness that enveloped the burgeoning city as lighted buildings whizzed past. He checked his watch. He tapped his foot. It was still not fast enough. Penh would have preferred to travel the short distance to his waiting plane by air. If only he had a helicopter.

That thought brought a shark-like grin to his face. Soon would be the day.

Penh's grand master plan was nearing completion. With his team of hackers from around the globe gathering in Mexico City, poised for their attack on the world's largest, most corrupt financial institutions and their top executives, Phase II was well underway. A few more manipulations of global currencies, combined with another series of precisely-timed hack-attacks on the exchanges, which would likely be followed closely by a prepared press release from the Chinese Minister of Commerce suspending all credit to foreign banks and calling in all loans due to their cash shortfall, and mass panic would ensue. It was only a matter of time before their ultimate goal was accomplished.

Once the clamoring started, it would be nearly impossible to stop. And with the right people, each with his hand–selected skill set in place in Mexico City, a coup there would add momentum to the collapse of the United States. One of the first moves of the new Mexican regime would be to stop trading their oil via the US dollar and move, instead, to the new currency China, Russia, and several OPEC nations had proposed. Moving oil trading away from the US dollar would cause the dollar's value to plummet even further and, consequently, compound the staggering foreign debts of the US government, preventing them from being able to print enough money to bail themselves out of this one.

The only thing they needed now to light the fuse for this devious chain of events was a fresh infusion of cash to pay his cohorts in crime. And Penh knew exactly where to go to get it. By getting back the $30 Million that was his, he would accomplish two goals with one stroke: put the down payment on the services to be rendered by the Mexican military and reverse the disgraces heaped upon him by Collin Cook. Once this transaction was finalized, Penh's end of the bargain would be complete, and the fall of Western capitalism would commence.

But first things had to come first. Embarrassment and shame must precede the calamities which were to follow. To start things off, Penh and his syndicate had already begun to unveil via online leaks a trove of stolen emails from the accounts of senior officers in some of the most respected banks, corporations, and government agencies in the United States. They would continue to be leaked in succession and would clearly outline the backhanded, secret deals that had been cut at the expense of investor returns and corporate profits. Soon, the whole world would have proof of how the executives had lined their pockets and hidden their vast fortunes.

Thousands of documents and several hundred recorded

conversations were making their way to cyberspace. News agencies, social media hawks, and political bloggers of every stripe were starting to pounce. Investors would react. Self-proclaimed experts had already begun to clamor for airtime to say, essentially, "I warned you." All the while, politicians would sling mud and insults aimed at discrediting the information, the sources, and the veracity of these scandalous-yet-true revelations, knowing full-well their cozy relationships and legislative influence aided these monsters. Indeed, many politicians, like the business executives they coddled and clung to, had much to lose. More than just the millions they garnered over the years of influence-peddling, their reputations and their very futures were beginning to crumble under the weight of this heretofore buried information, which Penh and his hackers were bringing to light—today. Yes, it would be a glorious day for truth and justice. It would be a horrible day for the greedy, pompous, and corrupt Westerners.

These stirring machinations increased Penh's heartrate and breathing. A wry grin spread across his tightly creased lips. He tilted his head up, pulled in a deep breath, and savored the moment.

Penh's satisfaction, however, was interrupted when the car began to slow. They were exiting the highway near the Sepang Circuit, the international raceway, using the side streets to get to the airport's private entrance where Penh's jet sat waiting.

His phone rang as the car pulled past the security gate. Penh answered, then listened with rapt attention, nodding his head periodically. The grin left momentarily, but returned as the man on the other end concluded his narrative. "All the pieces are in place, then? I will be there in approximately twenty-four hours. Schedule the meeting."

Penh listened for a moment, then added, "Assure the aides to the good senators of Mexico that their cooperation will be rewarded and their bosses will be the new conquistadores of the world after the United States implodes. Mexico will be redeemed, as will every other nation that has lived out their existence as subservient dwarves to the corrupt economic superpower for generations." Penh's voice exuded the supreme calm and confidence of a man who held all the cards in a high-stakes poker game. His royal flush was about to open the flood gates of opportunity for the oppressed of the world.

He listened again. "The power void is for them to figure out. I'm not concerned. Your interests will be covered—generously, I'm sure—when the dust settles and a true new world order takes shape."

The elegant black Mercedes rolled to a stop next to the private air strip on the far end of the airport, where all the high-powered business executives and government officials boarded their private jets. Penh had, with his fortunes and promises, secured himself a privileged place among the elites of the region.

He smiled broadly at the sight of the Gulfstream 650 that awaited his arrival. It was a beautiful jet and a symbol of his power and elevated profile. Soon enough, he thought, it would be upgraded. Lights flashed, windows glowed, and an entourage of support staff stood at attention at the bottom of the open stairway. A food service truck pulled away as the Mercedes approached.

Within minutes of Penh's arrival, the plane was in the air and on its way to Mexico City.

* * * *

Villahermosa, Mexico
June 17, 2:30 p.m. Local Time; 12:30 p.m. Pacific Time

With the pilot responding well to treatments and Collin's head beginning to feel normal again after rehydrating and taking a cool shower, Collin began to think through the events of the past twenty-four hours. It had been an eventful day, as they all had lately. Something in the back of his mind was banging around, begging for attention. What was it? Something forgotten. A nugget of usefulness that he tucked away in his mind and meant to remember later. But what was it? There was this something and it had gotten pushed to the background in the expediency of the moment—whichever urgent moment it was. He retraced his memories, his emotions, his reactions. Nothing jumped out at first, but that banging continued, like a kidnapee in the closet of some dark basement in one of those TV cop shows.

Collin remembered starting a conversation with Lukas while he was in the plane, on the first leg of the day's journey. It was early in the morning, and he was tired and cranky. That much he remembered clearly. His emotions were all tangled as he prepared to leave the hut on the beach—still were—being riddled with guilt and angst over the violence he had perpetrated on those who wanted to kill him. He started to confess to Lukas about killing Stinky and harpooning that diver, but Lukas had brushed him off. There was something else that lingered in his mind, something he felt like Lukas needed to know.

Then it hit him. As he paced the floor of the underground safe house, something in his pocket triggered a sensory stimulus and the light switched on. The weight of Stinky's satellite phone tapping against his thigh as the pockets of his cargo shorts swung with each step reminded him. He pulled out the yellow-and-black device and the sight of it rekindled those anxious moments in the boat when Penh breathed out his ominous threats against his mom and Emily through that very phone. He remembered the helplessness and anguish he felt knowing they were under the control of Penh's goons, sequestered in a dingy, abandoned warehouse in the middle of nowhere. Collin also recalled bumping into Stinky's bloated body in the submerged wreckage of the *Admiral Risty*, then pulling it back so he could fish the phone from the corpse's trousers. Reliving the scene brought back the squishy sensation of the grayish and plump flesh, causing him to fight back a wave of nausea.

The phone, Collin had surmised, could help them locate Penh.

He had to get a hold of Lukas and remind him of this salient fact.

Lukas sounded out of breath when he answered, but jumped right into the meat of the conversation. "I'm so glad you're safe, buddy. I thought Miriam was pretty amazing, but I think you're an absolute champ for landing a shot-up plane while you were fighting heat exhaustion and a sick pilot on your first ever solo flight. Amazing, man. Just amazing."

"It didn't feel so amazing at the time, I'll tell you that. It hurt—a lot."

"Probably something like your waterskiing crashes back in the day, if I'm picturing it right," Lukas quipped.

Collin shook his head and realized how good it was to have a friend on the other end of the phone, bringing him back to ground, keeping him attached to who he was. At the same time, it seemed strange to him that he had been on the ground for almost an hour, yet this was his first conversation with Lukas. "Thanks for that. And thanks for getting Miriam to help me out. I couldn't have done it alone. That was clutch."

"You've had a pretty wild ride lately. I wish I could offer you a long, relaxing vacation, but—"

"Hold that thought, Lukas. I have to share something with you before I forget. I think it's pertinent and I don't want to let it slip my mind again."

"OK, what've you got?"

"Remember how I started to tell you about the phone I pulled off the dead guy? You remember, that one in the boat? Penh's main guy there?"

"Yeah, I remember."

"Well, don't you want to pull whatever information you and your brainiac crew can from this thing? I mean, I've got it right here."

"Definitely. I couldn't have done much with it while you were in the air, but now that you're on the ground, we can certainly process whatever information is on it. Take it to the head IT guy there, he

Richard could pull his hand back, McCoy snatched the phone away. "And who is Rob?"

"Rob is a friend," Richard stammered, glancing at his parents for approval. They both frowned, but didn't say anything.

"I see. Who would like to tell us more about this 'friend' and why Richard has his cell phone?" asked Reggie, his eyes darting from person to person as he scanned the room.

Finally, Emily cleared her throat and responded. She knew the FBI agents would find out one way or another, so it would be most beneficial to not withhold information. "Rob Howell is Collin's best friend. They are very close—always have been. Rob and I have been friends ever since I met Collin our sophomore year of high school. When Rob found out that Collin was missing at sea, he came home to comfort the Cook's and me, knowing it would be hard on us. I expected him to be here this morning. We were supposed to talk. But he never showed up and never answered his phone, so Richard went up to the house in Huntington Beach to see what was going on since Rob was going to pick up the mail this morning before he came here to visit us."

"Thank you, Ms. Burns. If I remember correctly, this is the same friend who showed up shortly after Collin's disappearance and dealt with the media as the family spokesman, am I right?" asked Reggie, looking at Sarah and Henry.

"Yes, that's right. He was wonderful," said Sarah. "He took all the pressure off us and did such a nice job of helping us get more support from the community."

Looking back at Emily, Reggie continued his questioning. "And how long has he been in town?"

"A few days, I guess. All I know is that he said he had come by my office the day I was … I was …"

"Abducted?" interjected Reggie, with a delicate inflection.

"Yes. He said he came by to take me to lunch that day, but I didn't even know he was in town, let alone that he wanted to have lunch together. He said he feels terrible about it because if he had shown up ten minutes earlier, none of this would have happened." Emily stopped cold, looked at Sarah. "I'm sorry, that was selfish and insensitive of me, Sarah. All I know is that he was here, at the hospital, when I woke up and has been a huge comfort to me and a huge help to the whole family."

Richard stepped forward and added, "Yes, he was the one who picked me and my sister up at the airport and brought us here to see our parents. He also looked in on my dad when he was at the hospital in Huntington Beach. Rob is the one that informed us of what was going on and coordinated our travel schedules and pick-ups. He has been a God-send."

"And where does Mr. Howell reside?"

"He has an apartment in Los Angeles and, I believe, another one in New York," said Sarah. "But he travels all over the place. He's always gone. London, Sydney, Tokyo. He goes everywhere. He's hardly ever at home."

"And what does he do for work?"

"He's a venture capitalist," said Henry. "He's helped many start-ups hit it big and, in the process, has become quiet wealthy himself."

"I see," said Reggie. "So, he's been instrumental during all of these family crises. Does this strike anyone else as odd?" Reggie surveyed the room. "Mr. Cook, were you aware that Mr. Howell was in town prior to his showing up here at the hospital?"

Sarah squeezed Henry's hand and answered for him. "Rob made contact with us prior to when Emily and I were taken. It was shortly after Hurricane Abigail, when no one was certain whether Collin had survived. I never believed he was dead, but my faith was confirmed when Rob showed up and told us that he knew for certain that Collin was alive."

"How did he know, Mrs. Cook?"

"Like Emily said, those two are very close."

"So, Collin called Mr. Howell on the phone after the hurricane and told him he was alive?"

"I suppose so, though I never asked," explained Sarah, who suddenly seemed flustered and unsure of herself. "He just said that he knew Collin was alive and would be OK, eventually."

"Mr. Cook, do you have anything to add?" asked Reggie.

"Only that Rob asked us not to tell anyone of his involvement. The only reason I tell you now is that I fear he may be in danger. After what has happened here lately with all of us, I believe anything is possible. These people will stop at nothing to get what they want."

"So why was Mr. Howell here?"

"Like Emily said, he's practically a member of our family, has been since his father abandoned him, his sister, and his mother. They lived just three doors down. Rob and Collin were thick as thieves, as they say. I think Rob may have slept at our house as much or more than he slept at his own during those growing-up years. So, to answer your question, he came to support the family in a time of need."

"OK, if that's true, which one of you alerted Rob that Collin was in danger?" said McCoy.

No one answered.

"How did he know if no one told him?"

Again, no one said anything.

"It just looks strange to us as outsiders, maybe not to you because you know him. But why is it weird things happen to this family only when this Rob Howell is around?" McCoy let that sink in for a few seconds, then added, "You also know, don't you, that since this is an active investigation and since you all knew it was an active investigation since our first meeting back in what—November?—you could be arrested for obstruction of justice for failing to share relevant information about this active investigation with the proper authorities?"

* * * *

Villahermosa, Mexico
June 17, 3:20 p.m. Local Time; 1:20 p.m. Pacific Time

Mongoose had taken the device from Collin and rolled it over in his hands several times. He, like the others stationed at this safehouse, was of Mexican-American descent. He had short black hair, tan skin, and desert camo fatigues. After rummaging through a drawer, he found a power cord and a connector. "This is the good stuff," he explained. "Top of the line. Incredible range. Massive battery capability. And supposedly waterproof. I guess we'll see, won't we?" Mongoose plugged in the cord and connector and attached it to a PC. "How long did you say it was underwater?"

"I don't know, several hours. The ship went down in the early evening and I went back around midnight the following night."

"So over twenty-four hours?"

"Yeah, something like that."

"And how deep were you when you found it?"

"About a hundred feet," Collin said.

"Wow. This will be interesting. Even with this high-tech waterproof casing, I have my doubts about the integrity of the components inside. That's a lot of time and a lot of pressure."

"Had I been thinking more clearly while I was trying to escape with my life ..." Collin started to say, then realized the sarcasm may not play as well to someone who didn't know him.

"Let me run some analysis on the storage drive. Then we'll be able to see if there's any way to salvage the data on it." Mongoose's hands never stopped. If they weren't checking the cables and connections, they were drumming the desk or tapping on the keyboard or clicking the mouse. He was a bundle of kinetic energy. He talked fast, too.

That was forty-five minutes earlier.

Collin looked on in curiosity for the first few minutes. Rows of numbers began scrolling across the screen. Then a few blank lines, then more digits and letters rolled past. Mongoose typed a command of some kind when the cursor appeared and blinked at him. Then the progression restarted.

Collin's eyes grew heavy and he struggled to keep them open.

"Why don't you go lay down, man?" said Mongoose, pointing to a couch on the other side of the narrow room. "You look like you could use some sleep. I'll wake you up when I'm done with this."

At last, a line at the top of the screen read: system scan completed. 5223 files scanned. 4357 files damaged or inaccessible. It was accompanied by a loud beep.

The beep woke Collin with a start. He popped up to a sitting position and rubbed his eyes as he stood and moved closer to the computer.

Mongoose sat back and groaned. His fingers twitched above the keyboard, like they were dancing in air. He typed in another command at lightning speed and pounded on the enter key.

The monitor changed to a colored pie chart. The big red section took up most of the pie and was labeled "irreparable." The next biggest section was a narrow blue wedge. Its label indicated "readable." The smallest area on the chart, a tiny sliver in comparison to the huge red section, was green and said "accessible."

Another sigh emanated from the baby-faced IT guru. "Let's give it a whirl, shall we?"

He clicked the mouse and typed some more commands and the screen returned to black with line after line of small white text racing from top to bottom. Or was it bottom to top? Collin couldn't tell it was moving so fast.

"Ah-hah," said Mongoose when the scrolling stopped again. Another typed command yielded a white screen with boxes and text in black. "Looks like we have a call log, a text log, and a few IP addresses."

"Are those time stamps there next to the called numbers?" asked Collin, reaching in and pointing at a box.

"Indeed, they are," said Mongoose with an air of approval. "You're as sharp as they said."

Collin ignored the compliment and focused on the information in front of him. "Will you be able to trace those addresses and translate the text into English?"

"Should be able to do that better from HQ. That's why I'm going to do as your friend requested and upload all this information to his FTP site and let him and his team analyze to their heart's content. Meanwhile, I've got to prep my men for their mission." Mongoose stood and moved to a wire shelving unit on the wall behind him. He began sorting out small pieces of equipment that appeared to be bodywear cameras and microphones. There were also earpieces, handheld devices, and monitors that looked like they would be strapped onto the forearm. "You'd better go get yourself prepared, too. My understanding is that you guys ship out of here at eighteen hundred hours."

"Wait, what? Shipping out? Tonight? First I've heard of it," Collin stuttered.

"Yeah, you didn't expect to fly out of here in that plane, did you?" Mongoose chuckled at the thought. "It'll take too long to get another one in here and loaded up. You're heading out with four of our operatives in a truck right after chow."

"In a truck? How long will that take?"

"It's a long day's drive to Mexico City—maybe ten or twelve hours—but it'd take a lot longer, like I said, to wait for another plane that could carry all of you and the gear you'll need."

"Do you know what the plan is? Cause I certainly don't," Collin said, shaking his head.

"You'll have to talk to your friend in Washington. He's the one calling the shots. Kind of surprised he hasn't brought you up to speed."

chapter Sixteen

Lukas slammed his cane crossways on top of the desk in front of him. They missed him. An hour and a half into it and there was still no sign of Rob Howell. Either the blockade was set up too late or the searches were not thorough enough. In any case, Lukas was out of luck and Rob was certainly now in dangerous territory, location and exact destination unknown. One thing he did know, Mexico City was the focal point of a massive amount of communication and information flow on the dark net over the past several days. All indications were that Penh would show up sooner rather than later and that Rob would play a role in his plans. Lukas planned to use the data from the satellite phone Collin had taken to track Penh's whereabouts, but he figured Rob and Penh would end up in the same place very soon. He also knew Collin would, too. He had to.

Useful information from Lukas's cohorts in Mexico had been hard to come by until recently. When it did show up, it was usually late and sketchy. The working relationship between the intelligence communities of Mexico and the US were currently more strained than usual, due to a number of factors. Among them were an increase in savage violence on both sides of the border by the Mexican drug cartels, a breakdown in diplomatic relations, and, coinciding with the arrival of several of Penh's associates in Mexico City, rumors had begun circulating of a plot by the American clandestine network to assassinate the president of Mexico. Lukas's counterparts in Mexico had become wary and, at times, hostile thanks to the rising suspicions of US intentions regarding their neighbors to the south.

The overall situation made Lukas's blood boil. His two dearest friends in the world were now within the borders of the same country and he would have virtually no way to track, monitor, or surveille the movements of those who had taken Rob into Mexico without a level of collaboration between the two countries inconceivable just a month earlier. Lukas would have felt completely hopeless were it not for the small handful of cooperative cohorts with whom he had fostered healthy working relationships over the past several weeks. As a result of the voluminous data he had presented regarding Pho Nam Penh and his diabolical schemes, a new level of trust and cooperation was beginning to emerge, at least among this handful of open-minded individuals within Mexico's Center for Research and National Security.

Kevin interrupted his brooding. "Sir, I think you'll want to look at this."

Lukas sat forward, snatched up his cane, and pushed himself to a standing position, managing to hide the discomfort by keeping every muscle in his face frozen in the same look of consternation that had been there while he sat ruminating. Kevin displayed his findings on one of the large flat screens at the front of the room. It was a split screen with a face on each side. The one on the left was a portrait of Rob Howell—a picture Lukas had taken of him just before Lukas helped Collin disappear seven months earlier. It had a series of green cones and white lines with tiny numbers next to them at various points on Rob's face. The one on the right was much darker and grainier. It showed an older Asian gentleman leaning to the side. His face, too, was punctuated by the same maze of green and white. But they were flashing, indicating a match.

"Can you enhance the picture on the right?" Lukas asked.

"This is as enhanced as I can get it. The lighting is dim and subject is obscured enough by the passenger sitting next to him to make it difficult to get a clear view. But the software picks up the key biometrics and compares them, as you know. This man, though Asian in appearance, shares the same measurements along the key indicators as your friend, which leads me to believe his captors did a great makeup job on him to smuggle him into Mexico. You can alter appearances, but you can't change the distance between the eyes or from the eyes to the ears. This facial map is as close as you can get without an exact match. It simply shows us that they applied some makeup, but made no attempt to alter the key biometrics."

"Clever. Very, very clever. Not unexpected, I guess," Lukas said, pointing a finger at the screen. "We have a description on the vehicle he's in?"

"Yes, sir, we do. A handicap-accessible minivan. Blue Dodge. California plates."

"Can we run a trace?"

"The Mexican authorities are working on it, sir. But you know how it is with them right now."

"Unfortunately, I do," said Lukas, scratching his chin. "Are we able to hack their CCTV feeds?"

"Perhaps. I mean, we've done it before, but it's not undetectable. At some point, they're going to figure out what we did and will spike our efforts."

"I'm sure you're right. Let me make a couple calls to my contacts down there and see if I can get their help, but if they don't cooperate within the next hour, I may need you to hack in."

"That's a huge risk, sir," Kevin said.

"I know, but we can mend fences later. For now, we can't give Penh a free pass. This is about more than just my friends. This is about protecting our country and theirs from Penh's massive cyberattack aimed at crippling the entire banking system. The ripple effects would be global and catastrophic. If we blow it now, the world could be plunged into an economic depression that would make what happened in the thirties look like a birthday party."

* * * *

Oceanside, California
June 17, 2:39 p.m. Pacific Time

Reggie and Spinner were just finishing lunch at a quaint pub off the main drag in the beach town of Oceanside when Reggie's phone began buzzing on the table. He wiped his mouth and answered. "Tom?"

"Reggie," came Tom's gravelly voice between halting breaths and the rush of wind against the phone's mic. Reggie guessed he was walking outside.

"Have you got something for me?"

"Listen, Reggie. I've got to be quick here. I'm on my way into an urgent meeting to discuss your case. I can't believe it. First time I've heard of this guy Penh and your friend Cook was from you three hours ago. I ask a few questions and now I'm invited to high-level powwows to go over strategy. Unbelievable."

"That's a major shift in focus," Reggie said, trying to wrap his head around Tom's rapid-fire download.

"Your friends over at NSA ordered a blockade at the Mexican border, south of El Centro. The guy they're looking for wasn't found, so they're running all the images from the border patrol officers' body cams against facial recognition software."

"What'd they find? Anything?"

"Yeah, they found the guy they're looking for all dressed up like an Asian businessman being snuck over the border a couple hours ago."

"Hmm," said Reggie. "Sounds interesting, but what has this got to do with Collin Cook and Pho Nam Penh?"

"The guy who got smuggled into Mexico, the guy they were searching for, is Collin Cook's best friend."

"Rob Howell?"

"Yeah, how'd you know his name?"

"We just interrogated the family and girlfriend and learned that this guy Howell has been MIA since early this morning. They were worried, but hadn't bothered to tell us about him."

"Well, this guy Howell is now right in the middle of this whole brouhaha," muttered Tom.

"My partner and I figure he's being used as bait to draw Collin Cook into a trap."

"That's my guess, too, Reggie. Not sure what to do about it, but I'll let you know what I find out in this meeting."

"I hear you, Tom. Thanks for your—" Reggie said to a dial tone. Tom was already gone. Reggie sat staring at his phone for a moment, shaking his head.

Spinner shot him a curious look. "That sounded promising."

"Well, yeah, I guess you could say that. Tom is on his way to a 'high-level meeting' to talk about our boy Collin," said Reggie, using his fingers to make air quotes.

"So I guess the question now is what are we going to do about it?"

"What can we do? We don't have jurisdiction in Mexico. It's out of our hands," said Reggie, staring at something in the middle of the table, lost in thought.

"Is that what you want to tell Sarah Cook? 'It's out of our hands'?"

"Definitely not, but I'm not sure what we can do at this point. That's a different country and we have no authority beyond our borders."

Spinner locked Reggie in his gaze with a raised eyebrow. "Are you sure?"

* * * *

Scripps Cancer Research Patient Clinic, La Jolla, California
June 17, 4:10 p.m. Pacific Time

The Cook family had all departed for Emily's condo after reviewing and discussing what they had heard from Agents Crabtree and McCoy, leaving Sarah and Emily alone in their room to rest.

Sarah had closed her eyes and was settling in for an afternoon nap. She knew Dr. Navarro would be in to visit later to start planning her next round of cancer treatments.

Emily sat in the recliner near the window with her tablet and pondered the events of the day. A few searches on various government websites had yielded no new information about the hunt for Collin or about his connection with the Asian crime syndicate. She sat staring at the screen with glazed-over eyes when her phone interrupted her thoughts. The caller ID showed, "Unknown Caller." She hesitated as she held the phone up and studied the screen.

After the third ring, Sarah's groggy voice said, "Aren't you going to answer it, dear? Could be one of the FBI agents with an update on Rob."

Emily shrugged. It made sense. "Hello," she answered as she tapped the speaker button.

"Ms. Burns. What a pleasure to hear your voice. Our last meeting ended rather abruptly, don't you think?" The voice was smooth, with a proper British accent. Smug and arrogant, Emily knew she had heard it before, recently, but was having trouble placing it. When she didn't say anything, the voice continued. "Surely you remember me. Our common friend, Mr. Cook, brought us together. And now, we have another common friend. Mr. Howell, would you care to say a few words to Ms. Burns?"

That's when it clicked. The Asian man on the phone when she and Sarah were tied up in the abandoned warehouse. He was the one that ordered her and Sarah to be kidnapped and gave the two monsters permission to have their way. He had used her and Sarah to exert pressure on Collin to give up the codes for his hidden accounts, then left them as rewards for his dogs. As the memory flooded back to her consciousness, Emily felt faint and put a hand to her head. "Oh my—"

"Hey, Em. Don't worry about me. I'll be fine. Everything's under—" The connection was not good. Static and clicking made it difficult to decipher, but she was quite sure who it was.

Rob's voice cut out and was replaced by the smooth British one.

The level of background noise and interference disappeared, too. Emily guessed it was a conference call that had been ended. "Your brave friend may be fine now, but if you want to see him in one piece again, I suggest you cooperate and comply with my demands."

Sarah sat up in the bed across the room, a look of worry and dread spreading across her face.

Emily waited for her world to stop spinning, then replied. Rattled and angered by the unexpected threat, Emily's thoughts and words took off in a torrent. "What demands are you talking about? What is it you think *I* can do? You really think I can do much from this hospital room? Surely you know where I am. You're smart enough to know that I don't have the power to comply with any demand."

"Oh, now, Ms. Burns. Please try not to sound so hopeless and pathetic. I know the FBI and the NSA will help you in that regard, as they have done previously. Am I correct?" Penh waited a few beats, then carried on with his line of reasoning. "The problem is, if you don't follow my instructions exactly, Mr. Howell will lose a finger. One finger for every misstep or delay. If that doesn't work, we'll try something more drastic." Images of the goons who had tied her down flashed in her mind, sending a chill up her spine. She knew he was serious.

"Don't hurt him," Emily begged, barely able to keep her tattered emotions in check. "He's not part of this. He has nothing you need."

"Oh, but you are so misinformed. You know better than to say something so patently untrue. He has more knowledge than you do about our common friend, Mr. Cook, if you still consider him a friend after all he has put you through since your little get-together," Penh sneered, reminding her that it was Collin who got her involved when he showed up to her convention speech in Chicago just a few weeks earlier. "What kind of friend shares secrets, then runs and hides?"

"I told you already. He didn't share any secrets with me. I don't know anything about what he's involved in. I only know that Collin is afraid of something terrible—I assume that must be you—and is running to keep away from you. The only thing he said to me was, 'The less you know, the better.'"

"That may very well be, but nonetheless, he visited you and spoke with you. How am I to know what information he did or did not share with you at the time? Perhaps he slipped you a piece of paper or thumb drive without you knowing? You may be in possession of the very information I am looking for and not even know it. In any case, our dear boy, Collin, has thereby unwittingly brought you into this little game of cat and mouse. Either he will pay the price for his treachery, or his friends will."

Emily, struggling to keep her brain engaged so that her emotions would not run her aground, tried to think like a trained scientist instead of crying inside like a frightened victim of strong-armed coercion. *Examine the facts objectively and independently. Don't show weakness. Don't let him win.*

The mention of a thumb drive or piece of paper being slipped to her without her knowledge gave her pause, further shaking her confidence. In Chicago, Collin had managed to plant a cheap cell phone with prepaid minutes in her handbag unbeknownst to her and had used it several times since to communicate with her. Knowing that his mother was sick, Collin wanted information from Emily about his mother's condition, but shared nothing with her about what he was doing or where he was. He only told her that he was safe and healthy and asked her to pass the messages along to his mom. She was merely a conduit between Collin and his family. But she had not heard anything from him since that hurricane two weeks earlier.

By the simple fact that Rob had shown up when he did, Emily knew he had been much more involved with Collin's disappearance and subsequent life on the run than she had. The FBI had figured that out, too. This sudden revelation whirled through Emily's thought processes and knocked her back. Rob was more likely to have the information Penh wanted than she was, but knowing him, he would die before betraying Collin. Penh was using Rob to pressure Emily into talking. *He must be desperate*, she thought. She had to pretend to know something valuable. She had to bluff and do it now or Rob would be harmed and she would be to blame. She had to do something to stall and buy herself some time.

"Fine," she said. "I might have something, but you have to promise Rob will be safe."

"Now we're getting somewhere," Penh said with the aplomb of a man holding all the cards. "What is it?"

"A phone."

"A phone? Why would that be of any use to me, Ms. Burns?"

"Because it has texts on it from Collin. Some of them seemed pretty cryptic to me, but maybe you can decipher the code. Plus, with its GPS, I'm sure you can track him. Or even talk to him."

"Now we're getting somewhere. Give me the number to that phone."

Emily rattled off the number to Collin's secret phone from memory.

"Now, please make contact with your boyfriend and remind him that he owes me thirty million dollars, and while he's at it, I need his computer."

"Why would you need his computer?"

"Because he had information about me and about my money hidden in its memory."

"I have tried to reach him for days now, but he doesn't answer his phone. What am I supposed to do?" A mix of desperation and irritation constricted her larynx, adding strain to her tone.

"For Mr. Howell's sake, I hope his accomplices at the NSA and FBI do not try to interfere. If I were you, I would warn him," Penh said with a diabolic snigger.

"What are you talking about?"

"I am quite aware of the help he is getting from deep inside your government."

Emily tried to take in that information and process it as quickly as she could. The FBI? In on it? That didn't make sense. Did he also say NSA? That was a piece of breaking news. Shaking her head, Emily tried to inventory everything she knew. The FBI had just come and confiscated Rob's phone and interrogated the whole family. They had also taken the secret phone from Emily and cloned it before returning it to her. If they were helping Collin, they had a funny way of showing it. Seemed they were hunting more than helping.

Her attention snapped back when Penh cleared his throat. She had to rally herself to not get intimidated by his aristocratic accent or his dominating style. "The FBI thinks he's dead," she stated bluntly, looking back at the iPad on her lap.

"According to their website, perhaps, but I have it on good authority that agents of your government are in regular communication with Mr. Cook and are helping him return to the States, presumably to reunite with you and his dear mother."

"Why would he do that? He knows you're after him. He thinks the FBI want to arrest him. He knows he can't cross the border." She paused, still processing. "No, I don't believe you."

"Because I have video confirmation that he landed in a small plane in Belize just a few hours ago. That video was taken just minutes before runway cameras were turned off and all personnel removed from the area by the request of the NSA. He flew in and out in near-total secrecy, proving your government is aiding him."

"That doesn't mean he's coming here. Belize is a long way from California," Emily said, trying not to sound surprised or defensive. "Again, I doubt he would risk it. You're just probing."

"I am not probing. I am drawing a reasonable conclusion based on verified information and his pattern of rash behavior. He's alone and afraid. He's going to ground, despite the risks to you and his family, because that's the kind of person he is."

"I think you underestimate him, his resourcefulness, and his determination."

"Perhaps you overestimate his character. He's running scared, and for good reason. He's got some dirty secrets he's trying to hide from you and the world."

"He's not scared and he's got no dirty secrets to hide. You don't know him. You can't say that."

"Has he told you about the two people he killed?"

Emily gasped, as did Sarah from across the room.

"No?" said Penh. "Then, perhaps, you are the one who doesn't know him. Yes, he has killed two men and now is plotting to assassinate the president of Mexico."

chapter Seventeen

Tom's return call was not unexpected, just a bit tardy. Reggie and Spinner were enjoying another slow-roll through Orange County, this time, going northbound on the 405 Freeway through Long Beach. Reggie answered it on the first ring. "I hope you have some good news for me, Tom."

"Depends on your definition of good news, I guess," said Tom. His scratchy voice proceeding more slowly than usual. "From my perspective, much of what just happened is good news. More cooperation and information sharing between agencies on a case that has gone from obscure to high-profile in one day is a good thing when you sit in my chair, mostly. I only wish we had had this level of teamwork from the onset. It would have been much more productive, in my opinion. From your perspective, I'd imagine not much of what I'm going to tell you is going to sound like good news. The guy you've been after, Collin Cook, is, indeed, receiving aid from the NSA. At first, the aid was simply to get him out of harm's way. Then, when this Pho Nam Penh character upped the ante and posted pictures of himself with Cook, you guys were brought in. It appears that Penh was using the FBI to locate and flush Cook out of hiding, thus saving himself the valuable resources involved in such a manhunt."

"You're right," agreed Reggie. "That's not very good news for us."

"Anyway, the NSA team chose to remain silent for his safety. They figured they could get to him and hide him again, no problem. But Cook made a couple of mistakes and Penh latched on like a pit bull. Now, he seems hell-bent on destroying Cook, but not before he recovers his thirty-million-dollar settlement."

"OK. We're with you, Tom. Sounds like Cook's in trouble and

they need our help."

"Not exactly. Not the way they described it. According to the deputy director, there's a short window where Penh will be most vulnerable and they want to exploit it. They're trying to get their resources poised and in position while keeping Cook safe."

"I assume they know about Rob Howell."

"Yeah, they know about him. He's going to be a complicating factor because they have not been able to locate the vehicle that took him across the border, which means they've probably switched vehicles again. They don't know yet where Penh will take him, so they can't make final plans."

"What are the Mexican authorities doing about this? Shouldn't they be involved?" asked Spinner.

"That's a good question," said Tom. "Normally, I'd say they would be involved. The problem is, Penh's web has now spread to include certain factions within the Mexican government. They've got a group of very powerful political, business, and military leaders involved, working in secret to overthrow the current administration."

"That doesn't sound like good news at all," said Reggie, shaking his head as he drove. Traffic north of Long Beach Airport had thinned out and they were moving faster now, more like forty-five miles per hour, instead of fifteen.

"And that's not all of it," Tom said with a sigh.

Reggie picked up on the hesitation. "Go ahead. Tell me the rest of it."

"Well, they've just put out an alert with Collin Cook's name and picture on it, claiming that he is working for the US government as an assassin and plans to kill the Mexican president."

"What?" said Reggie and Spinner in unison.

"Yeah, they're looking for him right now. Claim he crash-landed in southern Mexico earlier today and is on the loose, being aided by a group of guerilla fighters funded by the United States."

"What next?" said Reggie in disbelief.

"Well, I'll tell you. There's an unknown portion of the Mexican military that has sided with the separatist movement, which it appears has been funded by none other than Pho Nam Penh. This group, working with Penh and his syndicate, is currently hunting for Cook. The problem is, no one knows at this point which military units are on which side—a problem the key personnel in the NSA are working on very closely with their counterparts in Mexico."

"Wow. You weren't kidding when you said good news was a matter of perspective. I assume there are high-level people on this thing?"

"Yeah, there's some whiz kid at NSA that is masterminding this whole thing. The director and deputy director seem to have full faith and confidence in him. He's the foremost expert on this Pho Nam Penh guy."

"Well, it would have been nice to know all this before we wasted so much time and effort. I mean, we've been made to look rather foolish."

"That was my initial reaction—not the looking foolish part; the wasting time part. It seems you were working at odds with the NSA guys, but they tell me that secrecy was all very necessary. That's not the way I see it, but I guess I have no choice now but to accept it and move forward. You guys have done an outstanding job, so don't feel foolish to any degree. OK, Reggie?"

Reggie hesitated, glancing at Spinner with an arched eyebrow. Spinner shrugged and nodded. "If you say so. I mean, we were given an assignment to find this guy and bring him in for questioning. That's all we've been trying to do for weeks now. But things are starting to make sense. Based on what you told me, it's no wonder we kept missing him."

"You're right. It's no wonder at all. At this point, Reggie, all I can say is keep your phone on. This may not be over yet." Tom paused a beat, then added, "And keep your guy at Interpol on the job, too."

* * * *

London, England
June 18, 12:45 a.m. Local Time; June 17, 4:45 p.m. Pacific Time

Nic struggled through a late-night brainstorming session with his boss, Alastair Montgomery. Tensions were mounting as the clock ticked forward while they rehashed the same tired data for the hundredth time. The meeting was quickly devolving into a blood-letting as Alastair expressed the pressure mounting on him from above. Nearly a full day and no further signs of Collin Cook, no trace of Pho Nam Penh, and nothing but gut instincts and suppositions about Collin's missing friend, Rob Howell. Alastair was fit to be tied and Nic was feeling smaller and smaller as the discussion wore on.

These meetings with his boss always involved a fair amount of browbeating, whether Alastair intended it or not. That was par for the course. Nic had grown accustomed to it and came prepared, usually. Not today, however. There was a dearth of new developments over the past six hours in one of Interpol's highest-priority cases. The British press had yet to relent on its coverage of the Royal Bank of Scotland hack attack and seemed to thrive on mocking Interpol's investigative drought. Because the latest online editions of the tabloids continued to denounce the investigators by name, Alastair's mood proved particularly foul.

Crabtree's incoming call was a saving grace that stemmed Alastair's deluge of profanity. Nic was grateful for the reprieve, though he suspected it would be short lived. "This is Crabtree," Nic said to Alastair, pointing at his phone as it rang in his hand.

"Good. Put him on speaker," Alastair demanded.

"Reggie," Nic said with a forced cheer in his voice. "I'm here with Alastair. What have you got for us?"

"OK. Good. Glad I got you both at the same time. Sorry to call at such an ungodly hour, but I figured you'd be awake and would want to hear this."

"Yes, Agent Crabtree, good to hear from you," said Alastair.

"We've got some new information for you ... and a request."

"Shoot," said Nic. "We're all ears."

Reggie went through all the facts that he and Spinner had collected that afternoon. He told them about Rob Howell's abduction and subsequent disguised border crossing. The news that Collin had been aided all along by the NSA brought Nic a measure of consolation, especially in front of Alastair. He informed them about Penh's expanded network and the plans that were coming to a head in Mexico.

"But we've got some major trouble brewing for our man, Collin, too," said Reggie.

"You mean beyond what you've already spelled out?" asked Nic. "Cause what you've told us to this point sounds pretty major already."

"Yes, yes," added Alastair, "What sort of major trouble are you referring to, may I ask?"

"He's been implicated in a plot to assassinate the president of Mexico and overthrow the democratically elected government."

* * * *

Highway 180, West of Villahermosa, Mexico
June 17, 7:10 p.m. Local Time; 5:10 p.m. Pacific Time

The accumulated heat in the back of the truck made it hard to breathe. Evening air was not necessarily cool air in southern Mexico, especially crammed in the tight space in the back of a covered pickup truck. Collin remained still, however, and tried to listen to the conversation. With his eyes closed, he concentrated on the Spanish words he could make out, then tried to piece together some sort of context. It was tough to make out the words from his vantage point at the bottom of a long wooden tool box. He lay under the false bottom with stacks of tools piled on the plywood ledge above him. Small gaps along the side allowed fresh air in for him to breathe, but that air was still hot, humid, and stagnant. It also smelled of mildew, soil, and rotting vegetation, with a hint of gasoline. This convenient space usually housed large weapons. The rocket launcher and sniper rifle were hidden in a similar box on the opposite side of the truck bed, wedged in with several other military-grade armaments.

Among the small repertoire of fears Collin carried, claustrophobia was near the top of his list. He loathed being confined in small spaces, but here he was yet again, forced to endure another round of torture for the sake of his safety and freedom. To avoid a panic attack, he focused on something other than his discomfort. The voices of the policeman and the driver, though muffled, gave him that something he needed to occupy his mind.

The pickup truck that carried him and four highly trained operatives was a gardener's truck. The driver and other passengers were Mexican-Americans. The guise was supposed to work, but here they were, having been pulled over by the *Federales* on a country highway an hour into their journey. The shell over the truck bed had concealed Collin and his movements from the view of the police while he hurriedly wiggled into place. One of the operatives had replaced the tools in the box and snapped the lid on tight, locking the two brackets along one of the edges of the hinged crate top.

From what Collin could hear, the officer was quizzing the driver about a number of things, including who his customers were, how he could afford to employee three other men, and what they were doing this far out in the countryside. In Collin's view, the driver could have asked that last question of the officer. The driver gave short answers, intended, Collin supposed, to make him out to be a simpleton who was merely following instructions from his *jefe*, or boss. This little speech had obviously been rehearsed and possibly used before. The driver never hesitated or sounded stumped. Each response was slow and measured, but seemed to follow a scripted narrative.

At length, the *Federale* officer grew impatient and let them on their way, but not until he had opened the back and inspected the boxes. Collin sensed that there were other men standing around, and assumed they had guns out and at the ready. When nothing turned up in their cursory search, the leader called to the others to load up and head out.

The truck pulled back out onto the highway slowly. "Riptide," as he was known, waited for the roar of the police truck to subside as it passed them before he opened the crate and began unloading its contents. Collin could hear each shovel and rake and hoe as they hit the bed of the truck. Finally, the plywood sheet above him was jiggled free, then lifted out of the way, breaking Collin free from his trance-like state.

Although the air in the back of the truck wasn't exactly fresh, Collin was glad to suck in a couple of quick lungs full. Sweat covered his face and had soaked his hair and shirt. Riptide helped him climb out of the coffin-like confinement, shaking his head all the while.

"*Tu es muy loco,*" Riptide snorted as he twirled his pointing finger in a circle around his ear. *You're crazy.*

Collin crawled toward the opening to the cabin where the air conditioning blew. "That may be true. It seems I've become crazier lately."

Riptide shook his head. "Remember, that was your idea, not mine."

"Yeah, I know, but it was worth it, wasn't it? This white kid would have caught their attention and brought on even more questions."

"I'm sure you're right ... what do we call you?"

"I don't know. I don't have a clever nickname like you do. Where'd you come up with Riptide?"

"Don't you know the Percy Jackson books, man?"

"I've heard of them, but never read them."

"Oh, man, they were my favorites as a kid. So it's all about gods and demigods and bad guys from Greek mythology and this guy, Percy Jackson, finds out he's the son of Neptune. Anyway, he's got a pen that turns into a sword and it's called Riptide."

"OK," said Collin, taking it all in. "But how does that become your nickname?"

"Because I loved Percy Jackson as a kid, I used to do swordplay with those fake nerf swords and I got pretty good at it. So, during basic training, my buddies started calling me that and it stuck."

"All right. That's pretty cool. What about him?" Collin asked, pointing to the driver.

"Butch? Now that's a funny story, but I'll give you the short version. We started calling him Butch when an argument broke out after watching the movie with Paul Newman and Robert Redford. This guy"—he chuckled, pointing through the back window at the driver—"has a steadfast belief that Butch Cassidy survived the shoot-out in the small mining town of San Vicente, Bolivia. He practically worships the guy. Knows everything about the legend of Butch Cassidy. Just ask him."

"I'll have to save that question for another time, perhaps." Turning to the driver, Collin asked, "What do you think that was all about back there?"

"Your friend in Washington says the government is searching for you."

"What? Me? How do they know anything about me?"

"The bad guys know where you are."

"How—?" he started to ask. Then it dawned on him. Penh was tracking him using his computer. It was the only explanation. On the boat, the long-haired guy had been working on Collin's laptop and must have installed some sort of tracking software. That was the only thing he could think of. He explained it to the others. "Mongoose told me to leave the computer with him so he could run some diagnostics on it. Do you think he can also remove whatever code that guy installed?"

"Probably," said Butch. "I'll call him." He thought for a moment before continuing. "It could also be the plane wreck. I'm sure it attracted some attention."

"Why, because I was flying so low or because people were shooting at me?"

"Maybe some of each," said Jorge, the man in the passenger's seat. Collin knew Jorge was a nickname, but hadn't yet figured out where it came from. "Our planes don't usually get shot at."

"Usually? So planes have been shot at before?"

"Yeah, but never hit. Of course, we never had one come in so low before, either."

"Do you know who these guys are, then?"

Jorge answered. "We keep an eye on them. They're rumored to be arms dealers, supplying the local drug lords. But they keep to themselves, same as us."

"So that's what you guys do down here? Watch the arms dealers and the drug lords?"

Butch smiled and said, "Something like that."

"I thought NSA was more about cybercrime and other nonmilitary threats," said Collin, furrowing his brow.

"Who says we're NSA?"

"I guess I just assumed."

"We're not. Contractors, really. No direct ties to anyone. Keeps things clean for the politicians in Washington," Butch explained.

Collin sat silent for a minute, digesting all this new information. "Why did they send me here with you guys?"

"We're your best bet for getting into and out of Mexico City undetected and unharmed. We're all ex-military. We do whatever needs to be done to protect our country. For now, consider us your escorts."

Collin's eyes widened and he pulled in a deep breath as he absorbed this information. "Military contractors? In Mexico?"

"Intelligence operatives, really."

"You mean spies?"

"Like I said, we provide protection when protection is needed. Let's leave it at that."

"What's the plan, then?"

"To keep you safe."

"Safe from what?"

"Any and all enemies."

chapter Eighteen

The war room was aglow with the bluish light of computer monitors and the large plasma screens on the wall when a wedge of light stretched into the room from the hallway as Lukas pushed open the door and hobbled to his desk at the back of the room. The three team members turned almost in unison to watch their leader reenter the room after a long absence. He dropped his computer bag on the chair and asked, "What do we know now that we didn't when I left for the meeting?"

Kevin swiveled in his chair, anxious and excited to share his findings. "Sir, we've managed to track the phone."

Lukas pinched his eyes shut and pursed his lips, like people do when they're trying to solve a riddle.

"The phone that was used to call the satellite phone that the team in Mexico cloned—the one that Collin took from the dead guy," Kevin explained.

"Ah, yes, that phone. Terrific. What do we know about it?"

"It's moving at five hundred sixty miles per hour over the Pacific. Looks to be en route to Hawaii." With the click of Kevin's mouse, a map appeared on one of the screens in the front of the room. It showed a red plane icon moving over a blue ocean with a yellow line trailing behind it and a white line projecting forward from its nose.

"That makes sense," Lukas said with a nod. "He's on his way to Mexico via Hawaii to refuel, I'd imagine. What else do we know?"

Carmen, the eager, intelligent blonde gal on the far end, started her assessment. "Sir, I've managed to track that minivan we believe is carrying Rob Howell."

Lukas looked at her and raised an eyebrow.

She tapped a key and another one of the wall-mounted screens came to life and showed a sped-up, grainy video. "This is a recording from one of our satellites taken earlier this afternoon. It seems that the driver and her two passengers pulled into a storage rental facility in Mexicali and swapped cars. The blue minivan pulled into one of the units and never came out. Instead, this black SUV emerged a few minutes later"—she wiggled the pointer on the screen to highlight the vehicle—"and has been traveling south on Highway 2 until just a few minutes ago. It stopped at a restaurant in Hermosillo, Mexico."

Lukas nodded and tried to suppress a smile. "Do we know if Rob is still alive?"

"He appears to be, although they transported him into the restaurant in a wheelchair."

"That figures. They want to keep him immobile, I'm sure. Keep watching them and let me know if anything changes. I'd bet my paycheck they're heading to Mexico City for the grand rendezvous."

"No grab team?"

"No. Too risky. We have to let this play out. Penh doesn't know that we know what he's up to. He's flying like a moth to the flame." Lukas turned toward the third member of his team. "How about our guys in Villahermosa?"

Without looking up or interrupting his typing, Marty replied, "The truck taking Collin to the city is behind schedule, but only twenty-five minutes or so. Got pulled over and searched by the *Federales*."

"The *Federales*? Oh no. That's not good," Lukas said with a frown.

"Yeah, that's what I thought," said Marty. "So, I called and warned our guys who stayed back at the shop in Villahermosa. Mongoose safeguarded the laptop and sent it north in another vehicle with another team."

"What happened with the *Federales* when they pulled over the truck?" Lukas's countenance had grown dark with worry.

"Cursory look through the back, but only found gardening tools, so they let them go," replied Marty, still consumed with this current task.

"What about Collin?"

"Stowed safely in a coffin-like toolbox in the back of the truck."

"They didn't check it?"

"Nope. Apparently Butch and his team were convincing enough."

"That's good news. What about the others back at the shop?"

"Packing up all the gear and electronics, preparing to leave."

"The sooner the better as far as I'm concerned. We don't know how much the *Federales* know about what's going on. It's possible that they are in league with Torres, our rogue senator, and are on high alert."

* * * *

Scripps Patient Clinic, La Jolla, California
June 17, 5:25 p.m. Pacific Time

Dr. Navarro arrived right on time, at the end of his shift as he had promised. He smiled cautiously as he announced that Sarah's test results came back and looked pretty good. Three days in the hospital with plenty of rest and a carefully monitored diet, and Sarah was back on track, more or less. He was pleased but guarded. "Are you feeling strong enough to go home tomorrow, Mrs. Cook?" asked the quiet, contemplative physician. "I worry about you negotiating the stairs in your home. You told me they are hardwood and that makes me just a bit nervous."

"I'll be fine. Most of my family is in town, so I'll have plenty of help."

"Nonetheless, we'll send someone to check in with you and take some more tests in a few days."

Dr. Navarro stood. When he smiled, his lips formed a straight line across his face. He looked satisfied but not enthusiastic.

When he left the room, Emily checked her watch. "You think we should call him now?"

"Yes, he needs to know," said Sarah matter-of-factly.

Reggie's voice came through the speaker of Sarah's phone, sounding tired. "Hi, Sarah. I wish I had some news for you—"

Emily jumped in. The nervous energy had made it difficult for her to sit still during Dr. Navarro's visit. It also caused her to talk fast. "Never mind that, Agent Crabtree. Mr. Penh called me and told me that if I didn't comply with his demands he would cut Rob's fingers off. He has Rob. I heard him. He started to say something, but Penh cut him off. What should we do?"

Reggie drew in a breath and held it for a beat or two before exhaling. "Whoa. Let me see if I got all that. *Penh* called *you*? What exactly did he want you to do?"

Emily thought for a moment. When she spoke again, she consciously controlled the speed of her words. "He just said that I had better make sure Collin complied with his demands. I'm to remind Collin that he still wants his money back and Collin's laptop. It's weird how he thinks I'm able to contact Collin to tell him these things." She paused to control the rising panic for Rob. "I haven't heard anything from him for weeks. I don't know what I can do. He's going to hurt Rob if I don't comply, but I don't know how to comply. Can you help me, Agent Crabtree?"

An awkward pause followed. Emily could hear a muffled, whispered conversation taking place, she assumed with Agent McCoy.

"I've got an idea or two. Let me relay this information to the appropriate people and see what kind of a solution we can come up with. OK?"

* * * *

Highway 145D, 300 miles southeast of Mexico City
June 17, 7:56 p.m. Local Time; 5:56 p.m. Pacific Time

"That's the fourth one I've seen in two hours," Butch said, pointing out the window at a military transport truck approaching from the opposite direction.

They had been on the road only two hours, ambling along on a northwesterly course toward Mexico City. Rolling green hills covered in trees were punctuated by lake-filled valleys on either side of the sparsely populated four-lane thoroughfare. Collin lay sleeping in the back of the truck on a bed of burlap bags and plastic tarps, catching up on some much-needed rest, while Riptide kept as alert as he could as he leaned up against the back of the cab in order to avail himself of what little air conditioning there was.

"Seems to be more than just a coincidence," said Jorge grimly.

"Yeah, it would seem so. I'm calling it in," said Butch as he handled his phone and searched for the number.

The pleasant voice of the young lady he had been dealing with the past few days answered in her usual calm but attentive style.

"We've got an unusual number of federal troop carriers on the road down here. Any ideas why?"

"At this point, we can't be certain which battalions are loyal to the current government and which are working for Torres. Since the loyalists are fortifying the capital right now, perhaps it's not too misguided to assume these units are rebels."

"Have you heard from Mongoose or the other guys in Villahermosa?"

"I haven't heard from them since I ordered the evac," Carmen said. The familiar background noise, including key tapping, filled the otherwise silent void. "They aren't responding to my texts, either."

"Is that unusual?"

"With Mongoose it is. He's almost always instant with his replies, especially when I'm asking him to check in. I'd better look into this. I'll get back to you."

chapter Nineteen

Pho Nam Penh fussed with his fingernails, checking that they were shiny and smooth and perfectly trimmed. One of the accoutrements he most enjoyed about having money. It could buy the nice things and allow him to spoil himself in luxury and fashion, thus enhancing his power profile. Money also bought people and loyalties, especially from those starving for power. Once tasted by some, even to a very small degree, the intoxication from the elixir of authority produced an addiction of mythical proportion.

Those in the middle to upper ranks of any government seemed the ones who fell into the power trap most often and most severely. That axiom was as true in Mexico as it was in any other country in the world. It just so happened that Mexico was strategically positioned in both time and geography to act on the suggestion of seizing its rightful spot atop the global stage. With the right mix of senatorial and military support, the coup within the country would be swift. Then, the necessary forces would be aligned to react quickly once the United States was weakened sufficiently.

Penh's brilliant plan was coming together nicely. And the evidence would point to Collin Cook as a coconspirator once the smoke lifted. He and his laptop were due to arrive in Mexico City just in time to join in. Penh marveled at the beautiful simplicity in his plan. Simple and elegant in presentation, complex and time-consuming to orchestrate.

Penh rolled the satellite phone over and over in his hand, occasionally tapping the end of it against his chin as he mulled his strategy. He scrolled through his contacts list, ready to dial the secure line of Senator Juan Miguel Rivera Torres.

Torres, a former military commander turned legislator, possessed the unlikely combination of leadership skill, technical savvy, high-level connections in all areas of government, and experience. What Penh liked most was his appetite for more power. Immensely ambitious, yet well-respected, Torres's reputation within the vaunted halls of the Mexican Capitol garnered him access to the right sorts of people to pull off the task. Among the many hallmarks of his distinguished career, he had also won the hearts of the people due to the image he portrayed as a loving husband and doting father.

Penh had discovered over time that every great champion had a chink in his armor. For Torres, a little-known penchant for expensive whiskey and exotic female escorts left him vulnerable to coercion from the outside. In public, he repelled all advances, suggestions, or appearances of evil. He had famously rebuffed the salacious approach of one of Mexico's most famous call girls, known to have dragged down many a high-ranking official on hidden camera. The speech he gave after the discovery of the recording where he censured the notion of cheating on one's spouse and piously proclaimed himself impervious to such vices had gone viral on YouTube in Mexico and much of Latin America.

His private life, however, painted a very different picture. A cool distance had secretly grown between him and his wife. Two of his children had not made contact for many months. His youngest was shipped off to a boarding school midyear.

Penh and his cadre of hackers were among the few to have discovered Torres's chink. Eighteen months of intensive observation had revealed it. Six months of threats and pressure had exploited it sufficiently to gain his full buy-in and participation. The man was hungry for power and desperate to protect his brand. The fact that he had managed to conceal this part of his life so completely from the rest of the world made him a candidate with an ideal skillset to be the front-man in Penh's scheme.

Months of meticulous planning and careful manipulation and intimidation had reached its glorious crescendo. The stage was now set for the phone call Penh was about to place.

* * * *

FBI Office, Los Angeles, California
June 17, 5:56 p.m. Pacific Time

"How are we going to manage that?" Spinner asked incredulously.

The two agents were back in the unadorned, but functional, borrowed office where they had started their day some fourteen hours earlier. Only now, their whole paradigm had shifted. Everything to do with this case had been flipped on its head, or so it seemed. After months of being stonewalled or ignored and coming up with nothing but close calls and missed opportunities, the past fifteen hours had produced a flood of new and actionable intelligence. The question now was how were they going to act on the information they had?

Reggie took his commitment to Sarah and Henry Cook very seriously. He had promised them at the beginning, back in November, that he would do his best to bring their son home, safe and sound. The case had taken several turns, including a long detour through a place that made Collin look like the criminal. Now, in the light of recent revelations, Collin's life and that of his best friend were in jeopardy. The solution seemed simple enough. Fly to Mexico, use the tracking device planted on Collin's computer to find him, then bring him home.

"We're going to call Tom, of course," said Reggie with a toothy smile. "Look at all the doors that have been opened to us since he got involved. He's like Aladdin's genie."

"Maybe so, but haven't we used up our three wishes?" asked Spinner, shaking his head.

"I only count two. The initial request to help us figure out what was going on and the second to pass along the message to Collin that Rob was in danger. That leaves us this one, the granddaddy of them all: Get us into Mexico to retrieve our boy and his friend and bring them home so we can do what we promised his parents we'd do. Pretty simple request, really."

Spinner continued to shake his head as a smile spread across his face. "You're indomitable. A true optimist and the embodiment of 'never say never.'"

"As they say, you get one hundred percent of what you don't ask for, so I'm asking for it."

Tom had called an hour and a half earlier and passed along another tidbit of information about the NSA pulling in operatives from every agency with assets in the country and converging on an area in the northwest section of Mexico City. So it seemed that they knew where Collin and Rob would end up. This left them with one minor detail to work out.

Knowing the bureaucratic red tape involved when two FBI officers wanted to travel to Mexico, it would take people in power on both sides of the border to make it happen. As sworn law enforcement officers of the federal government of the United States, their jurisdiction ended at the boundary line that separated the two countries. Getting beyond the border to perform their job functions required high-level clearance. The two problems there were obvious. Time and tip-off. It would take time to run through the approval process and, once approved, it would be like ringing an alarm to whoever it was in the Mexican government helping Pho Nam Penh set up shop there.

But the entanglements involved in international "business travel" for a Bureau man presented a problem. First, they had to prove Collin Cook was a suspected criminal. Second, they had to convince those in the know that he was not a spy with an order to assassinate Mexico's president. Third, they had to prove that he should be tried for his crimes in the US, not Mexico. Unless they could get over these three hurdles and obtain special permission from the liaison office in Mexico City to apprehend a suspect in an international cybercrime ring, they would be held at the airport upon arrival.

Crabtree was old school and believed in the power of being present when it came to investigating and solving mysteries. Plus, he didn't like to rely on others to do his dirty work. And maybe there was a bit of a trust issue, too. In any case, Reggie felt the need to get himself and Spinner to Mexico City as fast and as inconspicuously as possible. Glancing at this watch, he realized it was after 11:00 p.m. in Washington, DC, but he decided to ring his friend anyway.

Reggie knew they needed a break. Just a little luck, that's all he was asking for. The arrest warrant for Collin Cook sat on his lap. An electronic version had been sent to the liaison office fifteen minutes ago. It likely wouldn't get processed until morning, but he hoped that with Tom's help, it could be ready first thing when he and Spinner woke up.

He looked at Spinner with a raised eyebrow and half-turned smile. Spinner gave a silent, hopeful thumbs-up as Reggie tapped the call button on his phone.

* * * *

Villahermosa, Mexico
June 17, 7:56 p.m. Local Time; 5:56 p.m. Pacific Time

Mongoose sat in front of a computer in the back of the barn-like structure, typing away. A few strange noises erupted outside, followed by a dog barking. The barking stopped quickly, so he went on with his work reassembling the clone of Collin's laptop.

He had spent much of the day repairing the sections of Collin's hard drive that had been corrupted by Penh's men when they hooked it up to their equipment. They had managed to punch through one firewall to attain access to some of Collin's information, including his biometrics. That was bad, but not as serious as it would be if they got through the second, more robust firewall. Behind that electronic barrier lay a portal of sorts. Once accessed, the user could gain entry to the NSA's database if he was clever enough. That would be disastrous, but Mongoose was quite confident that Penh's group had not yet penetrated their elaborate cyberdefenses.

Luckily, Mongoose had sent Collin's laptop northward with a team that was to intercept Collin and the others and return the device to him. He had left the tracking software on, per the instructions he received from the German guy in Washington. That seemed odd, but the guy was adamant, so he followed the instructions he was given.

The last thing Mongoose did was update the piece of code he had created and built into every NSA laptop in the field over the past year, including this clone. It was a genius program that stored data about a user's keystroking nuances. Because every computer user had a unique pattern or rhythm to their typing, much like every human has a distinct gait, a clever program could monitor and analyze these metrics for each user over a period of time. The computer could measure and record the angle, pressure, speed, and cadence with which the user typed a certain sequence of keys. That pattern would become another identifier that would either lock or unlock the data and programs on a given computer system when the user typed a key phrase that included twenty-one different keystrokes.

Mongoose sat back and cracked his knuckles, pleased with his latest creation. It was well hidden and virtually untraceable within the computer's security protocol.

Next, he would upload this update to the NSA mainframe so that it would require a new round of tests for each login. But to make it less obnoxious, the user would only be required to type the predetermined, random text once per day.

An incoming text message grabbed Mongoose's attention so he didn't notice the front door open with a creak as he read the message from Carmen, asking for a status update. The fact that the door opened slower than usual didn't dawn on him until it was too late. He hit enter to save his work on his computer before responding to the text. He pivoted toward the interior door behind him just in time to see the muzzle flash. His blood splattered the wall, the table, and the laptop he was working on.

Mongoose's computer continued to send his code over a secured virtual private network connection to the NSA mainframe while his murderers surveyed the scene and went about fulfilling their assignment. His last act would prove a valuable contribution to the security of sensitive government data.

* * * *

Two sets of black boots stepped into the room. Two pistols, held firmly with two hands each, swept in all directions until the two men holding them were sure the room was otherwise empty. The boots proceeded to the dark wooden desk in the corner, where the body, splayed backward and facing the ceiling, partially covered a laptop computer. The pistols were holstered and the room was searched top to bottom. Everything that looked useful was quickly stacked into plastic tubs. When the tubs were full, two more men entered the room and hauled the tubs out of the building and into the back of a pickup truck. Electronic devices of all sorts—laptops, tablets, satellite phones, routers, even game consoles—were stacked into the plastic containers. Cables, connectors, modems, and mice were packed in, as well.

When everything was loaded in the truck, one of the men turned on the gas stove in the kitchen full blast. He was the last one out. After climbing in the back of the truck, he lit a cigarette. When the truck sped past the farm house, he flicked the cigarette into an open window.

The blast wasn't immediate. The truck had traveled the length of several football fields before it blew, but when it did, it was spectacular. Glass, splinters of wood, and chunks of plaster flew in all directions. Pieces of the tin roof launched high into the air and somersaulted down like strange acrobats in an aerial ballet. Some of it rained down around the speeding truck. The heat and flames spread in all directions as the fireball grew in size and intensity. As the truck came through a stand of trees and reached the distant road, all occupants looked back and saw a black mushroom cloud reaching into the sky.

The three Americans left behind to defend their safe house would have to be identified through dental records.

chapter Twenty

Carmen gasped in horror and covered her mouth with her hand. Lukas rushed to her desk from his position at the back of the stadium-style room. He came down two steps and leaned in for a closer look. Carmen pointed at the smoke that filled the center of her screen. "The safe house in Villahermosa just blew up," she said with the tone of forced detachment and emotional neutrality she had been trained to maintain.

"Ring them," Lukas demanded.

Carmen lowered her head and picked up her phone. She listened for a long moment. "There's nothing, sir. It's not even ringing."

Lukas sighed. "Do we know who was there?"

"We know most of two teams are escorting Mr. Cook to Mexico City. They left behind only Mongoose, Troy, and Clutch to guard the house and take care of Mamba."

Lukas shook his head and clinched his jaw. "Those are good men." He stepped away from Carmen's desk, shut his eyes, and pondered for a moment. "Call in the team from Guadalajara. Get them in there to back up Butch and his team. Who else can we bring in?"

Kevin spoke up. "We've got three men stationed in Cabo San Lucas, sir. They can be there in four hours."

"Do it. We're going to need everyone we can get. Anyone else?"

Marty looked up from his monitor and said, "We could get two guys out of Ensenada. The next closest is Tucson. Team of four there."

"OK. Make it happen. Things just changed. A group of *Federales* just attacked and killed three of our own." Lukas's brow was furrowed and his mouth pulled tight, showing the strain. "It looks like our crooked Mexican senator has garnered more support than we realized. This could be a bad omen. We need to get in touch with

General Aguilar and hope he's not in on it." Lukas muttered the last part under his breath.

"Will do, sir," said Kevin as he swiveled back and began to punch keys on this computer.

Lukas ran a hand through his bristly blonde hair as he turned and, leaning on his cane, strode back to his desk.

Carmen watched him. "Don't worry, sir. Our assets down there are professionals. They know what they're doing."

Lukas turned toward her, the wrinkles in his forehead pronounced. "I know they are, but Collin's just a civilian. I shouldn't have gotten him involved in this."

"He's with the best team we have. Remember, he volunteered to do this. He wanted to get involved. Plus, he has proven to be quick on his feet and very resourceful."

Lukas still had not sat down. Instead, he paced gingerly in the narrow space behind his desk. "I'll be back," he said, gripping his phone in his hand. "Continue coordinating the teams' arrivals and get them situated. They should each be given the signal for both Penh's phone and Collin's. We need to secure the perimeter around Collin. If they'll kill our agents in the field, they'll have little trouble killing him when they're done with him."

"But they won't be able to unlock the hard drive without him. They can't fake the biometrics data," Carmen said, hopefully. "Plus, since it's the money they're after, they will need him to get that money out."

"Yes, but that will only buy us so much time. They'll dispose of him and Rob without another thought. I can't let that happen."

"Our team will protect him, sir. No way they'll let Penh get to him."

Lukas stared at the screens on the wall for a long moment, his expression blank. He inhaled, held it, then said, "I wish I knew everything Penh had up his sleeve." He then shouldered his briefcase and waved his phone. "Call me with updates," he said as he pushed through the door to the back hallway where there was a service elevator to the basement. In the basement, there was tunnel he always used to enter and exit the building. A golf cart sat a few feet away, plugged into a charging station. He unplugged it and began silently working his way through the underground catacombs to the isolated parking area three-quarters of a mile deep in the forest of Virginia. A car with tinted windows and a professional driver awaited him in the tiny clearing.

* * * *

Orizaba, Mexico, 175 miles southeast of Mexico City
June 17, 10:35 p.m. Local Time

Collin was woken from his nap as they pulled into the quaint mountain village of Orizaba. An inky darkness had settled in. Flickering street lamps valiantly fought it back along the road lined with an assortment of buildings, most of them multiple stories. Some looked to be cathedrals built a century or two earlier. Others were newer office buildings with sixties-era stucco or concrete facades.

Collin instantly felt the chill of the thinner, higher altitude air as he rubbed his eyes and shook his head to bring his senses back to life.

As they ambled through the small town, Riptide informed Collin of the fate of those left in the safehouse of Villahermosa. Collin was in disbelief. "The lady who works with your German friend in Washington says she could see the black smoke from the satellite. No one made it out, except the *Federales* who torched it."

"Why would they do that?"

"They're working for the bad guys. If they think they're going to scare us, they're wrong. They only pissed us off. We're more ready than ever for a fight." The look on his face confirmed what he said.

He abruptly changed subjects and told Collin to listen close and repeat everything he said. Collin did so faithfully, committing to memory the things he would need to know.

Riptide was still rattling off the instructions when their gardening truck pulled into a Pemex gas station. Butch headed inside while Jorge prepared to pump gas. Collin clamored quickly out of the back of the truck while Riptide hurried him along. Wearing a hooded sweatshirt pulled down over his forehead, with his hands thrust deep into its pockets, Collin shuffled toward the bathroom. Given the chilly temperature, it was normal attire. Jorge came out of the store, turned a sharp right down the sidewalk, and continued toward a handled door near the end of the concrete building. As he approached the restroom door, a military jeep came barreling into the same gas station, headlamps blazing bright. It pulled up to a stop near the glass doors of the store entrance. Jorge glanced in their direction, but gave no indication that he was bothered by their sudden arrival.

Two uniformed men jumped out of the vehicle. Two others remained where they were, positioned in the back of the jeep, standing. All four men scanned the area, their heads stopping as if to take note of each person, each vehicle, and every movement. The two from the front seats stomped importantly into the building.

Collin felt his back straighten and his muscles tighten. He wondered if the soldiers in the jeep had seen him climb out of the back of the truck or not. Butch used a key attached to a loop of barbed wire to open the door. Collin stood outside the door and waited in the shadows. Trying not to act nervous as each second felt warped in a time stretching spool. He leaned against a wall next to the bathroom as casually as he could and kicked a couple of tiny rocks away as he stared at the ground. Something anyone would do when they were bored.

Less than a minute later, Jorge exited, handing the barbed wire loop to Collin. When Collin emerged from the restroom, the gardener truck was gone. Another man, wearing a blue T-shirt with the words "Either Or" on the front put out his hand for the key, saying in Spanish, "Just what I needed."

Following the cue, Collin sauntered straight out the door toward a gold-colored Toyota Corolla that had to be at least fifteen or twenty years old. It was at the pump adjacent to the one vacated by the truck. Banged up and rusty, the hood was up as Collin approached. A man stuck his head out from under the hood and called to Collin, "Hey, hand me the oil. It's in the front."

Collin opened the passenger door, picked up a quart of oil from the floorboard, and walked around the front of the car. On cue, the man under the hood utter the predetermined code in Spanish: "It's useless. This stupid car eats this stuff like a cow eats grass."

Collin responded with the Spanish phrase he'd been told to utter, "We don't get dream cars here. We get the leftovers."

With that, the man said, "Get in the car. We need to go. Now."

"What about my bags?"

"Already loaded in the trunk. Let's move."

As casually as he could, Collin climbed in the back seat. In the glow of the overhead lights, he could see there was another man back there. He was thick and muscular, with his arms folded across his chest. Collin was instantly intimidated, until the man smiled and tilted his head up slightly to greet their new passenger. Collin did likewise, saying nothing.

The man with the blue shirt sat in the passenger's seat and slammed the door. The man under the hood got in the driver's seat and started the car.

When they were a safe distance from the gas station, the driver spoke. This time in English. "How long they been following you?"

"The past couple of hours, from what I hear. I didn't see them because I was asleep in the back of the truck. But the guys told me they've just been using different vehicles and keeping a safe distance."

"That can't be good. They're up to something more than just protecting the local citizenry, that's for sure."

"If you say so. I've never been to this part of Mexico, so I don't know what's normal and what's not. I just know they've already pulled us over and searched the whole truck."

"Didn't find you, eh?"

"No. You guys have some clever hiding places."

"They've come in handy more than once, that's for sure," said the passenger in the front seat. Collin hadn't noticed it as they exchanged the key, but he had sculpted arms that sported tattoos on the biceps. Like the others, he looked to be of Latin American descent and spoke flawless English and Spanish. "We use those all the time to get assets and special equipment in and out of the area."

Collin started to ask something, then thought better of it and shut his mouth again.

"We better hope they don't pull us over. We've got no place to hide you in this thing," said the driver as he swept his hand in a semicircle around the interior of the car. "No place to hide."

As he drove, he checked his mirrors often. He pointed out several more military vehicles roaming the streets of the otherwise quiet town. Something was afoot, no doubt about it.

The conversation ended and they drove in silence for over three hours, until the forests, farms, and pastures gave way to more structures. Collin spent most of that time asleep again. His weary body and mind took advantage of the downtime.

The buildings started getting closer together and houses and apartments and gas stations began to appear more frequently. They all looked aged but cared for. These were the humble alpine hamlets that lay along the fringes of Mexico City, high in the mountains. A crescent moon hung overhead, casting its pale light over the little town and the towering mountains surrounding it. The driver pulled into a parking area in front of a low-lying building with a disheveled red-tile roof and cream-colored adobe walls. Unimpressive and poorly lit, this is where they stopped to get some rest. A shabby motel on a poorly maintained road on the outskirts of the small town of San Martin Texmelucan, Mexico. Collin shrugged. It was par for the course these days.

Checking his watch, he was surprised that it was almost two in the morning. Three hours crammed in the back of a Corolla had gone by quicker than he expected.

chapter Twenty-One

As the three men unloaded the items from the trunk of the Corolla, Collin's phone started ringing. Only one person it could be. "Lukas, what's up? You do realize what time it is, don't you? What makes you think I'm not asleep?" Collin spoke in a low tone, just above a whisper.

"Because I can see you moving. Listen, we've got a trace on the phone Penh used to call you when you were on the boat, thanks to the data on the satellite phone. I need you to do something right now. You ready?"

Collin walked into the dimly lit motel room, trying not to wake up anyone in the adjacent rooms. "You bet. What do you need?"

Lukas proceeded to walk Collin through the steps of installing an app on his phone, explaining that it was a tracking app. When the installation finished, a blinking red dot appeared on the screen, surrounded by a map showing names of streets and buildings. Most of them were very long names, but familiar. Collin adjusted his eyes. "Is that what I think it is? Is that Hawaii?"

"Yeah, he just landed in Honolulu, presumably to refuel. He's on his way to Mexico City. The rendezvous is happening, probably in the next twenty-four hours. Expect a call from him very soon."

"What do I tell him? What do I do?"

"He'll have instructions for you, I'm sure. He needs you, so he's not going to hurt you."

"Needs me? For what?"

"I'm only guessing here, but I'd have to say he wants his thirty million dollars back," Lukas said, mimicking Collin's usual sarcasm.

"Oh, yeah, right. Almost forgot about that. Seems he's still upset that his *insurance company* had to pay a claim."

"I'd also guess that he's running short on funds. From what my team and I have gathered over the past few days, he's had to line a lot of pockets and buy a lot of influence lately. He's got a substantial network of people working for him and his sources for stealing funds have run dry since the RBS thing. The banks have really beefed up their cybersecurity since then and the world's governments have been snooping and hunting for him, blocking access to the accounts he is suspected of having set up. I'd say he's getting desperate and will be coming for you and your money."

"That's really great news. What other cheery updates have you got for me?"

Lukas sighed. "You already know about the safe house in Villahermosa, I presume?"

"Yeah, I heard. How many were there?"

"Four."

"The pilot, too?"

"I'm afraid so." Lukas paused. "We have people and a plan in place to keep you safe, so don't worry."

"How are you going to manage that? In Mexico?"

"I've been working on this for quite some time. My whole team has. Trust me. By the time Penh lands, we'll have the assets we need in place."

"Great, so he'll come to Mexico to pick me up in his nifty little jet, run me down to Panama to get *my* money that he *thinks* is his, get me to use my fingerprint or retina scan to unlock the computer, then kill me?"

"It's more complex than that now. But … essentially you're right. Once he gets the money and gets into the hard drive, he can figure out how to access data on the NSA network. That may be just as important to the people he has enlisted in his cause as the money. Don't get me wrong. They're all a bunch of greedy slime balls, but the people he's working with want more than just money. Gaining access to our top-secret data, especially defense-related information, is even more important to them, I'm sure. But since he needs you to physically remove the money from the bank, we have leverage on him."

"So he'll keep me around long enough for me to give him back the money, then he'll dump my body in the ocean or something, right?"

"We're not going to let that happen, so don't think that way."

"Why do I hear so much background noise, Lukas? How are you going to keep me safe if you're not at your post doing what you do? I can't do this stuff without your help."

"I'm at my post, just not in my office at the moment. I've got a few things I have to take care of. The game has changed now that they've killed our men. I have to play it differently."

Neither one said anything for a long moment. Collin, lost in thought, had no words. Lukas, as always, seemed to have multiple balls to juggle. Collin could hear a steady droning sound and key tapping in the background.

"Collin, one more thing you should know, just so you don't go in thinking the wrong thing. They've got Rob. He's on his way to Mexico City, as well. They're going to use him as leverage, so be prepared for that. You and the team are going to need to be extremely cautious."

Collin inhaled loudly and held it. A few seconds later, he let it go. "Oh, that's just terrific. What am I supposed to do? They'll kill him if I don't give them what they want. If I do give it to them, they'll kill us both. There's no way to win here. No way …"

"You'll win. I'm working on the details of how, but you will win. You just need to stall as long as possible. Give our team enough time to set up the trap we're working on."

"A trap?"

"Yeah, I don't have time to explain the details, but Penh expects this to go down a certain way and we're going to catch him off guard and shock the hell out of him."

* * * *

Collin ended the call. All eyes in the room were on him. "Seems things are happening very quickly around here. Pho Nam Penh is on his way to Mexico right now." He scanned the faces of the other three men for understanding. All nodded knowingly, confidently.

Before anyone could speak, the driver's phone went off. He responded in short clipped phrases. When he was finished, he sat on the edge of one of the beds and explained that the call was from the leader of a team that had just arrived from Guadalajara. They would work together to coordinate security and protect the civilians involved, namely Collin and Rob. He looked Collin in the eye and said, "Things could get dicey. You ready?"

* * * *

Motel room on the outskirts of Mexico City
June 18, 2:16 a.m. Local Time

A knock came at the door. It was a forceful knock, the kind that authorities use when they mean business. Butch recognized the knock, as did the others. Riptide was the only one asleep before the knocking. He bolted straight up, instantly alert. Butch hunched over his computer at the little desk. Jorge sat on one of the beds, cleaning his firearm. They looked at each other, giving eye signals and hand gestures before moving into place quickly but noiselessly. By the time the second set of knocks came, each man stood or laid in position to do their part if things turned ugly. Weapons were hidden but accessible.

Butch took one last glance around the cramped, dim motel room. He got thumbs-up from each. Riptide lay stretched out on the bed farthest from the door. Jorge sat at the edge of the bed, as if he'd been woken from a deep sleep.

Butch opened the door hesitantly and peered through the crack. "*Quién es?*"

In Spanish, the reply came: "It's the Federal police. Please open the door."

Butch opened the door farther but remained cautious. "What is it? How can we help?"

"We are searching for a man believed to be an enemy to the country. Open the door so we can inspect your room."

Butch unlatched the chain and let the four officers enter. Three of them quickly canvassed the room, checking the shower, the closet, and under the beds. The leader eyed Butch suspiciously. He ordered the one closest to the bathroom to check the window. The officer grunted as he tried to slide the window open. After several attempts, he was only able to open it a few inches before it jammed. Unable to even stick his head outside, it became obvious that no one had escaped through the window.

The ranking officer then pulled out a photograph and held it in front of Butch. "Have you seen this man?"

"No," said Butch. "Who is he?"

"An American that has entered our country illegally. He is wanted for a conspiracy to assassinate our president."

"A conspiracy? To kill the president? Let me have another look." Butch examined the photo intensely, then passed it to his teammates. Each man studied the photo for a few seconds, shaking his head in turn. "We have not seen him, but if we do, we shall report it to the proper officials right away."

"No!" barked the commander. "You shall report him to me. I am responsible for his capture." Sensing, perhaps, the alarm in his own voice, he softened his tone and added, "I must succeed at this task that has been given to me. Please, call me directly." With a tight-lipped smile under his full mustache, the commander handed Butch a business card. He took a step back and clicked his heels. His men filed out the door and climbed into the truck.

As the engine roared to life, the three Mexican–American operatives looked at each other in stunned silence. After the military truck pulled out of the parking lot, Butch dug his phone out of his pocket and tapped the screen to make a call. "The *Federales* were just here. They're looking for him. Pretty intense about it, too." He listened for a moment, then added, "They seem to be a hired hit squad. The commander was adamant that I call him and only him if I were to see our guy there. My bet? You should expect a visit." Another pause. "It may have been random, but I doubt it. It seemed more targeted, which tells me they're following the signal from the two laptops. It's possible they've been watching you guys since the gas station. It's time for Plan B."

Chapter Twenty-Two

San Martin Texmelucan, Mexico
June 18, 2:18 p.m. Local Time

The driver, whom the other two passengers in the car called "Jefe," pressed the phone to his ear and turned toward the wall. He spoke too fast and too low for Collin to discern exactly what was said. But he knew there was something serious and that it was not good. The man pulled the phone away from his ear and tapped the screen.

Snapping his fingers, he ordered everyone to listen. "We have a situation. The *Federales* just searched Butch's room, looking for our man here. This is where Plan B kicks in. Freddie"—he pointed at the man who had been in the passenger's seat— "get the kit ready. You"—he pointed at Collin— "grab your things. Do you have any camo?"

Collin hesitated, shaking his head as he thought as fast as he could. "Uh, no," he said after he realized how woefully ill-prepared he was for anything beyond a ride in the car. He had his college-student-style backpack that had two changes of clothes, three sets of colored contact lenses, a couple of baseball caps, sunglasses, regular glasses, and his toiletry bag. He also had a computer bag, with the laptop, the satellite phone, a GPS unit, a dozen passports, a set of prosthetic teeth, and a pair of sandals.

Watching Collin's eyes rake over his sparse belongings, he said, "Leave the laptop with me. They must be tracking you with it and tracking Butch with the cloned one. So leave it here and we'll take care of it."

Freddie jumped up and headed out to the car. He pulled a knapsack out of the trunk and, stepping back through the doorway, threw it on the bed next to Collin. It was made of desert camouflage material. Sturdy but lightweight. Pulling items out one at a time, he described each in turn. "Listen up. You've got a nine millimeter, two mags ready to go, a standard-issue buck knife, binoculars, first aid kit complete with antivenom in case of a snake bite, six MREs, three liters of water, water filtration, personal hygiene pack, toilet paper and shovel, face paint, GPS, paper map, compass, flashlight with extra batteries, wool cap, GORE-TEX camo gloves, and desert camouflage fatigues—large."

Collin took it all in. As he watched each item come out and get tossed to the side, he visualized its use. It was interesting to him that the guy just assumed he knew how to use that 9mm handgun. Oh, well. He'd figure it out if he really needed to. It looked easy enough on TV and in the movies.

The kit was fairly complete for someone about to take a hike for several days. That thought intrigued him. Plan B was a hike, eh? Noticeably missing was footwear. Whoever put this kit together must have assumed the person who would be using it was smart enough to already be wearing, or at least own, sensible footwear for such a journey. A quick survey of the other men's shoes revealed just such sensible footwear. Each wore some variation of boot, either military-style or rugged hiking boots. His feet, however, were clad in a pair of lightweight black nylon athletic shoes—not the ideal things to wear in the rugged mountain terrain that surrounded Mexico City, or anywhere other than the street or a well-groomed running path.

"You look to be in decent shape, so we're going to drop you off up the road a ways and you're going to hike to the next meeting place while we and the other teams secure the perimeter," said Jefe.

Collin had no idea what exactly the man was saying. Where was the perimeter and how would they secure it? And, most importantly, where was this next meeting place? He began piecing Plan B together, even without an explicit explanation. It seemed that everyone assumed Collin was in on Plan B, so now it would be just a matter of executing that plan. Not wanting to seem like an idiot, Collin just listened closely and continued to build the visual in his head.

Freddie unfolded the map and studied it for a moment. With a ballpoint pen, he circled a spot along Highway 150D to the southeast of Mexico City. "This is where we'll drop you off, right here in Rio Frio de Juarez." He drew another circle around an intersection of two small roads in the mountains northwest of that location. The map showed a mix of green and tan, indicating thinly forested, dry land. "Here's where we're going to pick you up at twenty-two hundred hours," Freddie said, tapping the spot. That's approximately thirty miles, so you won't have much time to rest. We're at almost ten thousand feet here. This mountain here, this peak is over thirteen thousand feet. You don't need to go over the summit, but you'll be up pretty high going over the shoulder—here," he said as he pointed to another spot with his pen. "That elevation gain is going to slow you down, but remember, we have no time to lose, so you're going to have to keep moving."

The big guy from the back seat of the car approached and started helping Freddie repack the contents they had just inventoried. "You good? Know where we're going to rendezvous and when?"

Collin nodded his head, trying to keep his eyes from growing too large or glassing over. He wanted these guys to know, or at least think, that he was just like one of them. Apparently, that was their understanding and he didn't want to change that. "I'm good, but what happens at twenty-two hundred hours? Why can't I have more time? I mean, that's a long way to go. Why is it so tight?"

The three men exchanged furtive glances. Jefe leaned in, looking at the map, then at Collin. "Our intel tells us that your man, Penh, will be meeting with some big dogs here," he said, pointing at a spot in the northwest corner of the city, "at midnight. That will just barely give us enough time to get you prepped for the next phase."

"Right. And, I presume, that meeting includes me?" asked Collin.

"That's what we hear. They plan to launch some big cyberoffensive at midnight and expect you to be there with your computer to watch it happen," said Jefe, again putting his finger at the spot on the map. "This is also where they will be taking your friend."

Collin's eyebrows shot upward and he sucked in a breath. He held it for a moment while that information rattled around in his brain. "You know what that means? They're going to set me up for this, right after they take everything I have and right before they kill me." His eyes darted from one face to another as he spoke, confirming that they had the same understanding.

"You've got no time to lose," said Jefe, checking his watch. "Let's load up and head out. Once we drop you off, you'll want to make your way into the hills using your GPS unit. I've punched in your coordinates for the rendezvous point, so you should be good to go."

Again, Collin nodded his head. "Got it."

It had been years since he'd done any backpacking. Not since he was a Boy Scout in his midteens. He couldn't remember the last time he was this high in the mountains and wondered if he'd be able to breathe.

Already doing the math, he realized that he would have to average at least two miles per hour while he was in motion. That would give him very little time to rest—maybe a total of an hour or two. He sucked in another deep breath and nodded again.

Grabbing the pack by the straps and hefting out the door, he said, "All right. Let's get going."

"Drink up, first," called the big guy who had occupied the back seat with him, pointing at the sink. "You're going to need all the hydration you can get. Camel up now so you don't have to use up your supply and spend time filtering on the trail."

"Good idea," said Collin. Remembering what he had heard about the water in Mexico when he was younger, he turned and asked, "You sure the water's OK?"

"We drink it all the time."

Collin shrugged and filled the cheap plastic cup, drained it, filled it again, and drained it two more times.

Collin and Jefe loaded his pack into the car and headed out. It was a thirty-minute drive to the riverside hamlet of Rio Frio de Juarez, where they exited the highway and took a succession of backstreets until they had climbed uphill on a dirt road at the edge of town, amid tall pine trees and large boulders.

Without shutting off the engine, Jefe jumped out of the car and helped pull the pack out of the trunk. He gave Collin a few quick reminders about the timeline, about staying away from areas where cougars and bears might be active, and to stay hydrated.

Collin hoisted the pack onto his back. It probably weighed about thirty-five pounds, not enough to slow him down, really. Keeping up the pretense of being fearless and completely prepared for this, Collin switched on his headlamp, gave two thumbs-up, and strode out into the forest, almost immediately meeting a steep incline.

His mind was racing with the possibilities and ramifications. Knowing the *Federales* were hunting him was a scary proposition. Heading out into the mountains was a bit frightening, but not because he was a novice in the wilds. Certain that his training and experience as a youth would serve him well, he didn't fear being outdoors. But this was an area he was completely unfamiliar with, and he hadn't spent much time with a map and compass for at least a dozen years. Would he be able to navigate his way to the pick-up spot? What kind of weather would he encounter? Was there wildlife he needed to be afraid of? The snakebite kit packed away brought both terror and comfort. Things swirled around in his head, but he knew he had to focus and keep moving, so he decided not to think too much. Just keeping moving. With nineteen hours to cover thirty miles, that was his main strategy.

Ten minutes in and he was already feeling the effects of the altitude, so he stopped and checked his GPS. A trail weaved its way up from the bottom of the gulley he was in and headed in the general direction he needed to travel. Blowing out, he huffed as a way to summon his courage. Putting aside his worries about wildlife, terrain, and other hazards, Collin quick-stepped along the dried creek bed and continued his ascent through the rocky, volcanic terrain.

* * * *

San Martin Texmelucan, Mexico
June 18, 3:23 a.m. Local Time

Jefe expected the knock on the door, though it came sooner than he and the team had anticipated. Having just returned from his high-speed drop-off of Collin in the mountains half an hour to the north, he didn't feel as prepared as he would have liked to be. The three men had had enough time to review their lines, but only once. The *Federales* would be easy to handle. They just had to play it cool, like Butch and his team had done. Piece of cake. They knew nothing about the American's whereabouts and could, therefore, reveal nothing to the police. Nothing to worry about.

Jefe opened the door timidly after the unmistakable pounding. "Yes, sir, may I help you?" he said in perfect Spanish, widening his eyes and dropping his jaw in mock fear and surprise, pretending to have been woken from a deep slumber.

The officer in charge puffed out his chest as he pronounced his demands. "You arrived here with a passenger who is wanted in connection with subversion against the government of Mexico. You will bring him to us immediately."

Jefe wagged his head and looked shocked. He stammered as he spoke, animating the fear and dismay. "What are talking about, officer? I don't know anyone like that."

"My men saw your car at a gas station earlier tonight. There was a man there with a hooded sweatshirt. He climbed into your car at that gas station. We have surveillance video showing his image. It matches the description of the suspect we seek."

Jefe raised his eyebrows as high as he could and shrugged his shoulders in a gesture of innocence and naiveté. "He was a vagabond who only wanted a ride to the city. He offered us money, so we gave him a ride. As soon as we got here, he took off."

The officer narrowed his eyes, as if probing Jefe's innermost soul through his eyes. "Open this door. We will search this room and your car."

Jefe cowered in a conciliatory stance. "Of course, officer, please come in. We have nothing to hide," he said as he took a step back and opened the door wide. He stretched out one arm in a sweeping action. "Be my guest."

Freddie and the other passenger stood at quasi-attention, pretending to be frightened. The three military men stormed into the room and checked every square inch in less than thirty seconds. "Nothing," they each said.

"Show us the inside of your car, the gold Toyota there," demanded the lieutenant. Jefe picked up the key from the dresser. He shot his team members a sideways glance that told them to be ready. The soldiers who had inspected the room signaled for them to follow him out to the car. Pinging sounds from the gold Toyota's still-hot engine seemed to echo in the still night air. Pointing at the trunk, the officer in charge silently ordered Jefe to open it. As he did so, he could hear the sound of boots jogging across the dirt parking lot. He turned as he lifted the lid of the trunk to show its contents. At least a dozen soldiers now stood surrounding the cluster of men at the back of the car.

Jefe showed the lieutenant the inside of the trunk. Nothing but a few rags, a deflated soccer ball, a pair of old shoes, and a tire iron. The lieutenant reached in and picked up the tire iron. "Show them the picture," he ordered one of his soldiers.

Jefe became aware of two men moving very close to him, one directly behind each shoulder. He also saw soldiers taking similar positions behind his team members.

A young-looking man wearing a freshly pressed uniform stepped forward and displayed a photograph of Collin Cook.

The lieutenant asked, "Is this the man you brought here?"

"Yes," said Jefe, allowing his eyes to give the tire iron a wary glance. In the next few seconds, he would have a decision to make: save the mission or save himself.

"Where is he?"

"I do not know, sir," said Jefe, allowing his voice to express fear. "Like I told you, he took off right after we got here."

"Which way did he go?"

"I think he went to the side of the road to hitchhike. He said he had to go to the city, but he didn't say anything about where or why."

The tire iron came with blinding speed, faster and sooner than he expected, but he began leaning away from it and falling before it crashed into his skull, just above his left ear, reducing the blow to some degree. Everything inside his head exploded as if he'd been struck by thunder. The sound of bone crunching, a blinding flash of light, and intense pain expanded in waves through his skull. Then both sights and sounds turned fuzzy. He felt himself hit the ground, sending fresh waves of agony through his skull and shoulder. His cheek crashed into the dust and gravel. His eyes closed and he lay motionless. A surge of nausea rose and fell, while his body jerked and spasmed uncontrollably in the dirt.

Above the ringing in his ears, Jefe could hear the scraping and crunching of footsteps and excited movement all around him and knew there was a struggle taking place, though it seemed to be off in the distance somewhere, too far away to reach. He was powerless to do anything to help. Instead, he followed his Special Forces training and fought back the pain and the spinning to focus on what was happening around him, trying to at least maintain situational awareness.

There were more questions being asked, but he couldn't comprehend the words. His mind was too cloudy. Loud commanding tones were being used. There was more movement and more demands. The answers coming from his teammates were unintelligible, but he knew from their brevity that his two brave friends had not and would not reveal Collin's direction or destination.

The yelling intensified, but the short answers continued. After a marked silence, Jefe heard two soft *phht* sounds and knew what they were. Shots from a handgun with a silencer on it. Those sounds were followed by the unmistakable thuds of two bodies collapsing to the ground, one after another. Boots crunched against the dirt. Then two more *phht* sounds and he knew why. First to kill, second to confirm. First shot in the head, second in the heart. Classic, efficient executions.

Jefe expected to meet a similar fate as the boots approached him. But a *squawk* from the radio in the truck must have drawn away the men's attention. Jefe opened his eyes without moving another muscle, just enough to make out what was happening. He watched two sets of boots step over him and pound their way to the open door of the truck.

A conversation took place and the man in charge summoned his soldiers.

Several other sets of boots scuffled and scurried in the dirt parking lot. Doors were opened, then slammed shut. There was a cacophony of the thuds from thick rubber soles as they landed on the metal bed of the truck. A powerful engine roared to life. Tires spun as the engine thrummed. Another roar, followed by a screech of tires on pavement and a shower of gritty dirt landing on his face and the open wound above his ear. The noise grew steadily quieter as the engine raced into the distance.

A warm trickle ran behind his ear and down his neck. His face burned from the abrasions caused by the gravel. The world seemed to be spinning soundlessly all around him. Everything went dark, then came back into focus for a brief moment as he struggled to assess the situation, then it all turned black again.

chapter Twenty-Three

When Jefe came to, his only thought was to warn the others. The mission had to succeed because the consequences of failure were too dire. Numbness had replaced the oscillating waves of pain, though the hollow ringing in his ears persisted. Maybe he wasn't as injured as he originally thought. While attempting to push himself up, the sudden movement caused a sharp shooting pain in his head so severe he almost passed out. Slowing himself down, he crawled on his belly to check on Freddie and the big fella. They were dead, as suspected, but the skin around their necks where he checked their pulses retained much of its normal warmth. A sign that not too much time had passed.

Because moving his head brought on excruciating pain and nausea, Jefe used his elbows and dragged himself on his stomach, inch by inch, between the beat-up Corolla and an old Chevy pickup truck, both parked directly in front of their hotel room. The door was open and golden light spilled onto the cracked concrete walkway and the dirt parking lot. He dragged his body over the log that delineated the parking lot, across the broken walkway, and into his room. There, right where he'd left it, his phone lay hidden behind the TV. Getting it would require him to stand and he wasn't sure he could. The chair at the desk served as a halfway point and crutch. He pushed himself up slowly enough to avoid the wave of nausea, but quickly enough to cause his head to wobble.

Stretching around the old, boxy, cathode ray tube television set perched on the chest-high dresser, Jefe was able to reach his phone just before the dizziness caused him to collapse in the chair. With the phone clutched in his hand, Jefe steadied himself and surveyed the room. The soldiers had taken everything—their duffle bags, weapons, ammo, and, most notably, Collin's laptop. He closed his eyes as he fought off the pain and tried to focus. At length, he unlocked the phone's screen, scrolled to find the last received call, and tapped the icon to place the call. Butch answered on the first ring, sounding almost out of breath. "What's up?"

In a ragged, gurgled voice, Jefe answered. "No time to tell you. They came. The *Federales*. They shot the other two. Took off." His voice gave out and he had to catch himself on the desk.

"Son of a bitch," screamed Butch. "We're coming to get you now."

"No. Call for backup," mumbled Jefe, between gasping breaths. There were pauses between each word as he struggled to convey the message Butch needed to know. "They got the laptop. Cook will be at rendezvous point B at twenty-two hundred hours. Secure him and continue the mission with the Cabo team." Jefe mustered the last of his strength to focus on this one mission-critical task. If the runaway American guy didn't get picked up, it would be game over. Butch had to know that. He was the only hope this mission had for success. Jefe pulled up the map, made a screenshot, and forwarded it to Butch, just to be sure.

The room began to spin and his stomach clenched tight as the blood drained from his head. That's when things turned to black again and he felt his cheek collide with something hard.

* * * *

San Martin Texmelucan, Mexico
June 18, 4:08 a.m. Local Time

The gardening truck barreled into the motel's dirt parking lot and slid to a stop in front of the two prone bodies. Jorge and Riptide jumped out of the cab just as an inebriated man and a scantily clad buxom young woman in spiked heels and tousled hair cautiously circled the scene. The woman held a hand over her mouth, visibly shaken. Even the drunk john, too boozed up to know where he was, turned in horror. He looked dazed and ready to vomit. It was apparent that these two had certain business that had concluded. Most likely, they had come outside due to the commotion. There was a door left open in the direction from which they stumbled, so Jorge quickly pointed them back toward their room at the far end of the low-rise building. With all the authority he could muster, he told them this was government business and, if they wanted to avoid jail, they would move a little faster. The couple staggered away, stealing glances over their shoulders and whispering to each other as they did.

The two American ex-soldiers quickly loaded their fallen colleagues into the back of the truck and set about covering up the blood and gore.

Taking notice of another open door, this one on the near side of the U-shaped motel, Riptide pointed it out to Jorge and the two jumped over the log barrier and into the room. Jefe, the leader of Team B, was sprawled out on the floor, his phone two feet from his hand. Jorge grabbed his legs. Riptide, moving to his head, first collected the phone, then gripped Jefe under the armpits and hefted. "He's got a nasty head wound here. Looks like he got clobbered bad," he said, twisting his face and looking away.

Jorge grimaced. "Let's get him in the truck and get out of here."

"Better clean this place up, too," said Riptide. "Don't need to be leaving any clues behind. Now, let's move it."

After grappling Jefe's inert weight into the back seat of the truck, the two men went to work on cleaning the room. They moved quickly and efficiently, wiping down walls and surfaces and mopping up as much of Jefe's blood as they could. Ostensibly missing was the computer hardware each team carried with it. Eight and a half minutes after their arrival, they sped away from the cheap motel.

Jorge worked the phone while Riptide drove. The original meticulously laid-out plan had blown up and they had to come up with another one—quickly.

"Butch says we've got to ditch this vehicle, but first we've got to get him some medical attention," said Jorge, pointing a thumb toward Jefe, who moaned softly in the backseat.

"He give you any ideas?"

"Yeah, there's a dual-citizen doctor that does a lot of work for our guys locally on the north side of town. Says he can be trusted."

"Perfect. Did he give you an address?"

A *ding* sounded on Jorge's phone. "Yep. Just came in."

"What about Butch? He can't stay in the motel. These guys are obviously onto us somehow."

"He's been coordinating the other teams coming into town, but when this guy didn't answer, he got nervous and had another team pick him up. He's heading out to Rendezvous Point Charlie. ETA about twenty minutes."

A siren wailed in the distance. The two men looked at each other. The sound was coming toward them from the north and traveling very fast. Two federal police trucks sped past them. Riptide watched in his mirror. "Bet they're going back to the scene of the crime."

"Yeah, we'd better get out of here."

As Riptide pressed on the gas, the truck's engine rumbled louder and the speed picked up. Wind whistled inside the cab, but didn't quite drown out the moans of their friend in the back seat.

* * * *

Mt. Tlaloc, on the outskirts of Mexico City, Mexico
June 18, 4:34 a.m. Local Time

Collin had been steadily climbing for more than two hours. His heart was pounding and his breathing labored. The air was thinner than he remembered from his backpacking days as a young Boy Scout. Of course, he was now older and had not slept much over the past few days. And, as he recalled, very few of the mountains he had hiked in Southern California were this high. He paused to shine the headlamp in all directions, checking for hazards and getting his bearings.

He also checked his GPS unit. The good news: he was on course. The not-so-good news: he had only covered a little over three miles toward his goal along the pitched, switch-backing trail. Slow progress was to be expected climbing at this rate. As he removed the pack from his back, he noticed his stomach felt queasy. It was probably hunger, considering the fact that he hadn't had a real meal since before they had arrived at the motel in the early evening. Could be the altitude and the speed with which he had climbed. In any case, he set the pack down and rummaged through the pockets in search of food and water. He found an energy bar, dense with protein and carbohydrates. That seemed to be the quickest and easiest food to consume during a short stop. Just a few bites in and he knew he'd have to save the rest for later. The density and texture was too much for his stomach to bear all at once. A slug of water helped rinse down the chalky, chewy residue left behind.

After a few minutes of resting and refueling, Collin decided to press on. As he tightened the belt strap, the pain in his gut became more pronounced. No time to stress about a few cramps, he had to keep moving.

The quarter moon was now hidden from view as he wound through the folds and crevasses of the mountain. There were unfamiliar noises coming from the shadows and darkness and clumps of trees on either side of the trail. Thoughts of mountain lions, bears, and wild boar raced through Collin's mind. He hadn't gotten a full briefing about the hazards of the area's wildlife from Freddie and Jefe prior leaving the motel room. The primary objective was for him to become invisible before the police showed up. Pack a bag and get pushed out the door. That's how it went. Everyone seemed to assume that he had had the same training as them, whatever that entailed.

Collin realized he had no idea what types of animals lived in these mountains, which allowed his imagination to roam a bit too far. Feeling less than completely prepared, Collin stopped again and rummaged through the rucksack for the gun he had seen Freddie pack in there. Once he found it, he inserted the clip of ammo, checked to make sure the safety was on, and tucked the gun into an easily accessible side pocket. Just having a gun handy made him feel braver and somehow more prepared to meet a prowling predator.

Knowing he had little time for stops, Collin pressed forward up the mountain. At the top of a rounded knoll, an expansive meadow opened up in front of him. It was flat and mostly treeless. According to the GPS, the trail veered to the west and would eventually hook back around, presumably on the other side of the meadow, before beginning another zig-zagging climb northward. Collin pulled in a deep breath, drank some water, and started along the now-level path, hoping to pick up speed. Despite the wide openness of the meadow, he could hear things that caused his senses to go on high alert. Birds cawed and squawked from the trees at the edge of the meadow. Something rustled in the grass as he approached. A handful of small rocks clattered down the slope to his left as a furry, four-legged creature scurried away. *Probably nothing to be afraid of*, he tried to assure himself. But, the more noises he heard, the more he started feeling very alone and very exposed.

After skirting the edge of the mostly flat mesa in short order, the terrain grew much steeper and rockier. Collin's lightweight, stylish running shoes began to show their inadequacies. Traction was a problem, causing him to slip in the pitched gravelly areas and slide on the smooth rocks across which the path traveled. Making progress uphill became much more taxing on his energy reserves. Less than ten miles into his thirty-mile trek and he was developing blisters on his heels and between some of his toes. Next stop, he told himself, he would look for athletic tape or mole skin or some of that friction-reducing liquid bandage stuff. If none of that was in his pack, he would resort to duct tape, the fix-it-all solution.

Even with all the many things his mind had to worry about, ignoring the churning sensations in his gut became more difficult.

chapter Twenty-Four

Lieutenant Salazar hopped out of the passenger's seat as the truck skidded to a stop. Where there were bodies, now only footprints remained. From the looks of things, they were made by rugged boots. It hadn't been long since he left this same spot in search of the dead men's accomplices. At this time of night, it was unlikely anyone was awake to have noticed their activities. Who would take away three dead bodies? It seemed unfathomable to him, but a sinking feeling told him he should have been more careful, less rash. Leaving a few men to guard the bodies would have been the most prudent thing to do had he not been so focused on getting them all.

Salazar kicked around the area, shining his flash light in all directions, until the toe of his boot came back with something stuck to it. A clump of blackish mud. The more he kicked, the more the dirt clumped up and turned darker. He squatted down and touched the substance with his index finger. Pulling his finger and hand back toward his face and rubbing it with his thumb, his finger turned dark red. It was blood. Someone had covered it with loose dirt, but it was definitely blood, the only evidence that remained. No bodies. His head jerked in a circular pattern like a sprinkler, looking for someone to question.

To his right, he noticed a smear of blood on the log at the edge of the parking lot. He followed the trail to the room where the three men had been. The door was locked, so he reared back and stomped against it, right next to the door knob. Shattering splinters of wood flew in every direction. The door rattled against the wall behind it as it swung violently on its hinges, then rebounded toward him. He blocked it with an outstretched arm as he planted his boots inside the room and scanned it.

Empty. Cleaned out. Wiped down. The smell of disinfectant wafted past him as the cool night air rushed in on a breeze and mixed with the air in the room.

The lieutenant clinched his jaw and slammed a fist into the other palm. "I knew it. I should have trusted my instincts that told me they were professionals. We've been tricked."

One of his soldiers stepped in behind him and surveyed the room. The lieutenant put out an arm to hold him back. Pointing at the floor next to the chair, he said, "More blood." He knelt down again to touch it, just to confirm his suspicion. "Gather up all the guests. Someone must have seen or heard something."

"Yes, sir."

The lieutenant cursed himself for his impulsiveness. He should have kept those men alive for questioning. His superiors would surely be upset with him if they were to find out what happened. Perhaps this mistake wouldn't matter if he could glean some useful data from the computer they had confiscated from the room. Surely there must be some information on the hard drive about these soldiers' operations and plans. He needed something to redeem himself. Without it, his future would indeed be limited and, perhaps, abbreviated.

* * * *

Through interrogations of every one of the thirteen guests staying in the low-budget motor lodge, most of them roused from sleep and some of the methods of questioning quite forceful, Lieutenant Salazar learned that there had been an unusual amount of nocturnal activity at this particular spot on this particular night.

As he processed all the information he and his men had gathered, it became apparent that his quarry, the American, had exited the room where the other three men were staying sometime shortly after they arrived, with a camouflage pack that he had loaded into the trunk of the gold Toyota. The two witnesses who had been awakened by loud noises said they saw the man as they peered through the curtains and that he looked prepared for a camping trip, except that his pack looked like something the military would use.

The gold Toyota sped away, they told Salazar, with the American and his large pack only to come racing back an hour later.

That meant half an hour out and half an hour back, roughly. Within that radius, from where he stood, rose the volcanic mountains that rimmed the Valley of Mexico in virtually every direction, dozens of small towns, and half a dozen bus terminals that could take him anywhere in the country. _The man, this fugitive, could be anywhere,_ thought the lieutenant.

As he pondered his dilemma, one of his soldiers called out to him from the open door of the gold Toyota. "Sir, we have something here," the young soldier said excitedly. He held out a palm-sized device. "Look, sir, a GPS unit."

Salazar quickly snatched it from the soldier's hand. He turned on the power and waited for the screen to come alive. When it did, he scrolled to the trips file and opened the most recent one. It showed a round-trip to and from the foot of Mt. Tlaloc at the outskirts of the tiny town of Rio Frio de Juarez, just thirty miles to the north.

In a cloud of dust and the cacophony of roaring engines and peeling rubber, the lieutenant and his men tore out of the motel's parking lot, following the course the Toyota had taken just two hours earlier.

When they arrived at the spot the GPS unit indicated was the right place, Salazar's heart dropped. He realized there was a vast wilderness in front of him and no way to know where the American had gone.

He couldn't dismiss the possibility that the man had hitchhiked or had switched to another vehicle like he did at the gas station earlier in the day. Knowing the group of men helping this American were trained professionals only confounded Lieutenant Salazar that much more. It opened up a number of possibilities, which led to a sinking sense of hopeless despair. It all added up to a bad omen for his career aspirations.

If this man had come to Mexico, as his superiors purported, with a plot to kill the president, why would he run away into the mountains? He dared not call his boss, but dared not let his man escape. His orders were simple. All he had to do was bring the American in, unharmed, before he had the chance to commit the atrocities he had allegedly planned.

Only select members of the high command had any knowledge of this American or his plans. Knowing he, Lieutenant Juan Hernandez Salazar, was part of that group caused his chest to swell with pride. His superiors recognized in him a man they could trust to do an important job and keep it a secret. The last thing he wanted to do was disappoint those who had placed that sacred trust in him. But the prospects of finding this American had grown measurably dimmer.

Of course, none of this would have come to light were it not for Salazar's relationships with the drug lords in the south. They were the ones who noticed a low-flying plane coming in to disrupt their business in some way, they supposed. Their lookout men had seen the plane crash in the field just to their north and reported it to Salazar in hopes of protection. It was Salazar's report and the pictures from the scene, provided by the drug lord's men, that had alerted the chain of command that something suspicious was going on in Villahermosa. Someone higher up matched the face of the American as an international fugitive and linked him to a plot to kill the president of Mexico. Now the American had to be stopped before he carried out his murderous plans.

Salazar realized he was in a catch-22 situation. Sure, he had helped uncover the illegal entrance of this would-be assassin into Mexico, but at the cost of revealing his tight relationship to the drug lord.

Lieutenant Juan Hernandez Salazar was momentarily overcome

with fear of the consequences of his failure. He stood stock-still, trying to think, but finding it difficult to latch onto a productive idea that would move his investigation forward.

The lieutenant's thoughts were interrupted by one of his soldiers. "Sir, have you considered the dogs? We could send dogs after this man. Maybe that is the only way to know if he went into the mountains or not."

Lieutenant Salazar turned toward the soldier and nodded his head, grateful for the distraction. "I did consider that, but we don't have a scent for them to follow. It would be a waste of time."

"Then we need a helicopter and a search team. It will be light soon. I'm sure the chopper could be airborne in a matter of minutes."

Salazar snapped his head and blinked his eyes several times, bringing his troubled mind back into focus. "That is an excellent idea, Corporal. Even better than using dogs. Call it in." He stopped himself. "Call them both in. Let's get dogs here as soon as possible. Maybe they can find something. We'll send men with dogs and radios and a helicopter in the sky to search for him. We must try everything we can to find this man before he carries out his awful mission."

The lieutenant swallowed hard, knowing this was his last and only chance to get it right. The quarry might be long gone, but he had to pull out all stops in his efforts to track and arrest this murderous American before it was too late. Many sins could be overlooked by one heroic act.

* * * *

Penh's Private Jet, over the Pacific Ocean
June 18, 6:00 a.m. Mexico City Time

Soft music played, coming from the phone on the polished cherrywood desk to his right. Pho Nam Penh woke from a rejuvenating six-hour rest in his fully reclined, soft leather lounge chair. An attendant immediately brought him an ice-cold water bottle as the motorized seat adjuster did its work.

After downing half the bottle, Penh stood and stretched and walked to the tail section of the plane to get the blood moving in his legs. As he walked, he checked messages on his phone. With each message, his rage built. Nothing but bad news, as far as he was concerned. Collin Cook was on the loose still, aided to an even larger degree than before, it appeared.

A splash of cool water on his face in the luxurious restroom helped reverse the rising anger and prepare him for what was to come. It would be much more effective for him to remain in complete control of his emotions while dealing with his Mexican coconspirator. He double-checked his watch. 6:00 a.m. in Mexico City meant that Torres would be awake, so it was time to confirm the changes that needed to take place had happened while he rested.

The knowledge that Collin Cook was receiving aid from the National Security Agency had far-reaching consequences and had caused Penh, Torres, and their accomplices to shift their priorities and hasten their planned attack. If someone at the NSA was bringing Cook to Mexico, it could be an indication that the US government had somehow learned of the coup that was underway and likely had plans of their own to stop it. The fear of a leak within Torres's camp had crossed Penh's mind before, but now seemed an undeniable conclusion. Penh had confronted him as soon as the knowledge of Cook's arrival in Mexico had been confirmed. Torres had denied it. Then came the raid at the compound staffed by the American mercenaries, revealing the depth and breadth of the American involvement and level of their preparations. Torres had vowed to get to the root of the problem and cut the head off the snake.

Penh wanted to accelerate the timeline and cut the Americans' prep time to zero. The faster they could launch their multipronged attack, the better. But Torres balked. He wanted the money he had been promised or, he had said, it was a no-go.

A stalemate had begun with the discovery of the Americans' safe house in Villahermosa. Torres was spooked and Penh was irate, convinced that Torres had run a sloppy and undisciplined organization. Torres accused Penh of being rash and hasty and bent on a personal vendetta to the point of arrogantly assuming they could and would be able to operate undetected. Then, there was the issue of Penh neglecting to fulfill his financial obligations. Trust between the two men had deteriorated at a crucial point in time, just prior to the culmination of their months-long preparations.

Now, on the eve of their grand launch, Torres demanded payment for himself and his men. Penh promised to deliver if Torres could bring Cook to the airport upon his arrival. It was a classic Mexican standoff scenario. Neither person could retreat, nor could the deal proceed unless each side met the other's demand to produce tangible results necessary to keep the plan in motion. Each person had to show his ability to keep his end of the bargain.

Fortunately, Penh's men were still tracking Cook and his laptop. It appeared he and his computer were now moving toward Mexico City again with a group of Torres's men. Penh would confirm this on the phone.

Penh salivated at the prospect of his men breaking in to the NSA database and finding out how much the Americans knew. The sooner Collin Cook's laptop could be accessed, the sooner they could counteract the Americans' strategies. That could take place while Penh and Cook were making their hasty round-trip to Panama City to retrieve Cook's $30 million, which he would present to Torres to keep his military forces on the job and to live up to his end of the bargain.

It was a chess game on steroids. Move and countermove with the stakes being world domination. Very few people understood now the ramifications this night would bring. However, in the morning it would all be clear. The Americans were about to lose their prominence as the dominant economic and military force in the world to be replaced by those they had victimized and abused for decades. It was a thought that Penh relished as much as any other.

With the raid and killing of the four agents in Villahermosa, Penh felt confident that he had taken much of the air out of the NSA's tactical team. And if he could strike quicker and harder than previously planned with the help of the information and gateway on Collin's laptop, he was sure he and his team could thwart any and all offensives.

The NSA—indeed the entire world—was about to receive a massive shock.

Senator Rivera Torres picked up on the third ring, which annoyed Penh. He knew he was sending a signal, but Penh pushed past it to concentrate on more urgent matters. When asked, the senator assured Penh that the combined members of their two teams were in place. They had all the equipment they needed and were working in an isolated fire-walled office in an otherwise empty building.

"How can you be so sure the building is secure?" Penh inquired.

"It has not yet been completed, so there are high fences with razor wire. We have troops stationed around the perimeter to restrict access. No one gets in or out of that building without going through our checkpoints. There are no tenants because none of the offices are ready for occupants, except ours. Plus, all construction work has been halted thanks to a clever and conveniently timed inspection delay. Work cannot continue until those inspections take place and the inspectors are all tied up for the next several days."

"Your bureaucrats living up to their reputation."

"Yes, indeed," said Senator Torres with a chortle, the first bit of levity between them in days. "On top of that, we have a dedicated fiber-optic trunk line running into a conference room on the twenty-sixth floor. It is the only fully operational suite, by my request. I know the contractor personally. It is I who made sure his company was awarded the job—a one-hundred-million-dollar job, I might add—so he has granted me certain favors without asking questions."

"Any updates on our hostage?"

"They are traveling as we speak and will arrive in the early evening. That will give your man plenty of time to set up, as you requested."

"Excellent. Then we are on-schedule and can commence our attack tonight." It was more of a command than a question.

The senator responded with an edge in his voice. "Do you have the payment we agreed upon? My men cannot continue to work for free, and neither can I. You gave me your word you would have it upon arrival and I, in turn, promised my men the same."

"I will have the money by the time I return in the evening. Rest assured of that."

"My men will walk away from this project if your promises are not kept. It is a bad precedent that does not bode well for promises of future fortune and privilege."

"I told you to have your men take Cook into custody and bring him to me at the airport upon my arrival. Is he not en route?"

"My men are in pursuit of him as we speak," said the senator. "I will have an update within the hour."

"I certainly hope so, for your sake." Penh paused to let that sink in and to allow the tension to build. He knew Torres anticipated the next question, so he let the moment drag on. "And what about the issue of the mole within your organization?"

"There is no mole. I know every one of my top advisors. I know of their loyalty and passion. None would betray me or my vision. Besides, Mr. Penh, in less than twenty-four hours from now the world will be changed forever. There is little anyone can do at this point to stop what is about to happen. You said so yourself. Please tell me you do not doubt what you have said."

The nerve of Torres. "I don't need to remind you that this is our most crucial time. If there is an infiltrator within your ranks, he had better be silenced immediately. Is this clear, Senator?"

"Absolutely. It will be dealt with immediately."

chapter Twenty-Five

Butch paced the floor of a new hotel room closer to the city and much more comfortable. It offered room service and Wi-Fi. That's all he needed right now. He had set up an array of computer equipment that cast an eerie light across the sculpted carpeting under his feet. One computer monitored the whereabouts of his agents, as well as the nameless American's progress over the mountain using the tracking device they had planted in the rucksack without his knowledge. On the screen was a map with blinking colored dots. Each dot represented a different person. He could see the American was moving, albeit slower than expected. He would have to pick up the pace if he was going to make it on time. Butch figured once he got to the downhill side, it wouldn't be too difficult for him to average closer to three miles per hour.

Another laptop listened in to police radio communications. A third was hooked up to the satellite phone the American had with him and fed data into it to throw off whoever might be tracking its whereabouts.

The other dots tracked the groups of contractors converging on the Mexican capital, their movements and efforts being directed by the secretive team in Washington and shared with Butch.

With each turn, Butch started a new thought as he paced. His mind flipped from one aspect of the mission to another, from one person and his role to another. Sorrow filled him when he thought about the two dead agents now being hauled away by Jorge and Riptide and the four who perished in Villahermosa. Families would need to be notified and transportation would need to be arranged, but that was secondary to the mission. They could wait. Another turn brought thoughts about the injured man and his prognosis.

He crossed himself and silently prayed for all six of his brave fallen comrades. They served their country faithfully, but due to the clandestine nature of their work, no one would know the particulars of their sacrifice. The government would spin a special simplified story that would find its way to the of the neglected middle pages of the middle sections of the hometown newspapers in their areas. He had seen it a hundred times. It would all sound very patriotic. There would be praise for their senses of duty and devotion to country and family. The single-column stories would be high on commendation, short on details. Regardless of what was said or how it was portrayed, those families would be no less devastated by the loss.

These mounting losses also added up to operational extremities. With six missing team members, he had had to make significant changes to each team's assignment. They had to be brought up to speed on the details of the mission while they traveled. Their training, fitness, and operational IQ, like all in this line of work, were superior. That was all he had to rely on.

A surprise train of thought hijacked his mind during one of the laps across the room: here he was, not far from where his parents had lived prior to leaving their homeland to try to provide him and his brothers with a better life, now working for his new country while it helped protect his old country. Everything about the current mission seemed odd. The fact that he and his team were infiltrating a foreign country, preparing to engage in combat with soldiers from a friendly nation without authorization or consent from the president or Congress, put him and his team in a very difficult position should something go wrong. They were, after all, independent contractors with no traceable ties to any government agency. That gave the president and Congress complete deniability and left them stranded and alienated in the case of failure. At this point, their options were limited. Win, die trying, or walk away now. With so much on the line, losing or walking away were not options that anyone on this team would entertain. It was a tangled web, but he was proud to help two countries that he loved at the same time.

Butch knew everyone involved sought nothing less than complete success. Sure, the average American would never know about what they had done and they would never receive medals or commendations, but their reward would be as much peace as a victory over a single enemy could buy. The knowledge that the world would, for the most part, go on as it had was its own prize.

Butch knew he had to keep focused on the mission, so he pushed that thought, although encouraging, to the background for the time being.

A ringing sound shattered his concentration. It wasn't entirely unexpected, except for the timing of it. He moved to the chair and pulled the laptop connected to the satellite phone a bit closer and turned up the volume. The voice that answered was familiar. It was the American whose name he didn't know. He sounded hesitant as well as out of breath. "Hello."

"Mr. Cook. Did I catch you during your morning workout?" came a silky-smooth, almost British accent that emphasized the ending consonants a bit too much.

"I try to stay in shape. What do you need?"

"I need *you*, Mr. Cook."

"Why do *you* need *me*? You have all the information you need. It's right there on the hard drive you cloned."

"Oh, don't treat me like some sort of fool. You are lying and you know it. Without your fingerprints and retinas, I cannot access the information I need. You were very clever to set up such stringent security measures. Or, should I say, your friend at the NSA was?"

Butch listened closely, wondering how Penh had put it together and how much he knew about what they had planned. The American hesitated long enough to let Penh know he'd struck a nerve. Butch was sure of it. "What friend are you talking about? I'm all alone out here, just trying to dodge you and Interpol."

"I don't think so. There is plenty of evidence to refute that."

"You're deluded," the American snapped back. "There is none."

Again, Butch wondered if Penh sensed the same level of defensiveness and evasiveness he did.

"Where shall I start? Shall I start with your escape from London? Or how you decided to leave Hamburg in the middle of the night? Or shall we discuss your prearranged flight out of Paris to Grand Cayman? Hmm? Any of these ring a bell?"

"I don't know what you're talking about. I'm living my life free and on my own. No one tells me what to do or where to go."

"OK. You want to play it that way? Then who saved your mum and girlfriend by killing my men in San Diego? How did a group of trained assassins just stumble into that abandoned warehouse in the desert at just the right time while you were thousands of miles away in the middle of the ocean, tied up on a sailboat?"

"You're asking the wrong guy. I'm sure you have plenty of other enemies. A guy like you would have no problem accumulating people who dislike him. You're not as invisible as you'd like to think." Butch admired this American's ability to think on his feet and bluff like a poker champion.

"I also find it suspicious that after your boat wrecked, you were magically rescued and carried off in an airplane, the same airplane that made an emergency landing in Belize after shutting down the entire municipal airport around its arrival and departure time. Curious that all of that could happen while you were working alone, living your life the way you want."

The American held his tongue for a few ticks. Butch couldn't imagine what he might say to all of this. It was pretty obvious that Penh had broken through the mystery that surrounded this "Mr. Cook." If nothing else, Butch knew the man's name now.

"Yeah, so what? The NSA approached me after you and I mysteriously met each other in the Bahamas and then again in London a few weeks later. Apparently, they've been tracking you. They wanted to know what I knew about you. They didn't believe that I knew nothing, despite the fact that it was true. So they told me that if I worked with them, I would get to keep the money that is, by the way, rightfully mine. Obviously, I refused to cooperate. That's why Interpol and the FBI are after me."

The British-sounding guy didn't hesitate. "So they fed you a lie and you believed it?"

"I believe that you're a power-hungry, soulless, psychotic head case. That's not a lie and it's not that hard to believe."

The guy with the accent breathed in audibly. Butch could sense the tension. "Mr. Cook, we have your friend, Mr. Howell. If you want him to remain alive and in one piece, you will stay right where you are."

The American's defiant voice barked back, "Why is that?"

"You are currently surrounded by federal police from the Republic of Mexico. They have a warrant out for your arrest."

"My arrest? What for?"

"For conspiracy to assassinate the president of Mexico."

* * * *

Mt. Tlaloc, Mexico
June 18, 7:20 a.m. Local Time

For the past several hours, cramps, blisters, and the steep terrain slowed Collin to the point where his progress was little more than crawling speed, so he removed the pack and sat on a rock and contemplated his condition.

The conversation with Penh repeated in his head. He had had to convince Penh that he was not in possession of his laptop and hadn't been since he landed in Villahermosa. Penh hadn't believed him at first. But, apparently, he got some sort of confirmation and switched the subject. He did, however, continue to threaten Rob's life. Collin had managed to buy some time by agreeing to comply to Penh's terms after Penh landed in Mexico City, but he kept his current whereabouts hidden. Penh was not happy with any amount of delay, but Collin negotiated as hard as he could, given the circumstances.

Worries about Rob and what Penh might do had kept his mind off his physical discomfort. Exertion had kept him warm enough to this point despite the chilly breeze and cool night air. But now, even with the morning sunshine, what was a chilly breeze had turned to gusty wind as he approached the high-elevation pass that marked, as nearly as he could tell, the one-quarter mark toward his destination. Temperatures hovered in the low fifties, according to the tiny thermometer attached to one of the pack's zippers. The cool air quickly turned his sweat cold, aided by the wind, causing him to shiver. Collin opened the main compartment of his backpack and removed the camouflage clothing Freddie had packed in there. The shirt was made of polypropylene material so it would wick away moisture. He pulled off his saturated T-shirt and put on the long-sleeved camo shirt. While he was at it, he decided he would change his pants, too, replacing his cargo shorts with camouflage long pants.

When he stood, his vision began to swim. Dizzy and light-headed, Collin sat back down before he was able to put the pants on and held his head in his hands. He was breathing hard because of the thin air. That was definitely part of it. Maybe he was a bit dehydrated, too. He swigged some more water and bit off another worthy bite of the compact energy bar, knowing it was perhaps contributing to the rebellion rising in his stomach. Expecting the feeling to fade as he rested and drank, it instead worsened until he was on his knees, retching. When he finished, he realized the retching had helped the queasiness in this stomach, but sapped his strength. He sat up on the rock and pulled on the camouflage pants, waiting for his insides to normalize.

A feeling lower in his gut wouldn't subside. He recognized the feeling and rifled through the pack for the toilet paper he had watched Freddie pack in there. This was Montezuma's Revenge. He had heard about it, but not for many years, figuring the water in Mexico was now OK to drink. Remembering the two full glasses he pounded down at the big guy's insistence, he now regretted using tap water from a cheap motel to hydrate. *But that water couldn't affect him this quickly,* he thought. Then he remembered drinking from a glass in Puerto Lempira, two days prior. And before that, he had been in Panama, Columbia, Peru, Bolivia, and Argentina, staying, at times, in dives in the not-so-classy parts of town. Maybe he had not been as careful as he should have been about water since he left Europe a month and a half earlier.

Walking back to his pack, Collin's knees were wobbly and his head felt like a helium balloon attached to a string. His watch told him he had eight hours to get to this destination while his GPS told him he still had almost seventeen miles to go.

With no time to lose, Collin tried to lift the pack so he could put his arms through the straps. The pack wouldn't budge. It felt like a thousand pounds. Carefully avoiding his own pool of vomit, he manhandled the pack up on the rock using what little strength he had left in his legs to help. He struggled to hold the pack in place while he maneuvered his body into position. His arms and legs felt like they were full of lead. A deep yearning from inside pulled at him like extra gravity, making him want to just curl up in a ball and sleep. Tempting as it might have been to lay down for a few minutes, his mind pressed upon him the importance of his mission. Penh's words rang in his ears. Rob's life hung in the balance, as did the security of the United States and, perhaps, much of the world. Pushing himself to keep moving, he wrestled the pack onto his back.

Once the shoulder straps were on, he leaned forward and pushed himself up to a standing position. Steadying his balance against the rock, it took him a full minute to stand up straight and tighten his belt strap, then another half-minute to get his bearings and coax his feet into motion. Collin shuffled forward, climbing ever higher up the shoulder of the mountain, his thin athletic shoes struggling to grip the rocky surface, his hollow body struggling to stay upright.

He persevered for as long as he could before Montezuma demanded more. In a fit of manic flailing, he dropped the pack, dashed toward a rocky outcropping, and prepared himself for the onslaught. The contents of his bowels exited with such force that he worried his guts would shoot out, too.

While he was at it, his stomach revolted again, just for good measure, making it hard to keep his balance and concentration. The shoes took the brunt of the onslaught from his mouth. Vomit splattered off the left shoe and onto the rocks in front of him. To add to his misery, his foot was now soaking wet and pungent.

This would not have been a pleasant experience in even the most luxurious setting, but to have this happen when he was all alone, twelve thousand feet up the side of a mountain in a foreign country with an ominous deadline looming, presented a severe test of not only his physical endurance and his desire to survive, but his commitment to stopping Pho Nam Penh "at all costs." Collin had to fight off the thought that rest and recovery were more important at this time than making the rendezvous and preventing Penh from wreaking whatever havoc Lukas thought he was planning. In his exhausted and depleted state, Collin questioned whether it really mattered and if what Lukas told him was true. He wondered why Lukas and his team couldn't just do it without him so he could rest. His body kept insisting on sleep while in his mind he heard Lukas urging him on and Penh threatening him. In the end, his trust in Lukas and his desire to do the right thing prevailed and his body reluctantly followed what his mind told it to do.

At roughly forty-five-minute intervals, Montezuma returned and a similar scene repeated. He was making less than one mile per hour. With so little strength left and unable to hold down food or water, Collin worried that he wouldn't even survive the day, let alone make it to the meeting spot.

With his mouth dry, his throat raw, and his body in pain from head to foot, it was time for Lukas's semi-regular check-in call. It couldn't have come at a more inopportune time, but Collin was always glad to hear from his wise and loyal friend. He answered the bright yellow satellite phone on the third ring and spoke to Lukas for less than ninety seconds, but his voice and his calm assurance added just the boost of courage and vision Collin needed to get himself going again.

chapter Twenty-Six

Nic found himself gathering his things and preparing to leave the office in the middle of the afternoon. This day had taken a strange turn, one he never expected, when Alastair called him into his office five minutes ago and informed him he was heading to Mexico City to take Pho Nam Penh into custody.

"What? Have you gone mad? Arrest Penh? Just like that? What makes you think he's even there?" Nic had questioned in his squeaky voice, which elevated in pitch whenever he got excited. "Last I knew we were still trying to get Collin Cook. We knew *he* was in Mexico, but not Penh."

Alastair held up a hand and Nic stopped the questions. "We have it on good authority from both the Americans and the Mexicans that he will be landing there just five hours from now and is meeting with some high-level government insiders later this evening. We're a bit behind the eight ball here, Nic, but the terms of the agreement between the Americans and the Mexicans is that Interpol is to make the arrest. So get to it. Your plane leaves at half four." Nic left the office in a daze and was called back in just seconds later. "Be sure you're carrying your firearm and your badge, Detective Lancaster."

Now Nic's head was spinning. He had no idea what prompted this sudden turn of events or how the information had come or how reliable it was. All he knew was that his boss ordered him to go and he was going to be on a special military jet flying over the Atlantic in less than an hour. He found it interesting how quickly things could change sometimes in this line of work, but how painfully slow they could be at other times.

With barely more than the clothes on his back and his laptop computer in its carrying case, Nic was whisked away in a company car with a company driver for the first time in his young career. Maybe he was back on the fast track after all.

* * * *

Mt. Tlaloc, Mexico
June 18, 2:38 p.m. Local Time

After the sixth or seventh episode with Montezuma—he'd lost count—as he lay on his side with his pants around his knees, wondering if he would be able to carry on, Collin began to feel something inside. Something like a surge of energy. Something like a call from his stomach and a cry from his muscles, asking for food, asking for fuel. But he was completely wiped out, unable to move. Every ounce of strength had been depleted. The surge continued, as did the call for something to eat. Answering the call, he crawled the few feet to where he'd dropped his pack and pulled out one of the MREs, the infamous military "meals, ready to eat." He read the instructions, tore open the packaging, and began to eat the food many vets had told him was inedible. He didn't care. It had calories and it filled the void and would give him energy that he so desperately needed.

The other thing his military friends had told him was that MREs had several nicknames. One of them that he remembered as he looked at the package was "Meals Refusing to Exit." If that was true, he thought, it might be exactly what he needed right now. Anything that could counteract what Montezuma was doing to him was a worthwhile and welcome solution.

His throat was so burned from stomach acid that he couldn't taste anything and his gut was so hollow it would accept even protein-fortified sawdust. Collin shoveled in the foodstuff and washed it down with a generous slug of water, flavored with some sort of electrolyte drink packet that tasted mildly of raspberry. Of the three liters of water he started with, he was now down to about half a liter. He knew he needed to find a lake or a stream to filter water and refill his supply.

Within minutes, Collin felt rejuvenated enough to continue. His hind end hurt to move. Too many of these violent episodes in too short a time. Walking was already painful, thanks to his feet. This problem would only exacerbate the trauma of moving his legs. Every muscle in his midsection was sore and tender from the relentless retching. His throat was raw and burning. Even his back was sore, probably a pulled muscle during one of the gastrointestinal revolts.

Despite his physical pains, a renewed sense of hope and power began to take hold.

Thoughts of his mother floated through his mind. He said a silent prayer for her, sensing deep inside that she prayed for him, too. At the same moment, an image of Emily tied up and gagged flashed through his mind. Penh and his men had intended to hurt her, as well as his mother. A dark anger welled up inside, fueling the renewed strength coursing through his muscles and veins. Pho Nam Penh had to be stopped and he would have to pay for what he had done. The real question was how and what could he—Collin Cook, an untrained, unskilled, civilian—do? Especially considering his current condition.

He was off the trail now and had been for the past few hours, heading cross-country as best he could through patches of open, rocky terrain punctuated by the occasional stand of trees and bushes. Dried grass and low-lying, flowery succulents surrounded the rocky outcroppings where he stopped for this latest break.

He checked his watch. A little more than seven hours until pick up at the rendezvous point. The GPS said he still had just under sixteen miles to go. Strapping the pack onto his back, he sucked in a lung full of the fresh mountain air and steeled his resolve to be there on time. He wanted to get back to civilization and find a comfortable place to rest, yes, but he also wanted to speak with

Lukas and learn all he could about what he had in mind for dealing with Pho Nam Penh and getting Rob back.

With the first glimmers of renewed energy finding their way to his muscles, the next big impediment to making good time now was his feet. Despite the duct tape on his shoes and mole skin on his feet, blisters were forming everywhere. The flimsy athletic shoes were not supporting his feet in the rugged, volcanic-rock-strewn terrain. His feet moved around inside his shoes, causing friction, which caused hot spots on his skin, which caused blisters, which caused pain and discomfort.

The shoes were not only creating blisters, they were showing signs of distress. Around the joints of his toes, where the most flexion happened, holes were widening in the lightweight, stretchy fabric. Along the sides of the big toes, the upper was separating from the sole on both shoes. Other tears had started every time he scraped against the rough edge of a rock. He had wrapped duct tape around the worst spots, hoping it would hold the shoes together long enough for him to get off this mountain.

The tread wasn't doing much better. It was getting carved up on both shoes by the metamorphic terra beneath them. Every jagged rock pierced through the spongy soles to the bottoms of his feet. The air trapped in the highly-touted cushioning was no match for the conditions, nor the additional weight Collin lugged on his back. With this kind of foot pain, he knew from experience with long-distance running events, that even standing was going to be a chore before this journey was through.

As the agony mounted in his feet and with his legs still not at full-strength, not to mention the beating the shoes were taking, Collin wondered how he was going to make it, especially considering most of the remainder of hike would be downhill and cross-country, which was tougher on the feet, legs, and shoes. But he had no time to stop or slow down. He just kept moving and kept praying.

As Collin pounded his way downhill, doing his best to follow the straight red line on the GPS, he heard something echoing off the peaks around him. It was a thumping sound, accompanied by a dull roar. He stopped to listen more carefully. The thumping grew louder, but he could not tell where it was. He knew that sound was from a helicopter somewhere in the area and it sounded like a big one, which could only mean one thing: the military was searching for him.

* * * *

Licenciado Adolfo Lopez Mateos International Airport, 40 miles south of
Mexico City
June 18, 2:50 p.m. Local Time

As the Gulfstream taxied to the private hangar on the north end of the busy airport, Pho Nam Penh was already working the phone, contacting members of his team who had set up in Mexico City. His first phone call was to Senator Juan Miguel Rivera Torres. In short guttural bursts, the senator assured him that his team was prepared and standing by. His voice was hushed, just above a whisper, and he ended the call hastily, explaining that he could not speak right now, but would call back shortly. Penh scowled at his phone after the call and tapped it on his knee repeatedly.

The senator, of all people, knew what was at stake. He had been recruiting and assembling his forces for months. They were moving into place, making ready to seize the moment and claim the ultimate victory. Of the senator's grand and devious ambitions, Penh could rest assured.

He let the moment pass without redialing as the flight attendant brought him his suitcoat and briefcase. Trust, though currently under strain, had been established between Penh and Torres because of their common hatred of the gluttonous, greedy capitalists that had pillaged both of their countries over the generations. That commonality propelled the relationship and the schemes from their earliest stages to this point—the brink of Western civilization's collapse. As the final details of Penh's plan drew near, his trust in Torres had begun to slip. Torres's personal agenda had shown itself, so Penh knew he would need to constantly remind Torres of the end goal they had agreed upon. Vision and execution, that was the name of the game and those two things would have to be made crystal clear to his fellow conspirator and all those working with them in order to bring about the long-awaited, fast-approaching culmination of those plans.

When the plane's door opened, the nearly deserted northern reaches of the private tarmac were bathed in hazy sunlight. Mexico City was as polluted as Los Angeles and many other major metropolises Penh had visited. Not as bad as Beijing, but it was bad enough for him to take note.

Penh emerged from the temperature-controlled luxury of his plane to the warmth of the mountain-ringed Valley of the Damned, as it was sometimes called. A sense of pride and the thrill of anticipation swelled within him as he sucked in a lungful of the thin, polluted mountain air. It was all very fitting. Being in this place, this aptly named mega-metropolis, as it became the epicenter of a true modern-day revolution, harked back to the days when the Aztecs dominated this hemisphere. Since their fall, they had become like Penh's people in Southeast Asia: forgotten, looked over, and betrayed. Now, as Penh's scheme worked its way through its final phases, the forgotten and the damned would rise again and claim the place where now stood the self-appointed, overindulged, hypermaterialistic gluttons at the top of the world's old-order. The old guard would soon be toppled. And Penh would usher in a new era, headed by the new guard, and there would be order. Or else.

Surveying the area, Penh could see no sign of Collin Cook or the guards that should have delivered him upon Penh's arrival. The senator had promised. Anger rose within him and a hard scowl overtook his countenance.

Moments later, when his phone rang, a deviant smile returned to his face. It was Senator Torres. "Where is Collin Cook?" Penh demanded of him. "We had a deal."

"My men found those responsible for hiding and transporting him. I am happy to report those men are now dead. They have confiscated the computer, but as of yet, they have not located him."

Penh clenched his jaw and sucked in a breath slowly and loudly through his nose. "My instructions were explicit. Have him here when I land."

"I know what you demanded, but I don't know how we can find this man who keeps disappearing. I know you have had your own troubles apprehending him, so please do not lecture me about his escape. We are working to remedy the situation as we speak."

"Do you know where he is? How did he escape?"

"We believe he escaped into the mountains east of the city. We have a helicopter in the air searching for him as we speak."

"Why was this not done sooner? We are wasting valuable time."

"Please understand the limitations we have at the moment. Though our forces have grown and will continue to grow, we do not yet have all of the military units under our control. Acquiring the use of a military helicopter for our purposes required time and persuasion. Then, once the helicopter was in the air, we have had to cover more than three hundred square miles with just one aircraft. It is a long and difficult process."

Penh huffed. "What is your estimated time of delivery?"

"We have not yet located him, so I do not have a firm time to give you."

Penh shut his eyes tight and held the phone in front of him to let the storm inside settle. "Remember our bargain: no Cook, no money. If you cannot deliver him, you will not receive the money."

"We will deliver him."

chapter Twenty-Seven

When he first heard the thumping of the helicopter, Collin was out in the open, eating an MRE at the crest of a ridge. The peak of Mt. Tlaloc towered above him to the right. Begging his aching body to obey, he had managed to hustle downslope a quarter mile or so to a gulley where a clump of trees stood. The trees provided cover from the overhead observers looking for him, but they only extended a few hundred yards. He checked overhead and listened closely in an attempt to locate his would-be captors. When he thought it was clear, he darted, as best he could, to the next copse of trees two hundred yards away. A similar pattern had repeated for the past forty-five minutes, greatly reducing his speed. Run to cover, stay under the cover for as long as possible, take a visual check, then run like mad for more cover. It was easier when there was a stream to follow, as in the gulley areas. But when he had to circumnavigate around a hill or ridge, it became more tedious and difficult and slow-going, as well as risky.

Now he was worried about the timing. It was almost three o'clock in the afternoon. The GPS said he was still over sixteen miles from his destination. He needed to check in with Lukas, so he stopped for a rest in a patch of six-foot-high bushes that gave him clear sky above to use the satellite phone.

When Lukas answered, he asked, "Where have you been? I've been trying to reach you."

"I switched the phone off to save battery. Plus, I was afraid Penh was tracking me."

"Good point. He probably would have. But I wish I could have reached you sooner."

"Why?"

"Because things are accelerating, my friend. Penh landed in Mexico about an hour ago and was expecting you to be there. He's pissed at Torres, the crooked senator he's working with. Torres told him they were looking for you in the mountains, so beware."

"I've been dodging a helicopter for quite a while. It's really slowing me down."

"You've done well to keep moving and avoid capture, because that gives us time. Are you still heading for the same rendezvous point?"

"Yeah," said Collin.

"Good. Keep doing what you're doing. Try to keep up your pace, but if Penh calls you, you've got to buy yourself some time, as much as possible. We need to get our guys in place before that helicopter lands."

"How do I do that? If I keep this phone on, and he can track me, he'll send that helicopter to my location. Game over."

"Not necessarily," Lukas said evenly. "It's late enough in the day that he'll know there's no way to get you to the bank in Panama before it closes. That's a three-hour flight, at least. So he knows at this point that he's got to wait until morning to go get the money. He has pushed forward the timeline, despite not delivering the money. According to our source inside Torres's advisory group, Penh wants to launch the first wave of his attack at midnight tonight. Torres is demanding payment before the launch, but Penh is pushing back because Torres didn't bring you as he had promised. It's a see-saw battle for supremacy between the two of them. Anything could happen at this point."

"What do I do?" asked Collin.

"You should expect Penh to call. He's anxious and impatient, but knows he can't finish you off tonight, so you have the upper hand."

"Why do I not feel like I do?"

"Probably because he will continue to threaten your life and Rob's. But listen, he's going to make some demands of you. It's OK to play along, with some resistance, of course. You give him a little, but ask for something in return each time. If you agree to one of his demands under the condition that Rob doesn't get hurt, then you maintain some leverage against him. If he doesn't agree, tell him you can survive out in that wilderness as long as it takes. By the time his forces find you, his deadline will be long since passed."

"You think he'll go for that? I mean, does he need my money that bad?"

"I think it's more than just the money at this point. It's saving face. I also think he has high hopes for getting into that laptop his men took."

"That makes sense, but how do I know he won't hurt Rob?"

"We don't. He's likely to hurt him one way or the other. You just have to negotiate the best deal you can to keep him and yourself as safe as possible for as long as possible. Time is our most valuable commodity at this point and Penh knows it. That's why he's stepping up the first attack tonight. He wants to catch us off guard before we can assemble the forces we need to deal with the forces he already has. Our inside source is risking his life to discreetly get the word out to several Special Forces groups, asking for help. Every hour gives him the ability to marshal more troops and for them to get in position. Understood?"

"Yes, I totally understand. That's the easy part. The hard part is going to be figuring out how to stall."

"Yeah, I know," said Lukas. "But keep in mind the advantages you have. He wants and needs money, but he can't access it without you. He wants to use that laptop to infiltrate our systems. We have it set up to recognize and respond to you and only you. He has figured that out, so he knows he needs you to get what he wants off it."

"I wish that made me feel better, but it doesn't."

"I know. Sorry. That's all I can tell you right now. Now, stay positive and stay strong. I'll talk to you again soon."

The call ended and Collin saw a chance to make another dash

for the next hiding place a little way down the mountain. While he was running, the phone began to ring again. This time, it was Penh. He made it to the shelter of another clump of bushes while the helicopter was searching an area farther up the mountain. He was reluctant to answer for several reasons, one of which was the location of the helicopter and the ability to put in some distance while it was circling miles away in vain. Another was fear of Penh carrying out one of his violent threats on Rob.

* * * *

Mt. Tlaloc, Mexico
June 18, 3:49 p.m. Local Time

Collin kept the conversation with Penh short and to the point, as he was fairly sure that the longer he transmitted, the better the chances Penh and his men could locate him, especially if the helicopter had the right equipment on it.

After Penh made a blustery promise to slowly cut Rob to pieces, Collin called his bluff. "Problem is, you still need me and you don't know where I am. If you did, your goons would have caught me by now. So let's stop playing games. You want my money. I get that. You must be running low on funds and your little army of hackers must be getting pretty expensive to support. You're coming after me because you think—or, at least, thought at one point—that I'm an easy target. I think I've proved you wrong. And because of the security measures I've taken, the only way to get that money out of the bank is in person. Mine is the only face they'll recognize and accept for withdrawal requests. If that wasn't enough, now you feel the need to hack my laptop, which you can't do because of the advanced biometric protocol installed on it. So you're kind of screwed without me."

"That is a very dangerous supposition, Mr. Cook, considering I have your best friend in my custody and care. If you want to see him in one piece, I would suggest you cooperate fully and immediately."

Collin continued, seemingly unfazed. "You also need to show your men that I cannot beat you. I get that, too. It's one of those macho ego things and, apparently, you have an enormous ego that must be fed raw meat regularly." As he spoke, Collin could hear Penh's breathing grow louder, even over the static-filled connection. "I have come to accept the fact that you are going to kill me and Rob no matter what I do. But your threats to hurt Rob are a disincentive for me to cooperate with you. See, if you are going to hurt him and kill us both anyway, what's the point in cooperating?"

"Your choice is whether I kill you quickly and spare you and your friend the agony of a long, torturous death or whether you get to watch the world change right before we hand you over to the governors of the new world order and let them decide your punishment and fate."

"Again, that's not much of a choice. I'm ready to survive out here in the wilderness long enough to watch your whole diabolical scheme collapse on itself."

"I'm afraid, Mr. Cook, you overestimate your bargaining position. Your friend will pay a heavy toll for your callousness."

"Do I really? I don't think so. You need me. You hate to admit it, but you need me. And because you need me, I can make a few demands. Yes, I realize you have my best friend and you want to maim him as a way to get to me. I completely understand all that," Collin said with all the confidence he could muster. "I'll call you in an hour to see if you have come up with a better scenario." With that, Collin ended the call and shut off the satellite phone to avoid being traced.

* * * *

Clutching the 9mm tightly in his hand, Collin barreled down the side of Mt. Tlaloc toward his rendezvous point. Around every corner, he half-expected an ambush from a mountain lion or panther or whatever type of predator lived on this mountain. Hence, he held the gun firmly in hand as he moved swiftly past rocks, trees, and bends in the trail. The helicopter continued to sweep above the ridges and slopes to the east. He was under near-constant tree cover now that he had descended from the rocky upper climes, thus less worried about being spotted from above. Keeping an eye on his watch, he tried to cover as much distance as possible before he made the promised return phone call. The GPS indicated he had less than fourteen miles to go. Every muscle screamed under the exertion and the aftereffects of Montezuma's Revenge, which had thankfully passed.

Although it hurt to run downhill, he knew it was less stress on his muscles than trying to go slow and control his downhill momentum. Instead of focusing on the pain, he focused on the end goal. Collin was operating purely on willpower and determination at this point. Events of the past few weeks awakened in him a competitive drive and desire to win he had never experienced. Maybe it was out of necessity. Never had he wanted so badly to beat someone.

Collin seethed at the idea that Penh now had Rob held captive somewhere that only he knew. Penh was a sick dude and Collin worried about his best friend. Questions swirled in his mind about whether his tactics would backfire, fearing that Penh would mangle and torture Rob.

Thoughts of Emily rolled through his mind, as well, remembering what Penh and his goons had done to her and what they had threatened to do. He cringed at the image of her tied to a table with one of Penh's goons wielding a hunting knife. One of them had already cut her beautiful face by the time the last video was broadcast to him aboard the *Admiral Risty*. That image was seared into his mind and the savagery of it brought his blood to a boil, even now.

Then there was his mother. Penh had stooped as low as one can go when he kidnapped Collin's ailing mother as a poker chip in his little game. Only the dregs of humanity could sink that low. Despite his fine apparel, his aristocratic accent, and his Oxford and MIT education, Pho Nam Penh was still a scumbag in Collin's eyes. He deserved what he had coming and more.

Having found a seldom-used path, Collin had picked up the pace as it wound down through canyons and gullies on the forested western slopes of the mountain. Only the roughness and narrowness of the path prevented him from running faster. It took a great deal of effort to continually push thoughts of fatigue and his painfully abused feet to the background as he focused on saving Rob.

Half an hour after the last conversation with Penh, Collin paused long enough to pull out the phone and call Lukas's secure mobile line.

"Did you hear the conversation with Penh?" Collin asked.

"Sure did. You did great. That's just what we want, to plant the seeds of doubt in his mind. Let him know you're not going to just bow to his demands."

Collin had slowed down to talk, but continued moving along the edge of an open field for the sake of better reception. "I'm supposed to call him in half an hour. What do I say then? Do you think I give him a victory this time, just to keep him from getting too desperate and doing something cruel to Rob in retaliation?"

"I don't think he'll do that," said Lukas.

"How can you be so sure?"

"Because Rob has not arrived in Mexico City yet."

"How do you know that?"

"We know he's being transported there by car and, given the distance, there's no way he could have arrived there yet."

"So Penh is bluffing?"

"For now, yes. But in a few hours, when Rob arrives, he may not be. The best thing you could do right now is keeping buying yourself and my guys enough time to get set up. You need to get off that mountain, but if we time it right, your arrival could be enough of a distraction to keep Rob out of his focus."

"OK. How do I manage that?"

"Just keep playing it like you did on the last call. And keep moving toward that pick-up zone."

Collin switched off the phone again and practically galloped down a set of switchbacks. He was exposed on the side of a steep, rocky cliff. Each hairpin turn caused a new round of pain through his feet, but he had to get down to the cover of the trees below.

Most of the blisters on his feet had burst, soaking his socks with the ooze and blood from them. The flimsy athletic shoes were barely holding together, and that only because of the duct tape. Their tattered soles were missing chunks of the soft foamy material and the uppers had ripped in numerous places.

Hunger pangs stabbed at his gut. His lungs burned. Cramps knotted his midsection and thighs. This was like the first long-distance race he ran years ago. The middle section of that race, similar to the middle section of this trek, posed one trial after another, testing every ounce of his fortitude, grit, and commitment. None of this pain mattered. Only finishing the task at hand mattered. Getting to Penh in time to save Rob. As far as trying to halt Penh's hack attack on the United States, that would be up to Lukas and his crew. Collin was spent and would be virtually useless once he got to the pick-up zone. But he knew the pain he felt now would go away. The pain Penh planned to inflict on the civilized world would not.

chapter Twenty-Eight

From his hotel room-turned-command-center, Butch coordinated the comings and goings of several teams. He watched Collin's progress down the western side of Mt. Tlaloc using the transponders planted in the rucksack. And, with the latest input from the source within Torres' organization, he had additional information that buoyed his flagging spirits. The last thing he did before going underground to save his life and the lives of those he had recruited, the source sent a second helicopter, filled with Mexican Special Forces troops, to aid in the search for Collin. Despite the setbacks of losing the services of six trained and combat-tested operatives, Butch felt a solid plan coming together.

Now it was time to listen in to the conversation Collin had scheduled with Penh. As he did so, an instant message popped up from the team in Washington. A private helicopter had just picked up Rob Howell and his two travel companions along Highway 15D, north of Guadalajara, and was rushing him to the meeting spot in Mexico City.

Butch listened as Penh confirmed that fact with Cook. He heard the tenor of Cook's voice change, the bravado stolen. Penh urged him to make his location known immediately if he wanted his friend to remain intact. Wisely, Cook demanded to speak to his friend to verify that he was still whole and unharmed before he agreed to cooperate. Penh had ended the call in a huff, promising dire consequences, just to have Cook put it back in his face that Penh still needed him and if he wanted him to cooperate, Rob had better remain unharmed.

Cook promised to call back in one hour, thus giving Butch and his team more time to gather, organize, and get in position.

* * * *

Mt. Tlaloc, Mexico
June 18, 7:48 p.m. Central Time

Though he couldn't see it, he knew the sun was low on the western horizon because the shadows had grown long and the light had grown thin. Plus, the air began to chill. What he did see in the sky was just what Lukas had told him to expect, a second helicopter. It hovered above him, making tight circles, signaling his location. Soon, the first chopper made its way over and the two moved in tandem.

Following the agreement he made with Penh, Collin stepped cautiously into a clearing with his hands raised in the air. Of course, he had packed away the gun and left the rucksack under a tree several miles back. He had taken all the food and water he felt he would need and decided to go as light as possible in order to make up time on the trail. It had worked. Ignoring the pain, he had managed to jog or run for the better part of three hours to arrive at this flattened spot big enough for two helicopters to land.

The lactic acid had built up in his leg muscles, stiffening them. His feet were bruised, blistered, and bloodied. All of that combined with the cool air and caused him to tread gingerly and robotically. No one could mistake him as a flight risk or as a combative threat.

A helmeted man stood in the open doorway of a large green helicopter and pointed ominously at Collin as he stopped in his tracks, feeling like hunted prey with nowhere to run. Collin watched the UH-1 Huey as it hovered a few feet above the grass, then promptly set down. The second one landed a hundred yards beyond it, so Collin's view of it was obscured by the first chopper.

The road where he was to meet up with Butch's team couldn't be more than three miles away, according to his calculations. He just hoped he had stalled long enough. Perhaps, it was too long, because now he had to hurry. Penh would start chopping Rob into pieces in eighteen minutes, according to his watch, and there was no way he could let that happen to his best friend. He just wanted to get in the chopper and get in front of that computer like Penh demanded.

The soldier started yelling in Spanish and pointing the rifle at him while he swiveled his head behind him and back to Collin repeatedly.

Shots rang out. Lots of them. There were multiple bursts of gunfire. They seemed to be coming from all directions. Collin dropped to his knees immediately, covering his head, expecting to feel a flash of pain any moment. He checked himself and realized he had not been hit. Wanting to know why the Mexican soldiers were firing at him, he looked to the helicopter. That's when he realized they weren't looking at him. They had been thrown into total confusion. As the scene unfolded, Collin realized he hadn't heard any ricochets of bullets near him, which made him wonder who they were shooting at.

As he swiveled his head around to survey the scene, he saw the three gunmen in the helicopter pointing their rifles in the direction of the trees ahead of Collin. He swept his gaze to the rear of the chopper and saw a group of men running toward the Huey in a crouched position, weapons drawn. The three armed Mexican soldiers were too busy returning fire to notice the swift incursion from their flanks. Six men in camouflage were upon them in no time. One pointed his rifle at the head of the pilot before he could maneuver the helicopter out of harm's way. The others did the same thing with the copilot and the three gunmen in the back.

Another camo-clad group rushed forward from the second helicopter, guns drawn and trained at the occupants of the first one.

The shooting stopped and the helicopter landed softly back on the ground as one of the commandos on the ground signaled with his hands. Collin couldn't see anyone hurt, but saw plenty of baffled looks on the faces of the men in the first helicopter. A third group in camouflage rushed out from the trees ahead of Collin's position and from rocks on the edge of the meadow, quickly surrounding the first chopper. The Mexican soldiers had their hands up as these two new waves of commandos approached. The speed of the attack created instant bewilderment that the aggressors capitalized on.

Collin rose to his knees as the action dissipated. Being caught up in the drama, his heart skipped when a large hand planted itself on his shoulder. He whipped his head around with a start. The man pulling him up was none other than Jorge, the guy from the truck that had carried him out of Villahermosa.

"Come on, we've got to go," Jorge said. "We don't have much time."

"What just happened?"

"We got some help from one of the units that Torres thinks is on his side. These guys" he pointed at the first helicopter— "obviously had no idea we were coming."

"Now what?" said Collin, unsure whether to move or not.

"Now we get these gentlemen to understand what is happening and we convince them to give us a ride to the meeting location," said Jorge as he began to push Collin toward the chopper.

Collin could see Butch leaning into the cockpit of the first helicopter. A dozen or more camo-clad soldiers with weapons drawn formed a circle around the chopper. The original occupants were being unloaded at gunpoint, hands in the air. They were lined up in a row. Collin thought it looked like an execution was about to take place. Instead, they were being given some sort of instructions from one of the commandos in charge of this hostile takeover. The men were quiet and focused and seemed to be listening intently as the man shouted over the noise from the whirling blades.

When he caught sight of Collin approaching, Butch motioned for him to come quickly, so Collin tried to jog, instinctively ducking his head as he approached the rotating blades above him. Jorge followed.

"These men have your laptop," Butch yelled over the roar of the rotors and the engine. "We need to show Lieutenant Salazar here why it is we're commandeering his helicopter."

The Mexican lieutenant's eyes narrowed as he took in Collin. Collin became very self-conscious about his bedraggled appearance. After sizing him up, Salazar said, in Spanish, "This man does not look like an assassin."

"That's because he's not. You've been told a lie and I can prove it," replied Butch, also in Spanish, assessing the lieutenant's reaction with narrowed eyes.

Salazar glared at Butch, but said nothing and gave no indication that he would cooperate. "You killed my men back there in that motel. Give me any excuse and I'll put a slug in your brain, you understand?" Butch's trigger finger trembled as he pointed the handgun at the lieutenant's face.

Reluctantly, Salazar handed Butch the laptop and Butch handed it to Collin with a gesture to open it and get it going. Then he turned and continued speaking loudly to the Mexican lieutenant and his pilot. "From here on out, you're taking your orders from me, understand? We are here to protect both Mexico and the United States from a hostile threat. You can choose to cooperate and possibly reduce the charges of treason, or you can resist and die right here, right now. What's it going to be?"

"Show me the proof," Salazar demanded, stone-faced.

Collin punched in all of the codes and applied his finger to the print reader and put his eye in front of the camera lens. The screen soon flashed as the programs engaged.

Butch pulled the computer close and toggled to a black screen. He typed in a series of commands, then spun the screen toward Salazar and continued his explanation. A series of recordings played while an audio spectrometer, with its dancing and jumping bar graphs, appeared on the screen. Voices could be heard in both English and Spanish speaking in hushed, conspiratorial tones. It took several minutes for Butch and the information on Collin's computer to convince the lieutenant that Butch's story was true. Lieutenant Salazar was then ushered over to the row of his men kneeling on the ground. He added to what the commander had said, telling his men that they had the choice to be part of the problem or part of the solution. Each of the men nodded as the realization of what had transpired dawned on them.

Three minutes later, Collin was on board the chopper with a headset over his ears and a seatbelt fastened around his waist. Then they were airborne and racing toward the northwest section of Mexico City.

* * * *

Seventy-Fifth Floor, Unfinished Office Building, Mexico City
June 18, 8:12 p.m. Central Time

Rob awoke with a start, which caused waves of pain in his limbs. They wouldn't move. His rear end ached, as did his shoulders and the backs of his legs. He wanted to stand and stretch, but the restraints around his wrists and ankles prevented him from doing so. The urge to rub his eyes and itch his nose was overpowering. Being restricted was new to him, which only served to amplify the rage building inside.

He looked around and realized he was alone in a cavernous room. It was unfinished. Construction materials lay scattered in heaps and piles throughout the space. The floor was bare concrete. The ceiling was a maze of pipes, wires, and ducts, some dangling, between two-foot steel I-beams. A framework of aluminum studs indicated where walls would eventually be placed, but for now, there was only one solid wall on the entire floor that he could see. It was in the distance to his right. A single light bulb hung from a lone strand some ten feet to his right. A few feet to his left, a floor-to-ceiling plate of thick darkened glass looked out over some sort of park. There were trees and patches of grass interspersed with winding pathways, all visible in the golden-orange glow of a collection of street lamps. If he had to estimate, he would say he was at least sixty floors up, based on his experience, having had many meetings in tall buildings.

Rob wondered where his beautiful Asian abductor and her wiry boyfriend had gone. He tried to figure out where he was and what was going on, but his mind was still sluggish.

Before he could formulate a theory, a distant mechanical noise grew louder. He guessed it was the elevator, which meant somebody was either coming or going. The mystery and terror around this unknown caused his pulse to spike. A fresh round of perspiration broke out across his forehead and under his arms. Things could go very badly for Rob, based on what had happened with Sarah and Emily a few days earlier.

Rob wasn't sure that Lukas knew where he was or if he would be able to send in rescuers as he had for Sarah and Emily. Surely Penh was using him as bait to lure Collin in and exact his revenge. Collin had his money and had disgraced him. No doubt, Penh had a plan to deal with that.

He swallowed hard at the prospect of what might lie in store for him. *Be brave*, he told himself. *If you must die, die like a man.*

Then the sound faded with a faint clicking sound that reverberated off the uncovered concrete and echoed through the empty building. A door had been opened and shut. Now he could hear footfalls approaching. He was pretty sure there were three sets of shoes bumping, scraping, and clicking as they walked. And the voices. Muted but urgent. And accented. They were speaking English, but he had to strain to understand anything.

As expected, they came closer. Rob decided it would be best for him to still be in his drug-induced coma, so he slumped his head down and relaxed his body, subduing the urge to scratch his nose. He wasn't sure who these people were or what they intended to do with him, but keeping the status quo seemed like his best option.

Beads of sweat kept forming and rolling down his face and back. His shirt was damp around the neck, under his arms, and on his back. He feared it would give away the fact that he was conscious.

The footsteps paused some distance behind him. It was tempting to venture a glance to see if he recognized anyone. More unintelligible words were exchanged and a lone pair of shoes sauntered toward him. Heels, definitely stiletto heels. They had a distinctive sound on hard surfaces. as the heel struck, then the ball of the foot padded down. As the stilettos came closer, they veered in a semicircle in front of him, then stopped. Another utterance in a language he could not comprehend but from a voice he recognized. It was the pretty Asian girl.

Rob fought hard not to react, to stay perfectly still. But he could smell her perfume and imagine her face and eyes and skin. She grabbed a handful of his hair and pulled his head up from his chest. Rob added no resistance. His head lolled under the light pressure she applied. When she let go, his head flopped to the right, swung down unabated across his chest, before settling in roughly the same position it was in before. The beautiful girl rattled off some more words and the two men behind Rob continued their conversation, in accented English. One had an almost British accent with very proper enunciation and a certain high-brow eloquence. The second voice was deeper, grainier, and Latin. This man was older and most likely spoke Spanish as his native tongue. His R's rolled gracefully and his J's had a soft *jha* sound. This man, however, had an equal command of the English language.

Bound and drugged, Rob began to realize that he was at the epicenter of some big unfolding event. In his drug-induced fog, he couldn't be sure what was happening, but he knew he was completely helpless.

That's when an Asian man in a silk suit and fine Italian leather loafers stepped into his view. When Rob saw him, the realization dawned on him: this was Pho Nam Penh. Penh bent forward so his mouth was close to Rob's ear and whispered in his proper accent. "I told your friend Collin that you're going to lose a finger for every five minutes he is late. I guess we'll soon find out whether he really cares about you."

chapter Twenty-Nine

The footsteps retreated. Rob listened intently as the *click-tap* rhythm of the stilettos faded in the distance along with the scuffing of a softer set of shoes and the hard-soled crunching of grit under the third pair. He opened his eyes and surveyed the room, first without moving his head. Once he was certain he was alone, he studied his surroundings more carefully.

His buttocks and thighs burned with the pain of being sedentary for hours. He flexed the muscles just to keep some blood moving and relieve some of the pressure from the wheelchair he had been strapped to since morning.

Rob stared out the window and thought. But his thinking led him nowhere. Without the ability to move or communicate, Rob could do nothing to warn Collin or involve Lukas. There was no way to tell his friends where he was. His lack of mobility and freedom was making him crazy. He thrashed against the restraints, trying with all his might to break the bands of tape. It was no use. There were too many layers and the drugs had zapped too much of his strength.

His violent outburst had masked the *click-tap* approach of the stilettos. When he came to rest, he sensed he was no longer alone in the room. He swiveled his head right and left and caught a glimpse of her, standing behind him at the five o'clock position, maybe twenty feet away. She waited for him to settle. Once he did, she approached with a sauntering gait. As she entered his field of vision, he could see the hips sway and the calves flex as she rounded a circular pattern across the floor. She cast a stunning silhouette, backlit by the single bulb hanging somewhere behind her, a perfect hourglass in a tight knee-length skirt with a slit that exposed most of her left thigh. He couldn't see her face in this light, but he remembered it well and imagined those lips painted with bright red lipstick and those round eyes highlighted with black liner. Maybe a splash of color on the lids and a little something to make the cheeks stand out.

Rob had to force himself to hate her. It was difficult, made more so by the sultry voice. "There now, Mr. Howell. No need to be so angry. This will all be over very soon. You and your friends and all this pain and suffering will just be memories. Gone with the wind." She snickered.

"Maybe. But maybe you and your friends will be the distant memories," Rob shot back. His voice had no volume. The dryness in his mouth and throat stole it all.

"Do you think your friends are going to come and save you?"

Rob said nothing.

She stepped closer, angled her knees toward the window, and crouched down so her face was just a foot away from his. Her light-colored blouse caught a trace of light. Rob's eyes stayed focused on her face, though. "Thing is, we know they're coming. We'll be ready for them. Mr. Penh has it all planned. He is a mastermind, you know. A genius. Your friends will be too late and, I'm afraid, outnumbered. Many of them have already lost their lives attempting to help you. I think they have underestimated the size of our revolution, both here in Mexico and around the world."

Rob pinched his eyes shut and clenched his jaw.

Her delicate fingers first traced lines along his cheek bones to his temples, then down along his jawline to his chin, first on one side, then the other, ending at the center of his chin each time. She followed with a soft, damp cloth working against his skin with increasing intensity as she gently scrubbed the makeup from his face. When she was done, she dabbed here and there with a dry towel. Her voice, just above a whisper, brought him back from the dream-like state he had slipped into. "Look at me. I may be the last pleasant image you see before you die."

Her fingers ran the length of his jaw again, and tilted his chin upward until his eyes opened.

"There now. Take it all in." She smiled as she rose. Rob watched as she pivoted on the balls of her feet and sauntered for a few paces, the hip sway in full effect. She pivoted again so that she was facing him. This time, she made sure the light fully illuminated her figure. The tight black skirt with the slit showing a generous portion of her leg. The open silky blouse that accentuated her curves. The necklace that dangled a sparkling gem against her bare sternum. She tapped a watch on her elegant wrist. "Exactly ten minutes, Mr. Howell. That is when Mr. Penh wants your pinky finger brought to him."

Rob swallowed hard. Never had he felt so powerless, trapped, or terrified. *Take it like a man.* There was nothing to say and nothing he could do. He just shook his head slowly, forcing a smile at her before closing his eyes and lowering his chin to his chest. Surely Lukas had an even better plan in place.

The *click-tapping* came toward him quickly and forcefully. His eyes sprang open and watched as she marched, fists clenched and arms straight down by her sides. She slapped him across the face, then whipped around to the back of the wheelchair and yanked it backward. Once she had some momentum, she spun him around and thrust him and his wheelchair forward with hostility. She parked him in front of a window that was boarded up with a sheet of plywood. The plywood had pieces of wood fastened to it to fashion a sort of handle in the middle, presumably to make it easier to lift and move.

The *click-tapping* of her stilettos pounded purposefully away from Rob and into the interior of the building. They returned shortly with the same determined *click-tapping* rhythm. She moved into his line of view again, locking eyes with him. She had one hand behind her back, but there was a metallic chinking sound emanating from the hidden hand. After three or four repetitions of the clacking noise, she brought her hand around to the front and showed Rob what it was she held. A pair of gardening shears, the kind used for pruning trees and bushes. She snapped the sharp beak-shaped scissors a few more times, just for effect. This tool could snap a half-inch thick branch. Or a finger.

Rob's heart sank as the implications settled in.

She looked at her watch and said, "Eight minutes."

* * * *

Onboard the Huey helicopter
June 18, 8:22 p.m. Local Time

Collin closed his eyes and leaned into the hard seat, trying to recalibrate his thinking. Just moments ago he was running full speed down the side of the mountain, thinking only of rescuing Rob from the clutches of Pho Nam Penh. Now he was in a helicopter, a hijacked Mexican military helicopter, surrounded by Mexican soldiers and Mexican-American ex-soldiers now operating undercover on foreign soil. There was much more at stake than just saving Rob from Penh's demonic torture, but that was still of key importance to Collin.

Collin was roused from thought by someone pushing on his shoulder. "Come on, man. No time for naps right now. There's a call for you," said Jorge as he tapped on his own headset, indicating that Collin needed to press a button on his in order to talk.

Collin shook his head quickly to try to focus on the moment. He pressed the button and heard Lukas's strained voice. There was crackling and hissing on the line, which made it difficult to hear him. "Are you all right, Collin?"

"I'll be fine, I guess."

"Good. In about seven minutes, you're going to arrive at the location where Penh is holding Rob prisoner. The Mexican soldiers on board with you now have called in to their bosses and alerted them to your imminent arrival. Thanks to you and Butch and our inside source, the group that is with you is now aware of Penh's and Torres' subterfuge. No one is quite sure just how many of the Mexican Army have been seduced to follow Torres, but he has promised wealth and power to a great number of officers and the soldiers if they participate in this coup. We're working to gather as many as possible who are still loyal to the government. Again, you need to stall when you get there. Penh's going to want to hack into our system using your laptop. That's fine. Let him. We've got firewalls in place to contain him and to slow him down. He'll get access to a bunch of documents and such that are completely bogus, but he won't know that. The objective is to make him think he's winning and to slow him down while we get people in place."

"How much time do you need?" asked Collin as he pinched the bridge of his nose and squeezed his eyes shut. He was trying to imagine what he could do, but his mind was blank.

"An hour, at least. More if possible."

"I don't have any idea what I'm going to face. I don't even know where I'm going."

"Don't worry about that. When you get there, you need to insist on seeing Rob. Do anything you can think of to stall."

An idea popped into Collin's head. "Got it. I'll do the best I can."

* * * *

Seventy-Fifth Floor, Unfinished Office Building, Mexico City
June 18, 8:24 p.m. Local Time

She circled. Although the heat of her anger had begun to dissipate, there was a seething in her breath and a subtle fury in her gait that let him know she was still upset. For the past several minutes, Rob had replayed the scene in his head a hundred times, toying with an alternate ending each time. Endings that didn't include a slap in the face and losing fingers via a sharp gardening tool. Instead of something painful, he imagined her sidling up next to him, cooing, and tracing her fingers across his face again or pressing her lips against his or whisking him off to safety while the powerful men in the other room were busy. The last scene played well in his mind, so he repeated it with slightly altered variations each time.

But now that she stood in front of him, gripping and squeezing the handheld shears, he decided on the desperate, but sometimes effective, stratagem of flattery and charm. "I forgot to tell you how beautiful you look."

She glowered at him. If laser beams could shoot out of her eyes, she would have burned a big wide hole in his head.

"I mean it. I haven't seen someone look so good in a very long time. I just wish you hadn't said that part about cutting off my fingers."

She continued to stare at him, but her eyes softened slightly, growing wider.

"If I'm going to be tortured here, and likely die in some cruel fashion tonight, I'm really glad I got to see you looking so ... so, can I say it? Hot. You look sexy and beautiful, like the kind of girl I wish I could take to dinner at a fine restaurant."

She cocked her head.

Maybe that was too far.

The faintest trace of movement crossed her lips.

Maybe not.

"I know just the place I'd take you. You like French cuisine? There's a place in New York City. You ever been there?"

A slight shake of her head, the lips still battling to remain motionless.

"Fabulous town, New York. Full of sophistication, glamour, romance. If you know your way around, New York is the best."

Her lips lost the battle and turned up slightly. She shifted her weight. A little bit more of the thigh shone through the slit in her dress.

Rob smiled as he let his eyes wander. "After dinner, a Broadway play. You ever been to a Broadway play? Talk about classy and sophisticated. An elegant gal like you deserves to be treated to classic French dining and a night on Broadway. That's what I wish I could do with you. Not just stare at your form-hugging outfit and your perfect face. I'd like to have you with me when I go to fabulous places."

The jaw muscles were flexing, trying to keep the face rigid. The calves tightened, too. She watched his eyes as they moved up and down her body.

"A beautiful woman like you deserves that kind of treatment. That's why it's hard for me to look at you. I don't want this to be the last time I see something so perfect."

That did it. To hide the tremors taking over, she balled her fists and marched out of the room again. But Rob saw it in her face. He knew he'd penetrated her armor. She wasn't the hardened lackey she wanted him to think she was.

But it was a meaningless victory. The wheels were turning and chances were good she could not stop them from rolling forward and sealing his doom. Collin still stood a chance, but not him. The hourglass of his life had only a few more grains in it. He was convinced of this.

His chin returned to his chest and he replayed the previous scene one last time. A clatter erupted from somewhere in the distance. A bucket was kicked and metal pieces tinged on the cold cement. More bumping and banging and dragging. An armload of stuff dropped to the floor with a dull thud ten feet behind him. Rob tried to turn around, but couldn't crane his neck that far.

The wiry guy emerged from the echoing darkness behind Rob, talking in his high-pitched foreign tongue. He had changed out of his suit and into jeans, a thick hoodie sweatshirt, and work boots. As he talked, he tied a knot in a rope, forming a loop. The loop was opened wide, then draped over Rob's head until the strand was centered around his stomach. Sounds continued to emanate from behind him as the wiry guy shuffled around and talked and tied. Metal clanked now and then and things banged together and the rope tightened. Then there was more fussing around the back of his wheelchair. Next thing he knew, the rope was jerked tight around his torso and he was yanked into the air, facing the ground three feet below him. He was swinging left to right, a foot or more each side of center. The weight of the wheelchair rested against his back until his squirming caused a shift. Now he was at an angle and the chair felt like it was pulling him downward to his right, the tape holding him to the chair ripping at the hairs and skin on his arms and ankles.

The Asian guy clucked his tongue a couple of times and lowered Rob until the front wheels were barely touching the ground. Rob heard him strain, and then he came forward and positioned the chair with the wheels down. He kept a foot against the armrest to maintain the attitude he wanted. A little more straining and the chair dropped to the ground. The jolt jarred Rob's back, shooting long pulses up his spine and down his legs. Rob's eyes clenched shut until the pain rolled through. When he opened them, the Asian guy stood before him with his chin in his hand, as if assessing his handiwork.

The process was repeated twice, until the guy nodded in satisfaction. Rob expected the drop the second and third times, and was able to lean forward enough to keep the impact from being absorbed primarily by his spine. Instead, his rear end and legs took the brunt of the force.

Once satisfied, the wiry Asian guy disappeared. Rob was once again left alone in the dark chill with nothing to look at but the plywood wall and the construction debris scattered around. His mind had a lot of scenarios to play out. The suspense might kill him before Penh did.

* * * *

Onboard the Huey Helicopter over Mexico City, Mexico
June 18, 8:25 p.m. Local Time

Butch's team, along with the Mexican soldiers aboard the helicopter, were crammed into the tight space inside the Huey UH-1. The chopper had room for thirteen, plus the pilot and copilot, but Butch had insisted on bringing twelve of his men on board to help the three Mexican riflemen. With Collin, that made sixteen men on board. The thin mountain air and the increased weight put a strain on the Huey's powerplant, but it managed to handle the load after a shaky takeoff.

En route, they divvied up assignments and roles for each man. They expected the helipad to be heavily guarded upon their arrival, but hoped to persuade the security detail that the group on board the helicopter would take the prisoner to the bosses and help with rooftop patrol.

If that didn't work out, there could be a shoot-out. Butch's men prepared themselves by checking their weapons, vests, and ammo supplies. Most of them were either former Navy Seals or Army Rangers. Their training and experience had pulled them through many dangerous missions. Butch knew this mission would rank up there on the danger/insanity scale. They had less-than-ideal intel to go on and even less time to formulate a combat plan. With only nine minutes in the air between takeoff and landing, this hastily formed unit had to rely on gut instinct born of intense training if they were going to succeed. Their objective was clear: get inside the building with Cook and keep the camera on his vest rolling for the benefit of the German guy and his team in Washington.

As the helicopter approached the darkened tower, standing like a sentinel guarding a village, Butch crossed himself and kissed the crucifix around his neck. He noticed other soldiers doing the same thing.

The pilot circled the glass-and-steel structure that rose higher than anything in sight, allowing Butch and the others to get a birds-eye view of what was going on below. Street lamps and house lights were switching on as twilight descended, but there were no lights coming from inside the towering structure. There were four troop carrier trucks on the ground, parked nearby, and at least a dozen armed men taking up defensive positions around the perimeter.

Lieutenant Salazar provided all the intel he had on the situation, which wasn't much. Since he was the officer tasked with delivering Cook, he insisted that he do all the talking once they landed. He understood the gravity of the situation and assured Butch that he felt it to be his sacred duty to do everything he could to prevent a *coup d'état* to right the wrongs he had done. He loved his country too much to see it thrown into upheaval and chaos.

chapter Thirty

Collin tried to get his bearings while also listening to the conversations between Butch and Salazar, as well as between Butch and the rest of the team. His Spanish was good, so he understood much of it, but not good enough to catch it all. They spoke so fast and used words—which he assumed were military oriented—he'd never heard. So he sat shivering and stiffening in the cold—confused, hungry, and exhausted.

The chopper was making one last pass around the building. Over the radio, Collin could just piece together the words the pilot was uttering to someone awaiting them at the landing site. He used words like "strong wind" and "safety" and "very dangerous" to explain the reason they had not yet landed. A wind sock at the helipad showed the proof that it was windy out there.

The chill air swirling through the cabin and the adrenaline surging through his system kept Collin shaking and jittery. The unknown lay before him, dark and ominous. How would he react to meeting Penh? What had Penh and his men done to Rob? Was Rob even still alive? Would Collin be able to stall long enough for the reinforcements to arrive and prevent the calamities Penh had planned? These thoughts ping-ponged around his mind, keeping him revved up and on edge.

Butch looked at Collin with a raised eyebrow, seeing his constant, nervous fidgeting. He pounded a fist against Collin's knee and spoke to him through the headset. "You're going to do just fine, Mr. Cook. We've got your back if something goes wrong in there. Don't worry. Do the best you can to take as much time as you can. A little more time and we'll have numbers here, ready to take this place with overwhelming force."

Collin nodded slowly, trying to absorb the meaning behind the words. The whole message seemed to bounce off him, though. He was on overload. The enormity of the situation was too much to process. But the thought of returning home, no longer having to live life on the run, brought a sense of calm and resolve that quickly took over and emboldened him.

Butch pulled a tiny flesh-colored piece of plastic from his shirt pocket. It had a thin clear tube protruding from it. He motioned for Collin to put it in his ear. When Collin didn't respond, he removed his headset and placed an identical piece in his own ear canal. Collin nodded and followed suit. Butch handed one to the soldier seated next to him, whom he referred to as Pepé, as well as one to Lieutenant Salazar in the front seat.

"We'll be able to hear instructions coming from the team leader, your friend from Washington, and from Jorge here, who's going to keep a lookout on the roof," explained Butch as he slapped Jorge's shoulder. "That way, we know what's going on around us."

"Testing, testing. We all good?" asked Jorge.

Butch and the others gave a thumbs-up, so Collin did the same.

Out the open door, Collin could see that the newly constructed building stood at one end of a roundabout and plaza at the intersection of two great avenues in the new part of the city. The side of the building faced the street at an angle. Its architectural design gave it a sleek, modern feel and a nonboxy shape. The structure rose into the sky, towering over its neighbors like a teacher in a kindergarten class. Gray stone accents marked the divisions between large smoked glass windows, adding to its high-tech feel. A few lights flooded the area inside a fenced perimeter. The fences looked to be quite high and topped with razor wire. Maybe that was the norm in Mexico. He didn't know.

Collin spent half a second wondering what the architecture looked like in the daylight. Seeing it at night was eerie. This gargantuan building had a ghostly, menacing quality about it.

There were several other high-rises nearby with a smattering of lights glowing in windows. But none was as tall or as ominous as the building Penh had chosen as their meeting place.

The helicopter slowed and gradually pulled into hover mode. As it began to descend, Collin's insides continued their churning. The hunger, the fear, and the adrenaline combined to make him feel sick. The urge to fight met with the urge for flight. He wanted to run away and beat the crap out of Penh at the same time. It was the strangest feeling he'd ever experienced and he wasn't sure what to make of it.

Two military guards stood post at the edge of the helipad. Two more uniformed men, presumably from the Mexican Army, stood at attention next to a door in close proximity. All four moved in closer as the helicopter landed. Butch knocked the side of Collin's leg again and gave him an encouraging nod of his head. "We got this," he said confidently.

Butch jumped out first, as soon as the landing skids touched the pad. Lieutenant Salazar and Pepé followed close behind. Butch turned inside and motioned authoritatively for Collin to exit the helicopter. The two men stationed at the pad looked confused. They had rushed forward to accept the prisoner, but Butch had bluntly ignored them as he and Pepé escorted Collin toward the door. Salazar walked behind with Collin's laptop tucked under his arm. He stopped in front of the ranking officer stationed at the helipad, leaned in, and conveyed a message over the racket. The man listening seemed confused at first, but Salazar pulled away and continued his march with his men and his prisoner.

The two men at the door looked at each other, then at the other two men who had been waiting for the prisoner's arrival. Butch saluted and shouted in perfectly accented Mexican Spanish, "Our orders are to take this man to the boss. Show us the way."

Lieutenant Salazar confirmed this with an authoritative nod.

The man who was presumably in charge of the rooftop

welcoming committee took two steps toward the door in front of Butch. Another man opened the door and the three soldiers and Collin pushed through the doorway in formation. The man in charge on the roof went first, followed by Butch, who held Collin's left elbow, followed by Collin, followed by Pepé, holding Collin's right elbow. Salazar trailed. Collin had no restraints on his hands or ankles, but this minor detail was overlooked while expediency overruled the need for inspection of the prisoner.

Boots clattered and rumbled against the metal stair treads, reverberating off the bare concrete walls, as the group pounded their way downward. Each step was a painful reminder of the ordeal Collin's feet and legs had endured over the past eighteen hours. His first movements were stiff and mechanical. Collin gritted his teeth and turned his face upward, trying to ignore the agony each movement caused.

Fluorescent fixtures overhead cast a ghostly light in the tight space as the company descended, turned, and descended some more. Three floors down, they stopped at a locked door with a "76" emblazoned in black paint against the off-white steel veneer. The officer leading the group knocked. Immediately, the door swung inward and another soldier appeared. His rifle was held tightly across his chest and a scowl formed on his face when we saw the large contingent accompanying the American.

Lieutenant Salazar stepped forward and explained the difficulties they had experienced finding and capturing this man, adding that every precaution had been taken to guard the prisoner and bring him safely from the mountain to this meeting with General Torres and Mr. Penh.

The grim-faced guard eyed each man in the group warily before commanding them to wait and disappeared behind the door that closed, leaving the group packed tightly on the narrow landing in the stairwell.

* * * *

Seventy-Fifth Floor, Unfinished Office Building, Mexico City
June 18, 8:38 p.m. Central Time

The wiry guy tried to hide the Cheshire cat grin on his face, mumbling in an animated tone as he resumed his work. He had stopped to smoke a cigarette and watch in rapt fascination as his beautiful girlfriend went about her work. She had come gripping the handheld pruning shears tightly and marching in her high heels in a military cadence. *Man, that was sexy.* Without a word, she went to work, quickly and efficiently fulfilling her assignment from the boss. No expression crossed her face as she snipped off the American guy's left pinky finger right at the base as if it was an errant twig on a manicured shrub. She had sprayed the wound with some sort of disinfectant and wrapped it in gauze, knowing Mr. Penh preferred to keep things neat and tidy. She had then stood staring at the man strapped to the wheelchair for a long minute before sauntering back out the way she had come. All business, no feeling.

Can't find a woman sexier than that, he thought to himself as he snuffed out his smoke.

Rising slowly as he eyed the American, a hint of admiration spread through him. The guy didn't make more than a muffled grunt and some fast and hard breathing through his mouth during the ordeal. No pleading, no whining, and no screaming. He had to respect a man like that.

Flicking the butt of his cigarette away, he set about to finish what he had started. First, he dragged a heavy load of thick black cable across the floor, leaving it in front of the wheelchair. He knelt down and began to uncoil the cable and string it through the wheels of the chair. The guy moved quickly, back and forth, in front and in back. Grunting sounds and the rattling of tools being plucked out of a metal box and dropped back in moments later echoed throughout the empty space. Next, he moved to the window, unraveling more cable as he went, making satisfied rumbles in the back of his throat from time to time.

A five-foot-tall wooden spool, used to transport the thick black electrical cables, was rolled into place near the window ledge. The wood panel in front of the window was removed and the wiry guy set to work tying ropes and cables to the spool, then running them through pulleys and tying them off. He worked quickly and efficiently.

This design was genius. His ingenuity would surely garner him some favors in Mr. Penh's new world order. A high school dropout like him didn't get the big opportunities some of the other members of the team got. The guys with the computer skills were revered while a lowly mechanic like himself was given the grunt jobs and ordered around like a monkey. But this contraption would display his usefulness and talent. Yes, Mr. Penh would be pleased when he saw what happened to his victims once the wire was tripped.

* * * *

Seventy-Sixth Floor, Unfinished Office Building, Mexico City
June 18, 8:58 p.m. Central Time

The wait was excruciating. Every possible scenario rattled inside Collin's head. Maybe they figured out that Butch and his guys were American and planned to shoot them when they returned. Maybe Rob was dead. Maybe Penh had already launched his plan and the *coup d'état* had already commenced.

Lukas's soft Germanic accent flowed through the earpiece in a whisper, bringing much-needed reassurance. "We've got eyes on you. Tracking your movements. Remember, once you get in there, keep trying to slow things down if you can. We need some more time."

Just then, the door opened and the same guard stepped into the stairwell, holding the door open and motioning for the group to proceed.

They took a sharp right once they came through the door and followed a pathway covered in thin industrial-style carpeting. It led them through a jagged, unfinished hallway of aluminum studs with no wallboard on them. An occasional single light bulb hung down from the open ceiling, casting pale yellow spheres of light through the otherwise dark and empty space.

Collin, who looked a wreck, spoke up. "Excuse me."

The officer in charge halted the company, then whirled around and shot him an incredulous look.

"I need to use the bathroom. You know, the baño." He pulled a pained, urgent expression.

"We meet the boss first," said the officer. He turned on his heels and continued marching down the path through the bowels of the building.

Disappointed in his failed attempt to delay the inevitable, Collin dropped his head and shuffled forward reluctantly. Butch and Pepé practically dragged him a few steps, barking *"andele"* several times as they urged him on.

* * * *

The only walled-in area Collin could see in the wide-open interior of the building, other than the stairway and the elevator shaft, had only one entrance. The group approached a set of elegant dark-wood double doors. They halted when the commander in front held up his hand. He rapped on the solid door and waited. The seconds stretched out to an uncomfortable length, causing the commander to shift his weight and glance behind him twice.

Finally, the door rattled open. A well-dressed, confident Asian man, standing maybe five foot eight, wearing patent leather loafers, a blue silk suit, and an orange tie with a matching pocket square stepped out of the room and into the faint light. There was a buzz of frenetic activity and urgent voices in the room behind him. He was flanked by two other Asian men wearing dark sweaters and equally dark expressions. The second one quickly pulled the door closed behind him.

The perfectly-tailored suit shimmered in the yellowish glow of the single bulb overhead. His black hair was slicked back, and his dark eyes jumped out. An air of assurance and power radiated off him like heat from a gas lamp. It smacked of the kind of smugness and arrogance and entitlement that Collin had learned to hate growing up among ultrarich kids. He knew upon seeing him that it was Pho Nam Penh, the lurking monster from the pictures that he had been trying to avoid all these months. Collin's jaw clenched, his fists balled, and his eyes narrowed. It also made his heart beat in a heavy rhythm and his breathing grow quick and shallow. In that moment, Collin felt like a bull meeting the matador. Butch and Pepé each tightened their grips on his elbows as Collin tensed and lunged toward Penh. All five of the guards around Collin closed ranks to hold him back and shield Penh.

The contrast between the two was sharp and incontrovertible. Penh was slick and sophisticated. Collin was dirty and disheveled. Penh was free and relaxed. Collin was restrained and agitated. Penh was cool and in control. Collin was hot and fierce.

Penh eyed him from head to foot and back. "So I get to meet the infamous Collin Cook, in the flesh once again? My, how things have changed since last we met. You've grown a legend of mythical proportions." Penh's voice dripped with disdain.

Collin's heavy breathing was a testament to the surge of adrenaline that had yet to subside.

Penh looked past him to Lieutenant Salazar. His gaze went directly to the object he held against his side. "The computer?" he said, with his hand outstretched and his fingers curling toward him in a "give-that-to-me" gesture.

"Show me where Rob is first," Collin said as forcefully as he could.

"Mr. Cook, you are in no position to make demands," Penh said with a sneer. He clicked his fingers and one of his guards approached Salazar and motioned for the computer.

Salazar dutifully handed the Asian guard the laptop.

Penh stepped forward, staring Collin down. Collin didn't break eye contact. Penh's clean-shaven face was regal and serene while Collin's stubbly face was contorted.

Stepping directly in front of Collin, Penh continued to glare. "You tried to outsmart me, but you failed," Penh hissed, emphasizing the word "failed." Then he pulled his head away and took a step backward. His nose scrunched up as he winced, a look of revulsion crossing his smooth face. "You smell worse than an animal." Looking at Salazar, Penh barked, "Get him cleaned up. I don't want this filthy pig near me."

Penh motioned to the guard holding the computer and signaled him inside with a few words that Collin could not understand. The guard spun on his heels to reenter the room.

"Speaking of filthy animals," Collin said angrily. "You made me a promise. You said that Rob would be released if I gave you what you wanted. There, you got what you wanted, now let him go."

Penh shook his head. "Still trying to bargain while the odds are stacked so heavily against you? I admire your pluck, Mr. Cook. But if you know what is best, you will make no further demands until I have *everything* I want, including *my* money—every one of the thirty million dollars you stole from me."

Collin spat as he reacted. "*Your* money? What makes you think it's yours?" Collin stopped himself, realizing there was no arguing at this point. Words were meaningless and so was money. He held his breath a moment and shook his head in disgust as Penh eyed him warily. "Listen, I really don't care about the money. I'd much rather have my family than that stinking money, but you're not going to get a dime of it until I know for sure Rob is OK."

Penh held Collin in an icy stare. His dark eyes locked onto Collin's, revealing his contempt. Then he snapped his fingers while still glaring at Collin. He refocused his gaze toward Salazar. "You are the one who captured this animal, correct?"

Salazar looked surprised, but answered, "Yes, sir."

"Good." Flicking his eyes toward Collin, then back to Salazar, Penh said, "Take this dog to see his friend, then get him cleaned up. Return him here in ten minutes. We will commence our work immediately."

Salazar nodded confidently and said, "Yes, sir."

"One last thing before you go, Mr. Cook," said Penh, as if suddenly remembering something he had almost forgotten and fixing his eyes on Collin's once again. "Just to show that I am a man who keeps his promises, I have a little memento for you to keep." He held a hand out and nodded at Butch until he loosened his grip on Collin's arm.

Collin cocked his head in confusion, then slowly raised his hand to accept Penh's offer. Penh dropped a long cylindrical object wrapped in white gauze into his hand. The object was warm and firm, but malleable. Curiosity forced Collin to break eye contact at last and brought his gaze to his palm. The gauze was stained a deep red on one end.

"You were late, but I kept my word."

Collin felt the blood drain from his face as he realized what he was holding. The memory of Penh's threat over the phone flashed back to the forefront in that instant and he knew he was holding his best friend's severed finger.

chapter Thirty-One

After Penh and his guards disappeared through the double doors, Lieutenant Salazar stood taller with his chest out and said, "You heard the boss. Let's take him to his friend." Looking toward the man who had led the group from the helipad and squinting at the name embroidered above his chest pocket, he added, "Please lead the way, Sergeant Hernandez."

The sergeant cocked his head and furrowed his brow, but started to push his way through the group, nearly knocking Collin over as he stood, ashen faced, staring at the object in his hand. Collin's stomach turned and his head spun. Butch and Pepé steadied him and began to turn him around. Butch calmly took the finger from Collin's hand while no one was looking and put it in his breast pocket. He squeezed his elbow to add some reassurance.

The sergeant led them back to the stairway they had come down moments earlier. Collin staggered as Pepé and Butch practically dragged him. They descended one flight to the seventy-fifth floor. A gust of cold wind greeted them as the sergeant opened the door. Collin strained to see his lifelong friend, but he found it hard to move and even harder to see. In the dim glow of a distance light, he could see Rob strapped to a wheelchair only a few feet from the edge of a missing window. Collin stopped cold at the sight.

At the sound of the door opening, Rob's head popped up and looked toward the door.

Collin tried to call Rob's name, but his voice was so weak, it was barely audible.

There was a hesitation before Rob replied. When he did, his tone startled Collin. It was fierce and pointed. "Don't come near me, Collin. I don't want to see you right now," he shouted through clenched teeth. The angry words echoed throughout the empty space, carried by the whipping wind.

Collin tensed at the reproach, speechless. Rob was a hundred feet away, immobile and helpless, but Collin couldn't move. He had wanted to run to him. Maybe give him a hug, maybe untie him.

"There's nothing to say, Collin. Just get out. I don't want you here."

Lieutenant Salazar snapped his fingers and pronounced the meeting over. "Let's get this filthy American clean. Sergeant Hernandez, where shall we take him?"

Hernandez gave Salazar a puzzled look but said nothing.

Butch nudged Collin to turn around. Collin's movements were sluggish. In his earpiece he heard Lukas say, "Don't worry, Collin. He'll be all right."

Butch grabbed a wad of Collin's jacket, just under the collar, and said in Spanish, "After you, Sergeant."

When they reached the landing for the seventy-sixth floor, Hernandez marched them through a maze of scattered tools, saw horses, and construction materials that lay about until they reached another walled-in area with a sign on the door indicating it was a men's bathroom.

Collin staggered straight to the sink and bent over, propping himself up with his hands on either side of it. He ran the water, and splashed his face. Butch stood next to him with Pepé next to the far wall. Salazar and Hernandez were stationed just inside the entry. A knock came at the door just before it swung open. A bright-faced Mexican soldier with a neatly pressed uniform and shiny black boots paused awkwardly just after he entered. It looked like he hadn't had time to finish basic training before being assigned to this duty. He stopped in his tracks, sizing up the five men congregated in the bathroom. His eyes scanned each man's face and uniform. A troubled expression appeared as he looked over Butch and Pepé. Their uniforms had no insignia on them—just desert camouflage fatigues, boots, and combat vests. Butch interrupted his silent search. "What do you need, soldier?" he asked in Spanish.

"We are here to escort the prisoner back to the conference room, sir," said the young private.

Another young army man in a new uniform stepped in behind the first, looking straight ahead, keeping his eyes away from any of the men in restroom.

"Mr. Penh demanded that this man be cleaned up before returning. As you can see, he is still filthy," said Butch. "Mr. Penh ordered him to be returned in ten minutes, but that was only four minutes ago."

"We're just following orders, sir."

"Understood. So are we. Give us a few minutes and he'll be ready."

Lukas's voice could be heard again in the earpiece, saying, "I need more time. Stall if you can."

Collin splashed more water on his face and took off his shirt. Using liquid soap from the sink dispenser, he began to wash his hands, arms, and neck. The lather turned brown as he worked. He continued soaping and scrubbing his upper body, producing more brownish rivulets. He cupped his hand under the faucet and splashed the cold water all over to rinse off. As he blotted the water off his skin with a wad of paper towels, another Mexican soldier, this one a lieutenant, barged into the crowded restroom. "The prisoner is wanted, at once," he barked.

Sergeant Hernandez snapped to attention. "Yes, sir," he said. Pointing at Butch and Pepé, he ordered, "Bring him now."

"But, he's not clean, as Mr. Penh ordered," said Butch.

The new lieutenant shook his head. "No matter. He is wanted immediately. Bring him at once."

Two more armed soldiers elbowed into the room and seized Collin by the arms and briskly escorted him out of the restroom, shirtless, damp, and partly soapy.

* * * *

"Collin," said Lukas in a whisper through the earpiece as Collin marched down the rubbery carpet strip toward the conference room at the far end of the building, an armed guard firmly holding each of his elbows. "Penh needs you to log on to your computer because of the biometric identifiers we put on it. His hackers have not been able to get past the login protocol. Go ahead and let them in. We've got a little maze set up for them. It should keep them busy hopefully long enough for the rest of our forces to get into place. So stand by and be ready."

Collin and his armed entourage finally reached the double doors of the long, walled-in room. Bare sheetrock walls extended to his right as they stood in the dim light and waited for someone to answer the knock. One of Penh's bodyguards opened it cautiously and stepped out. He eyed the bare-chested Collin curiously, then signaled for him to come in and for the others to wait right where they were. The guy had powerful hands. He clutched Collin's sturdy arm in a vice-like grip, as if he were trying to deflate the biceps.

As Collin was pulled into the room, he couldn't help but notice how overcrowded the space was with people and equipment. The far wall was occupied by two racks of computer servers with flashing and glowing lights—green, blue, and red. Thick blue and yellow wires trailed out of the backs of the slim modules, each hooked in to its own shelf. Each rack was six feet high and stuffed full. Collin was shocked by the scale of the operation.

Computers and monitors were lined up on long plastic stow-away tables, the kind people keep in the garage and set up for outdoor barbeques or parties. These tables lined the walls on either side of the long rectangular room. Fans stood on wobbly legs between some of the tables, oscillating and blowing warm air around the room. Diligent people sat on folding chairs and pecked away at the keys and murmured among themselves. Supervisors lorded over them in the narrow space between the rows of tables and chairs, pacing back and forth between three or four people, barking an occasional command or answering questions. It was like a veritable beehive buzzing with workers and activity. Collin estimated thirty or more people crammed into this workspace. Some wore uniforms. They appeared to be Mexican nationals. Others appeared to be Asian. They were not in uniform, but neatly dressed. All were men. Smoke filled the air and Collin coughed and sputtered as he was dragged into the middle of the room.

Penh stood, at the center of the action, waiting for Collin to be brought to him. He, too, gave Collin an inquisitive look when he saw him without his shirt. "We have work to do, Mr. Cook. Please, have a seat." He pointed to the rack of servers at the far end of the room.

"Before we start, let me get this straight. I log in to this computer. You get what you need from it. Then you set Rob free. Did I miss anything? I mean, that was the agreement, was it not?"

Penh smiled a cat-like smile at him. "Yes, indeed," he said as he led Collin back into the room. A chair was ready for him in the far corner. Penh swept his hand in front of him, guiding Collin toward the seat. "You missed the part where you turn over the thirty million dollars to me. We leave for Panama as soon as we are finished here. You were clever enough to make that money so secure that only you can withdraw it and then, only in person. Clever but potentially detrimental to your friend because if anything goes wrong, he will suffer even more than he has already."

Collin hesitated, scanning the room before he sat down. It was a long way back to the door and there were a lot of people between him and his escape route. Penh impatiently pointed toward the empty chair in front of the table where Collin's laptop sat open and ready. The login screen silently waited for him.

As he maneuvered his legs under the table, his thoughts strayed as he recalled all the time he had spent typing away on that very keyboard. He thought about the photo journal he had started for his late wife and the pictures of all the cool places he had visited. Penh nudged his shoulder, thus ending his nostalgic musings.

Collin typed in his username and password. The computer began scrolling through its security protocol. Collin realized as he watched it do its thing that he hadn't logged in to his computer for weeks. When the security protocols ended, a window popped up and Collin was asked to swipe his right index finger across the ID pad, which he did. Then he was asked to scan his retina. This task required him to put his eye close to the camera at the top of his monitor and hold still. Next was the special phrase he had to type. This was not only a password, but it measured the rhythm, pressure, and cadence of his typing. After passing all three phases of the identity verification, Collin tensed up. He felt Penh leaning closer, his breath hitting the top of his head and trailing down his neck. It was uncomfortable. He began to wonder what Penh would do to him if his login failed.

"Open your bank account. Let's make sure you haven't moved the money," Penh enunciated calmly.

"I can't. You know that. This bank does not allow Internet access. It's strictly in-person, old-fashioned banking for the rich and paranoid."

Penh huffed as if he didn't believe what Collin told him. Just for good measure, Collin tried to find the bank online. No luck. Penh huffed again and straightened up. A moment later, the two bodyguards crowded in on either side of Collin's seat and forcibly stood him up and moved him behind the chair. A skinny, bespectacled Asian guy slid into his vacated seat. He began typing furiously.

White words on a black screen began to scroll at a blistering pace from the top to the bottom, line after line. Occasionally, the lines would stop and the cursor would blink until the Asian guy typed in something else. Then, the scrolling would continue. After several minutes of this, the NSA logo filled the screen. From here, the nerdy operator used the mouse to maneuver through the site. Penh leaned in closer and began directing him where to go. He was visibly enthused by what appeared to be top-secret documents, blueprints, and memos. Penh asked the nerdy guy to open one after another.

Penh was enthralled and asked the nerd to stop every so often so he could look more closely. Before Collin knew it, an hour had passed. The bodyguards never relinquished their hold on his arms, but their grips did loosen. A quiet whisper came through the earpiece. "Be ready."

chapter Thirty-Two

The room suddenly went dark, except for the glow of the laptop screens running on battery power. Gasps turned to panic as the sound of firecracker bursts erupted in the empty expanse outside of the conference room. High-speed projectiles began slamming into the wall, causing everyone to duck and drop to the floor, including Collin and the two guards.

Collin used the opportunity to free himself from their respective grips. Because he was closer, the guy on Collin's right got an elbow to the gut as he pulled Collin to the ground. In the darkness, Collin spun and smashed his fist into the man's side over and over as fast as he could, landing three solid blows to the ribs before the man curled and rolled away. The second guard had moved forward to cover Penh and pulled him and the nerd to the safety of the floor.

With both guards occupied, Collin began clawing his way over bodies and between chairs toward the double doors on his hands and knees.

Crawling as fast as he could through the darkness and confusion toward the room's only exit, Collin was at the door and had begun opening it when he felt someone grab his ankle. The muted light revealed the outline of the bodyguard he had pummeled. Without thinking, he drove the sole of his free foot straight outward and felt it connect with the guy's head. He heard a pained grunt. The grip slackened. He struck out again at the head, then slammed the same foot down against the wrist that held him. Finally, it relented and he shimmied through the crack of the door and into the cavernous expanse.

Butch, Pepé, and Salazar were gone and pandemonium reigned in the open space of the unfinished floor. Intermittent bursts of rapid gunfire erupted from a group assembled a few yards to his left. A moment later came the answer from somewhere farther inside the building. Bullets whizzed through the air and ricocheted off hard surfaces. Glass popped and shattered in the distance.

Collin remained on his hands and knees and scurried to his right, away from the gunfire, in search of an escape route. The muzzle flashes continued in the distance to his left and seemed to be pointed in the general direction of the stairway he and the others had come down earlier.

A smoky haze and the smell of spent ammunition filled the air. The commandos were systematically securing the building under Lukas's direction. Butch and his team were busy securing the stairway and the helipad. He could hear their frenzied exchanges through his earpiece.

"Collin," he heard Lukas calling through the earpiece. "Get to the helicopter. The team will take you to safety. Hurry, while the stairway is secure."

Collin had no microphone, no way to communicate back to Lukas. With all the gunfire going back and forth, the stairwell did not seem very secure. Instead, he moved into the inky darkness to his right. As his eyes adjusted, he began to move more quickly, avoiding the construction mess as he did.

Lukas and Butch and their team were executing their mission to thwart Penh and disrupt his plan. That was their top priority.

But it wasn't Collin's. Getting Rob was. No way would Collin board that helicopter without Rob.

Collin worked his way through the dark until he saw the columnar shape of what he guessed was another stairway. It was a good guess. Once inside the stairway, he stood again and descended the steps as fast as his aching body would go. One level down, he cautiously peered through the door, surveying the area for guards or shooters. Seeing no one and hearing nothing, he stepped out into another unfinished floor, expecting to see Rob off to the left, like he had before. But he wasn't there. Neither was the broken window. There were no windows around because this stairway was situated close to the center of the building. He took a moment to orient himself. Vast, empty space spread out in all directions. The clatter of guns and bullets from above was ominous and made it hard to think.

Collin moved out guardedly, trying to be orient himself. He noticed a light in the distance, near the corner of the building. He remembered the light from his brief encounter with Rob, so he moved through the scattered debris toward it. On his way, he kicked and stumbled over an aluminum beam lying across the floor. The *clanging* reverberated through the hollow building. Collin paused, half-expecting someone to show up and shoot him. Nothing happened, so he scampered forward in a crouch, picking his way through the debris, more carefully now.

As he neared the hanging bulb, wind hit him in the face, so he moved into it, remembering the missing window next to Rob. After maneuvering his way between the framed sections, the buckets, the spools of wiring, and randomly strewn pallets, he saw Rob's inert figure still sitting in the wheelchair, not more than six feet from the edge of the window. His heart sank seeing his best friend like that.

He approached Rob from Rob's right side. Rob looked to be unconscious, chin against his chest, motionless. The wind howled through the opening. No wonder Rob didn't react to all the noise Collin had made.

Collin eased up next to his best friend, noting the left hand wrapped in white gauze and stained with blood. A flood of memories and feelings wanted to run wild in his mind, but he pushed them back. Holding his emotions in check, Collin tapped his buddy on the shoulder. Nothing. He shook the shoulder. Nothing. He paused while a wave of terror washed over him. What if they had killed him already? Fear, followed by anger, chased away by grief, finished with a gut-wrenching sickness that swept through Collin's heart and body in that instant.

Collin moved around until he was kneeling in front of the wheelchair. First, he checked Rob's pulse along his carotid artery. Relieved to find it, he grabbed Rob's face with both hands and pulled his head up from his chest. What he saw horrified him. Blood dripped down from Rob's nose and mouth. Both eyes were swollen and purple. Bruises and scrapes covered most of his face. Gently, he shook him again, trying to wake him.

A crunching sound came from somewhere behind him. "It's no use, Mr. Cook," echoed the arrogant, accented voice of Pho Nam Penh. More crunching as he stepped into the light. "You see the cost of friendship with you? It will be quite some time, I'd imagine, before he revives. But, by then, it will be too late. For him and for you."

* * * *

Mobile Command Center, Mexico City, Mexico
June 18, 10:28 p.m. Local Time

Lukas watched the gun battles via helmet-mounted video feeds. It didn't look promising at the moment. Although Collin had done an admirable job of stalling, it wasn't quite enough. Lukas and his Mexican counterparts needed more time. He knew the forces loyal to the democratically elected government of Mexico outnumbered those whom Torres had misled with his silvery promises of a new world order and the resurgence of the mighty Aztec nation as the rightful rulers of the American continent. But the truth was, Penh, Torres, and their band of dreamers had the upper hand in this battle while the loyalist troops continued to gather. He bit his lip and continued to watch both the video feed of the skirmish up in the tower on one screen and the progress of the amassing troops on another. He just hoped the groups inside the building could hold on long enough for the reinforcements to arrive.

His phone buzzed with an incoming text, which brought a sigh of relief. The commanding general of the Mexican Army was on his way with a hand-selected brigade of Special Forces commandos. Their estimated time of arrival was eleven minutes out.

Lukas felt like a sleeping giant had been awakened. Perhaps broadcasting the unfolding events over a secured network to those who had remained skeptical of the intel he and his counterpart had provided was making the difference. Some people will only believe once they see. The question now was whether their acceptance of the facts and conversion to full-fledged support was too late.

He smiled a wistful smile as he shook his head slowly. His team needed some good news right about now, so he spoke words of encouragement through the microphone to all those wearing the communication gear, hoping the prospect of additional troops joining the fray would bolster their spirits and give them courage to hold out a little longer.

* * * *

Seventy-Fifth Floor, Unfinished Office Building, Mexico City, Mexico
June 18, 10:29 p.m. Local Time

"You're a sick bastard, Penh," Collin snarled as he rose gracelessly to his blistered feet. He tried not to hobble in front of his enemy, but his legs were stiff and his midsection was sore. He stood, nonetheless, reaching his full five-foot-eleven-inch stature. Even in the faint light of the single bulb overhead, the taut muscles of his exposed chest and abdomen were obvious. The veins in his arms bulged with the adrenaline the ongoing skirmish produced.

Penh watched him through narrowed eyes. He practically spat his condescending words at Collin. "Maybe you think so, but I'm a winner. Always have been. You? You are a loser. Always have been. You may have thought you could beat me. Catch me unaware.

Somehow come into my fortress here and escape with the victory. Tssk. Tssk. Tssk."

"Doesn't look to me like you're winning. Looks more like you're surrounded and about to lose," said Collin as he rigidly stepped backward toward a larger more open space behind the wheelchair.

Penh chuckled. "Trust me, Mr. Cook. We have more troops at the ready that will soon overpower the pitiful force your friends at the NSA have assembled. You see, I have spent months planning for every contingency and have gathered vast support, which you will see in action momentarily."

"You might be the most arrogant, delusional, and twisted piece of human garbage I've ever encountered." Collin spoke slowly as he continued to back away from Rob's wheelchair, hoping to lure Penh some distance from Rob. "Even while you're getting crushed, you think you're winning. Unbelievable."

"Crushed? You call *that* getting crushed?" Penh sneered, angling his arm toward the commotion above them. "Your handful of commandos against our hundreds of soldiers? I believe you might be the delusional one, Mr. Cook."

"Think what you want, you prick. Truth is, you're going to lose tonight."

Penh shook his head slowly. "You have no idea what you're up against, Mr. Cook."

"Maybe, maybe not. Another thing I know is that you don't have the guts to face me, so you pick on my mom and my friends." Collin was backing up as he spoke, moving into the open but darkened space in the corner of the building behind Rob. With each step backward, Penh moved closer. "You catch them off guard and use them against me. You're a slime ball and I've been looking forward to this moment since your goon shot my friend Tug. I just didn't think you had the balls to show up and face me like a man." Collin raised his fists, calling Penh in for a fight.

"I see you are unarmed," said Penh, stepping carefully through the aluminum frames, six feet behind Rob. "I am, as well." Penh held out his hands so they were visible.

"Yeah, but your two little buddies aren't. I'm sure they're around here somewhere. You can't seem to face anything on your own. Not even a loser like me."

Penh removed his suitcoat and draped it over an aluminum crossbeam in the framework he'd just stepped through while Collin rolled his shoulders and head, trying to loosen the muscles. Penh then removed his tie and set it on top of the coat. "My bodyguards are preoccupied at the moment," he said as he unbuttoned his top button. "So it will be just you and me. *Mano y mano*, as they say around here. This will be most gratifying."

Penh bent his knees slightly, moving foot over foot gracefully in a wide arc, rolling up his sleeves as he glided, looking like a panther on the prowl. Collin circled haltingly, his aching body struggling to match Penh's movements. With his fists raised in a boxer's classic defensive pose, Collin looked and felt clumsy next to Penh's refined and practiced moves. But he had a secret he hoped would make up the difference. Buried in his right fist was a nail he had scooped up as he knelt next to Rob and heard Penh's footsteps. It was his only hope of besting Penh in a fight he knew he couldn't otherwise win, even if he was feeling 100 percent.

Penh closed the gap, tightening the circle. Penh weaved this way and that. Collin reacted sluggishly. He kept moving and felt his muscles warming up as he did. After two or three circles, Penh lunged at him. Collin couldn't dodge quickly enough to stymie the attack. Penh drew first blood, landing a vicious blow to the side of Collin's face. Collin managed to push him away before he could strike again.

Collin licked his mouth and tasted the coppery tang of his own blood as it dripped from his lips. Penh backed away and laughed mockingly. Penh swaggered, his supreme confidence and superior training on full display while Collin regrouped. Feeling like the lowly

Rocky Balboa facing the venerable world champion, Apollo Creed, Collin raised his fists again and tried to shake off the additional pain.

Penh seized the moment and launched himself forward. Two quick shuffle steps and he had breached Collin's perimeter. He kicked out, chest high, but Collin dodged deftly to his right and deflected the leg as he twisted his body away from the incoming kick. He jabbed the leg downward with the butt of his right hand. The nail was too concealed in his hand and didn't make contact with Penh's leg as he'd hoped.

Penh appeared to be mildly surprised as he resumed circling. Maybe he didn't expect any resistance. He seemed content at the moment to just toy with his prey. That could be his undoing. Collin decided to continue to look sluggish, even though he could feel his body responding to the renewed adrenaline surging through his veins. He suspected he was tougher than Penh presumed. Plus, he had a nail in his hand, which he tried to position better in his grip as he purposely lumbered around the circle.

Penh swooped in again, this time with his fists. Collin kept his arms up in front of his face, but Penh landed two blows, one to each side of his head that sent him reeling and staggering backward. Again, the stiff muscles showed an awkwardness that Penh seized upon, lashing out again with another barrage. But Collin saw it coming. He ducked and dodged and blocked a right-handed arcing punch with the pointy end of the nail sticking out. Penh cried out in pain as the point ripped his shirt and slashed his skin. He retreated a few steps and surveyed his forearm, pressing on the bleeding gash. This only made him angrier and he flew at Collin again, kicking out with his legs. Collin moved left and jabbed out again with his curled right hand, sticking the point of the nail into the side of Penh's calf. Penh pulled back again, a stunned look on his face. His pant leg was torn and blood was running into his silky blue dress sock.

Fire built in Penh's eyes, a rage Collin had never witnessed in person. He came full-force, and although Collin tried to protect himself, Penh's powerful kick to the chest knocked Collin on his back. It took the air out of his lungs and shot pain through his torso. Penh fell on him with savage hostility, pinning Collin to the ground. Penh's knees were on Collin's biceps, holding down his arms while he repeatedly punched and slapped Collin's face. Collin wiggled and twisted under Penh's weight, eventually freeing his right arm as Penh struck him with a right across the cheek. Collin swung his right fist into Penh's left thigh. This time he let go of the nail as he stuck it in the muscle. In one swift motion, Collin hammered the nail deeper into the quadricep with his balled fist.

Penh howled and grabbed his leg. As he did, Collin reached up and grabbed Penh by the throat with both hands. Penh reacted by grabbing each of Collin's wrists, trying to pry them away. But Collin was stronger than Penh had credited him. Collin rolled to his left, pulling Penh to the ground and reducing his leverage. As Collin tried to scramble to pin him, Penh kicked hard, hitting Collin in the ribs and knocking him back.

Collin's muscles were warmed up now and responding better. He spun around and regained his feet. He tried to clear his head while Penh was down. Collin was dizzy and a bit nauseous, but he fought it back. Penh stood and dug the nail out of his leg, glaring at Collin as he panted and fumed.

chapter Thirty-Three

A knock came just before a guard stuck his head in to announce the arrival of Señor Billy Bob's guests. Lukas stood and shook hands with each of the three men as they introduced themselves. Of course, he knew who they were and what they looked like long before this, but he indulged in the pleasantries nonetheless. He gave them a brief and rapid-fire recap of Collin Cook's story, starting with the accident that claimed his wife and children and moving quickly to the $30 million settlement paid out by Pho Nam Penh's shell company, Pacific Casualty Insurance, an offshore reinsurer. He spoke quickly and avoided minutia. When he saw the confused looks, he explained that a reinsurance company is one that insures the primary insurance companies when they take on risks that are larger than they are comfortable with. He explained how lucrative this had been for Penh and how he had used the profits from it and other shell companies to fund his syndicate and launch his malicious cyberattacks.

Lukas also explained how he had first met Penh at MIT when they were both graduate students at the vaunted technology school. They joined the same club and studied in many of the same groups. Lukas watched Penh closely because of the vibe Penh gave off, even then. Lukas explained briefly their association and dealings at the time.

Lukas admitted that Penh had given him the shivers back then when he spoke. The man had a coldness and a hardness about him that left little doubt that he wouldn't stop until his vision became reality. When Lukas was recruited by the NSA, he unfolded for his superiors the depth and breadth of Pho Nam Penh's intentions and the lengths he had gone to, even in graduate school, to recruit tech-savvy dissidents. With recordings and writings and one of Penh's dark net websites as proof, it didn't take long before Lukas was granted permission and resources to keep tabs on Penh. As the threat grew, so did Lukas's stature and budget. He explained how his death in Afghanistan was faked so he could go deep undercover.

One of his guests asked why he had to fake his death. "Because of an argument that got out of hand the day before graduation," Lukas explained. "I opposed him openly and disagreed with him vehemently during one of his secretive recruiting events and he swore that if I ever got in his way, he would ruin me. Well, it didn't take long. He knew I was wary of him and knew I was determined to stop him. That's why he planted evidence at a mutual friend's house that cast suspicion on me as a contributor to my friend's death."

"How'd you exonerate yourself?"

"By that time, I had friends in high places. My technical prowess and die-hard loyalty had won me many friends. Their words, not mine. They went to bat for me and cleared me of any and all suspicions."

"It's good to know the right people, isn't it?"

Lukas paused, choosing his words carefully. "I enjoy using my talents to help keep people safe, especially the country that has given me so many opportunities and gifts. I know there are plenty of imperfections in our system and in our history, but this country has allowed a poor Austrian kid to grow up and pursue every dream he's ever dreamed and more. And my friends have been part of that from the time I arrived. I'll do anything I can to save this country and my friends."

"Very well," said the tall, experienced gentleman. "We'd better get to work."

With that, Lukas quickly laid out the plan of attack. He equipped each man with an earpiece and mic as well as a GPS tracker and camera attached to the bullet-proof vest he wore. The GPS units, they were told, would allow them to see where all of Lukas's commandos were, including Collin. Each man was marked with a different color. They were also given night vision goggles, gloves, and beanie caps to keep them warm in the chill nighttime mountain air.

As they exited Lukas's temporary headquarters, a large military command truck on loan from the Mexican government, they stepped across a parking lot to the awaiting helicopter. With a thumbs–up, Lukas wished them luck through the earpieces they wore.

These three detectives had earned the right to be here and be part of this culmination. They had worked hard, applying the skills of their trade. He wanted them to participate in the biggest victory for freedom and democracy that no one would ever hear about.

* * * *

Seventy-Fifth Floor, Unfinished Office Building, Mexico City, Mexico
June 18, 10:38 p.m. Local Time

Blood dripped from the nail as Penh raised it to eye level. He peered past it at Collin, contempt flaring from his dark eyes. The nail made a hollow *clink* as it dropped to the bare concrete.

Collin crouched down and swept the area with one hand, searching for anything he could use as a weapon. Nothing but dust. He backed up as Penh staggered forward. A few feet later, Collin bumped into a bucket and fell backward, landing in a pile of debris. This gave Penh another chance to pounce. And pounce he did. Two limping steps forward and Penh dove on top of Collin again, punching as he came up to a kneeling position. Collin's left hand grasped something solid. A short 2 x 4 piece of wood that he swung at Penh's head. This slowed Penh down enough as he stopped punching to block it that Collin could strike at his midsection with his right fist. He aimed for the solar plexus and succeeded in knocking out some of Penh's breath. Collin continued to swing the

2 x 4 until Penh wrested it from his grip. With Penh preoccupied, Collin was able to push Penh off him and pull himself free again.

As he scrambled to his feet, he bumped into something solid. A thick hand came around his mouth and another one around his waist. Collin tried to struggle free, but it was useless. The man was too powerful and Collin was too exhausted.

Someone else walked to Penh's side and helped him to his feet. The bodyguards. Dark sweaters, dark pants, thick bodies. Confidence and victory in their eyes and smiles. Penh shook off the help and staggered toward Collin. They had moved close to the window along the wall perpendicular to the missing window by Rob. Pale moonlight, filtered by the smoked glass, outlined his form as he approached. His fists were balled and the rage in his eyes even hotter than before. Penh stood in the light, three feet from Collin, surveying the scene as if trying to decide exactly how to dispose of his enemy.

As he glared at Collin, shots rang out through the stillness. Penh dropped to the floor, ducking for cover. The bodyguard behind Penh lifted his machine gun, not sure where to aim. Then his arms flailed backward once, twice, three times as bullets ripped into him. His gun let out a final futile burst into the ceiling as he crashed to the floor, sending a plume of dust into the air. The guy behind Collin loosened his grip and dropped to the ground at about the same time.

Collin stood motionless, stunned, while Penh pushed himself up from the ground, clutching his injured thigh.

Crunching sounds in the darkness to Collin's left pulled him out of the temporary shock and back into the present. "Mr. Cook, are you all right?" said a deep American voice. Collin squinted in the direction of the voice. All he could see was the outline of a tall figure, two hands holding a gun straight out in front of his body, stepping slowly and cautiously through the space.

"Yeah, I'm OK. Who *are* you?"

The guy stepped into the light coming through the window, still training his gun on Penh. He was a tall black man with a few gray hairs showing at the temples. A second later he flashed a badge. "I'm Special Agent Reggie Crabtree. FBI."

Another man stepped out from behind Collin, wiping blood from a hunting knife as he stepped over the dead bodyguard. He was tall and husky and wore cowboy boots and jeans with a corduroy blazer. "Special Agent Spinner McCoy," he said with a grin and a Texas accent as he continued walking. He kicked the gun from the bodyguard closest to Penh.

A third guy approached Penh, gun at the draw. He had thinning reddish hair and a squeaky voice with a heavy British accent. "Detective Nicolas Lancaster, Interpol. Mr. Penh, you are under arrest for criminal acts perpetrated against the United Kingdom and other sovereign nations relating to cyberactivity, grand larceny, and the disruption of banking commerce." He grabbed Penh's arms and pulled them behind his back and bound his wrists with plastic zip-tie cuffs.

* * * *

Mobile Command Center, Mexico City, Mexico
June 18, 10:42 p.m. Local Time

Lukas pumped his fist in the air as he watched his three guests take Penh into custody and save Collin. He wasted little time celebrating, though. There was still work to do.

"Butch," he said into his headset's microphone. "Get your team downstairs to help secure the civilians. Your backups should be arriving any minute."

"I don't know if I can," responded Butch, who was breathing heavily and speaking haltingly. "We're pinned down here on the seventy-sixth floor. A whole new unit has joined the fight. There must be fifty or sixty of them taking up position around us. They've just about got us flanked."

"Hang in there, Butch. Use the gas and a flash-bang. That'll slow them down."

"Roger that."

Lukas heard Butch giving one of his men the command to "smoke 'em out."

"We're deploying every smoke can we've got so we can get back to the stairs," Butch said, still breathing hard.

"Reinforcements will be coming from up above and down below. They'll be wearing camo instead of Class B's. Should make them easier to spot. Don't shoot at those guys, OK?"

"Roger. Camo is friendly. Everyone we've seen in here is wearing B's."

Lukas switched his focus to another monitor that showed him exactly where everyone was. Four transport trucks of loyalist soldiers were taking up position on every side of the building, each a block away. Two helicopters were airborne above the building. Salazar's men had held the top of the building secure. Salazar's pilot was moving his chopper so the additional transports could land and unload.

Lukas was pleased, but wished they weren't a step behind Torres and his troops. It would have been so much better if the Mexican authorities had believed him sooner. But, he realized, that was the nature of the business when working with politicians. Their abundance of caution and reticence to move quickly often caused problems for him. This time, the political gears moved just fast enough to divert a disaster and just slow enough to complicate an otherwise simple operation.

Checking the monitor with the live-streaming thermal images, Lukas pressed the mic button on his headset to give his team members some warning. "You've got company coming up the stairs. Looks like at least two dozen unfriendlies. Be ready for it."

* * * *

Nic Lancaster looked very pleased as he hauled Pho Nam Penh to his feet and began to drag him away by the collar. Reggie Crabtree held Collin by the elbow until he was steady enough to walk on his own. Spinner McCoy followed behind.

Collin pointed to the missing glass pane on their right, the source of the wind that was blowing up dust and swirling it around them. "Rob is over this way," he said as he started off in the direction he pointed.

Following Collin's instructions, Nic guided Penh toward the windowless wall, using the light from his phone. He found an opening in the metal framing that looked to be for a doorway. He pushed the limping Penh through in front of him into what looked to be a future hallway. The others lined up to follow. He heard something in his earpiece. Something that sounded like a warning. "Come again," he said politely as he held a finger in his ear to block out extraneous noise. But he didn't press the mic button.

As Nic shone his light behind for the others to see, he noticed the looks on the faces of Collin, Crabtree, and McCoy. Then someone shouted, "Stop right there." A blaze of bouncing lights illuminated the empty space, approaching them from all sides. Nic swept his phone light in an arc to reveal at least two dozen Mexican troops with assault rifles aimed and triggers fingered. Each had a high-powered LED light fixed to the top of their weapons. They moved swiftly and surrounded the five men. Two pairs of soldiers moved out to inspect the fallen bodies a few yards behind the group and more men swarmed into their places.

A distinguished gentleman wearing soft Italian loafers, a long camel-colored wool trench coat, and a finely tailored suit stepped into the light. He had a shock of thick white hair, neatly combed, and a full mustache to compliment his handsome, tanned face. "You have no right to be here. This is my country, my jurisdiction," said the man. His R's rolled gracefully off his tongue and his J's had a *jha* sound to them.

"The hell I don't," cried Nic Lancaster in his high-pitched voice. "Interpol has worldwide jurisdiction in cases of international crime, such as the crimes committed by this man."

"He is in my country. My government will see to his prosecution," the man said. His voice carried a regal, authoritarian tone.

"And who might you be?" asked Nic indignantly.

"My name is Juan Miguel Rivera Torres. I am a senior senator in the Mexican government. You have overstepped your bounds and I shall see to it that you receive the punishment you deserve for violating the sovereignty of this great nation."

"I've done no such thing, Senator," Nic said, his pitch elevating with each word. He retained a firm grip on Penh's shirt.

"Release him to the proper authorities," demanded Senator Torres. Two of the soldiers stepped toward Nic, aiming at his head. Nic wouldn't let loose his grasp on Penh. He stared at the senator, jaw muscles tensed.

Torres repeated his demand. "Release him."

"I'll do no such thing," said Nic defiantly. His eyes flicked from one rifle to another. The men holding them tensed, but waited for their leader's command. Even with all of those muzzles pointing at his head, Nic Lancaster was determined to stand his ground.

chapter Thirty-Four

"Don't get any crazy ideas there, Senator Torres," barked Reggie Crabtree. He and McCoy had drawn their weapons when they heard Lukas's warning and now held them steady with both hands, aiming them at Torres's face. "Tell your boys to stand down or we'll blow your head off."

Crabtree had turned his mic on so Lukas could heard the whole exchange. Nic was obviously following Lukas's instructions to stall as long as possible. The guy had guts. Crabtree had to admire that about him. But he also felt compelled to take control of the situation—to the extent possible, anyway.

Torres raised a hand to steady everyone's nerves as he stared unflinchingly at the faces of the two Americans pointing .40-caliber Glocks at him. His comely features remained calm amid the tension. Clearly, he thought he had had the situation completely under control. Torres didn't know what Crabtree knew because he didn't have the same information Crabtree had coming in through a hidden earpiece.

"Aren't you the Senator Torres being investigated by the Federal Ministerial Police for acts of subversion and collusion with a foreign entity intent on overthrowing the duly elected president of Mexico?" asked Crabtree, trying to deflect some of the attention away from Nic.

Torres's eyes grew wide in panic first, then turned cold and hostile as he cocked his head and squinted at Crabtree. "These accusations have no grounds," he snapped.

"Oh, really? I beg to differ. I wouldn't be here by invitation of your government if there weren't suitable grounds," said Reggie. "Between our two governments, there's a mountain of pertinent data that suggests you are guilty as charged."

"They can prove nothing. Besides, in a matter of hours, there will be a new government in Mexico. At that point, the Policia Federal Ministerial will be under my command and their investigation will be irrelevant."

The soldiers aiming the rifles exchanged glances, but remained poised and ready to shoot.

"You seem pretty sure of yourself there, Senator. How confident are you in the coalition you've formed within the army? Are you sure you have all the support you think you have?"

Reggie paused, watching the senator squirm slightly. His men looked confused and unsure. Reggie listened as Lukas coaxed him through the earpiece saying, "We need two more minutes. Keep it going for just two more minutes."

"Maybe you are unaware of the four full brigades of soldiers loyal to the current administration—the only one with a legitimate claim to govern—who are, at this very moment, surrounding this building and taking control of it, floor by floor. Your forces, though impressive and surprising in numbers, will be no match for the overwhelming numbers under the command of General Aguilar. I'm sure you know him. He's the general over the entire Mexican Army. He's aware of your treasonous designs and has dispatched every available soldier to stop your intended coup."

"You're bluffing," snorted the senator.

"Am I? You want to gamble on that?"

"You know nothing, you American fool. I am good friends with General Aguilar. We spoke earlier today and I can assure you he knows nothing about what will soon transpire."

"How sure are you that he knows nothing?"

"Even if he knows, it's too late. The wheels have been set in motion already. There is a new world order coming online as we speak. Your American and British banks have been disabled as we have caused your currencies to collapse under the weight of your enormous debts. We have seen to it that our friends in China will be calling the loans they have issued because they know the United States and its allies are no longer suitable risks.

"By morning, the flow of money will have ceased. By the end of the day, businesses will choke due to their inability to pay for the goods and services they require because the credit markets will have dried up. American consumers will be unable to access money in their accounts. Their debit cards and credit cards will be useless because their accounts will have evaporated in a vain attempt by the banks to repay what they owe. And, because nobody carries cash anymore, the average family will shortly lose the ability to make even the simplest of purchases. Within a week, your entire system will be irreparably crippled and begging for relief. But who will loan money to a bankrupt country? Chaos will ensue and your murder rates will soar even higher than they already are. Your people will be turned into savages who will kill for a meal."

Crabtree listened patiently. When the senator stopped for a breath, he interjected, "Hmm. Maybe you missed out on that little power glitch earlier. Yeah, that was us throwing a wet towel over your system, so to speak, and rerouting all activity. Did you not realize that your systems have been completely shadowed and contained for the past several hours?"

Torres halted, visibly stymied. His face, illuminated by a sliver of moonlight shining in through the missing window, appeared to grow pale. Anger and uncertainty swirled together across his countenance as Crabtree spoke.

"That's right. There have been some very smart people, both in your Secretariat of Communications and your Federal Ministerial Police, who have been working around the clock with the good folks from our National Security Agency to intercept and contain all communications coming from this building via a cloned Internet environment. Pretty tricky stuff that I couldn't begin to fully explain. But the end result is that those wheels you referred to are not in motion, at least not out in the real world."

"Impossible. No one can do that."

"I admit, I don't know how it works," said Reggie. "I just heard something about 'bots' and 'cloning' and 'masking.' That's all I know. That, and the fact that all of your team's keystrokes were recorded somewhere so there is also evidence of your malicious intentions. I also heard that at least one of your trusted hackers was pulling double duty and sharing information with our team. That's how we knew where you were and what you were doing."

Before Torres could answer, a hail of gunfire erupted and echoed against the hard surfaces in the barren cavity. It came from the stairwell behind Torres, accompanied by screams of pain and shouts of commands in Spanish. Boots clattered against the steel treads of the stairway, drowning out the voices.

Torres ducked for cover, as did several of his soldiers. Others pointed their muzzles toward the clamor, jerking them from side to side, looking for a target. Amid the confusion, one man yanked Penh out of Nic's grasp while Nic was trying to back him away toward safety. He shoved Nic backward into an aluminum stud, stunning him momentarily. The soldier flicked out a knife and cut the zip ties that bound Penh's hands. He also waved it in Nic's direction in warning.

The gunfire stopped, but the pounding of boots didn't. Dozens of camo-clad soldiers poured into the empty space of the unfinished floor, rifles at the ready, commanding everyone to stay still in two languages. They came from every direction it seemed. Some appeared from the darkness behind them where Penh and Collin had fought. Others came from around the opposite side.

The soldier who had freed Penh took advantage of the confusion and pushed Penh forward down the unfinished hallway and through the framed doorway toward the open window. Penh was trying to say something over the din, but the soldier ignored him, intent on moving Penh toward the only possible escape route. He must have seen the ropes near the opening and expected to use them to escape.

The moment they breached the doorway, something clapped and Penh shrieked in pain. Penh's leg caught on a hook connected to a cable strung across the threshold at ankle level. He had tripped the wire intended for Collin, the one the wiry Asian guy had rigged. The whirring of rope spinning through pulleys echoed as Penh was yanked to the floor, pulled with such force that the soldier lost his grip on Penh's arm as he was dragged across the concrete toward the window. The large wooden spool, which had been teetering on the edge, held in place by the tension on the rope, had plunged over the window ledge when Penh tripped the line holding it in place, which then pulled Penh toward the empty window frame. Penh did a swimming motion on his back, trying to find something to hold on to, but there was only dust on the floor. He was picking up speed the closer he got and his flailing became more desperate. Penh contorted his body every which way to increase friction, hoping to slow his slide toward certain death. As his feet approached the lip of the window frame, the tension of the cable around Rob's wheelchair brought the cable from the back of the chair taut and propelled him and the chair over the edge just ahead of Penh.

Rob's wheelchair stopped with a jolt just after the back wheels breached the edge. He was facing straight down, held in place by the rope across his midsection and the tape around his ankles and hands, which gripped the armrests with every ounce of energy he had.

At the same time, Penh was pulled upward, dangling upside down by his leg in the center of the empty window frame. His body twisted while terror contorted his face and filled his eyes.

"You fool," he cursed at the soldier. "This was for Cook."

The Mexican soldier looked terrified and confused. In Spanish, he pled his innocence and ignorance.

The gunfire had ebbed and the room was now full of soldiers wearing camouflage systematically disarming those wearing their Class B uniforms. Their raised voices replaced the chatter of their rifles and the clamoring of their boots. As the weapons dropped to the floor, Collin ran to the open window and began tugging on the rope that held Rob's chair in place just over the edge of the precipice.

"Don't worry, Rob. I'm not going to let you fall," Collin called out.

Penh continued to twist, but was struggling to reach something. Collin looked to see what it was and noticed two ropes, one white, one black. Each had a loop tied to the end and each was roughly level with his face and just beyond Penh's grasp as the wind continued to spin him gently in circles. Collin followed the ropes' paths back into the building with is eyes, but couldn't see the ends of them. He did notice, however, that the rope attached to Penh's leg was white and the one attached to Rob's wheelchair was black. Penh continued to stretch out for the white rope, ignoring the black one that seemed to be more easily accessible.

That's when he figured it out. If his trap was meant for Collin, he was to be given a choice of whether to save himself or save Rob. Penh must have known the secret and was trying to save himself and allow Rob to plunge to his death. His fingers made contact with the white rope, but he rotated away from it before he was able to grasp it.

Now Collin had a decision to make: let go of Rob's chair and hope he could reach the rope before Penh caught ahold of it or hold on tight and hope he had the strength to pull Rob back to safety. As he contemplated this choice, a thunderous voice caught his, and everyone in the room's, attention. That voice rose above the scuffling of moving boots, the muttering voices, and the howling wind, ordering silence. A man stepped into the glow of the lights from dozens of rifles. He, too, wore a Class B military uniform with the insignia of a general on its shoulders. Torres's face dropped when he saw him. "Good evening, Senator Torres," the man said. "What have we here?"

Torres remained silent. His countenance grew cloudy, like he was trying to piece together a puzzle in his mind. "General Aguilar?"

Behind the general, another man crossed the threshold with a pronounced limp, a cane in his right hand. He remained in the general's shadow, surveying the scene, saying nothing.

The general spoke again. "Senator Torres, you are under arrest for acts of treason against the United Mexican States," he bellowed in Spanish. Turning to the men on either side of him, he said, "Arrest this man. Arrest all of these traitors."

Torres tried to say something, but words seemed to fail him as General Aguilar quickly took control of the situation, unceremoniously overthrowing months of meticulous planning and coordination. In that instant, Torres's dreams and ambitions blew up and left him unable to speak.

While General Aguilar's loyalist forces rounded up the treasonous followers of Torres and Penh, the man with the cane stepped out of the shadows and limped toward the open window.

Penh's eyes widened and his mouth opened when he saw the man's face with its steely grin and piercing blue eyes. "You? How did you …"

"It's been a long time, Penh," he said in his soft, Germanic accent. "I've waited for this moment all these years, patiently tracking your moves. I always knew you'd follow through with those plans you drew up at MIT."

"You used your friends for this?" Penh said in disgust.

"No. That was an unfortunate coincidence that set us on an inevitable collision course, I'm afraid," said Lukas as he continued making his way toward Collin and Rob. "I couldn't let you do to Collin what you had done to so many other recipients of your insurance company's settlements. I did my best to hide him and protect him, but you wouldn't stop searching for him, would you? You couldn't stand to lose, could you?"

"I should have known …" Penh began. Before Lukas reached Collin, Penh lunged with one last desperate effort and grabbed at the looped ropes. Lukas sprang as best he could, jabbing his cane to block Penh's hand. In the process, his cane whacked the white rope away as it made contact with Penh's wrist. But there was not enough energy in the jab to halt the wrist's forward progress. Momentum carried Penh's hand through its intended motion. Penh's outstretched fingers wrapped around the black loop toward the apex of his arm's arc. Then gravity took over. As Penh's body swung back toward the open window, his hand pulled the loop, releasing the black rope from the spool that was suspended in the air by both the black and white ropes. Rob's chair suddenly popped upward and inward while Penh's body was yanked downward by the weight of the dropping spool, his head and shoulder bouncing against the ledge with a sickening crack before free-falling seventy-five floors to the ground below.

The sudden jolt threw Collin off balance as he continued to pull on the handles of the wheelchair, causing him to lose his footing and rotate as he slipped toward the ledge. He landed at an awkward angle on his rear end, losing his grip on the wheelchair, which now had all four wheels on the floor. Momentum propelled him toward the ledge as his body continued to twist. He was on his stomach with his feet plunging over the edge as he continued to slide. His hands tried to find purchase on the grit that covered the floor, but they grasped futilely on the slick surface. His momentum was working against him, carrying his lower body over the edge at an increasing rate. Panic set in and his efforts became more desperate. As he eyed the fast-approaching end of the concrete floor, he felt a firm hand gripping his forearm. Nic Lancaster, sliding with one leg under him and one leg out to the side, clutched Collin's arm and prevented him from slipping over the edge. The two wrestled and struggled until Collin was back safely inside the building.

Spinner McCoy first lunged forward and grabbed the handles of the wheelchair, pulling Rob backward toward safety, then aided Nic and Collin. Reggie Crabtree clasped Lukas by the arm to secure him.

Rob grimaced and shook his head. His jaw rattled with cold and fear. His hands still gripped the armrests so hard they were completely white, the tendons popping above the skin with the strain.

Collin and Nic sidled up to the ledge on hands and knees and looked over, morbid curiosity getting the best of them. Penh's grotesquely disfigured body lay splayed out on the concrete hundreds of feet below, a dark pool growing around it. Fragments of the wooden spool lay in a circular pattern around the gore. Nic and Collin, strangers up to this point, embraced as the significance of the moment sank in. Collin thanked the man who, unbeknownst to him, had hunted him like an animal and cursed him repeatedly during the past several weeks. Nic, in typical British fashion, shrugged off the thanks and pointed to Lukas as the one who deserved the credit.

Collin then turned his focus to his lifelong friend. After cutting his ankles free, Collin expected Rob to stand so he could embrace him, but Rob couldn't do it. After nearly twenty-one hours strapped to the wheelchair, his legs were numb. He also shook uncontrollably. Collin, still on his knees, wrapped him up in a brotherly embrace. Lukas bent toward him from the other side and joined in. They stayed like that until one of General Aguilar's officers brought a warm coat for Rob and suggested they get him medical attention.

chapter Thirty-Five

The three friends sat on a postmodern black leather sofa in the lobby, the only space in the building that resembled anything close to being finished. Across from them, Agents Crabtree, McCoy, and Lancaster listened in. The floor had been tiled in gray granite with shiny black accents forming a stylish pattern. A bank of bluish-white LED lights, angled from mounts two-stories high on the wall, pointed at the fountains in the center of the foyer and gave an otherworldly, ultra-modern glow to the otherwise empty space. A small stream, lined with smooth, black rocks the size of a fist ran through the middle of the open-design, forty-foot-ceilinged first floor. The babbling water brought a peaceful ambiance that echoed throughout the entire bottom story.

Rob, who had been given medical attention, sat rigidly between Lukas and Collin—bandaged and bruised, but smiling. He was wrapped in a blanket, but still wore the suit his Asian captures had put on him, bloodstains on the shirt and lapel.

Lukas explained to the group of curious participants the unprecedented level of cooperation and coordination between the US and Mexico that had taken place over the past several months. He talked about how difficult it had been to convince General Aguilar of his friend's treacherous designs and to get him to fully cooperate. Fortunately, one of Aguilar's most trusted subordinates had caught wind of something fishy in Senator Torres's office during a series of routine meetings earlier in the year. That subordinate struck up a romantic relationship with Torres's aide and soon "joined" Torres's "cause."

"So it was just by luck that Torres got caught and this thing got stopped?" Nic Lancaster said.

"Not exactly," Lukas explained. "Beyond all of the evidence the NSA had gathered and presented, there were others who had heard some grumblings and whisperings. There was plenty of suspicion around Torres, but no one wanted to act on it. He's a national hero, you see. But once Aguilar's aide got in tight with his movement and began feeding information to his boss, people started to believe what I had been telling them. A small group within Mexico's Center for Research and National Security and I began to cooperate a month or two ago. It's been an uphill battle for support and resources, but finally, they came through."

"Not a moment too soon, from what I gather," added Reggie.

"You're absolutely right. The last thing anyone wants is to be wrong in a situation like this," said Lukas. "I have to commend all the guys I've worked with these past few weeks. Butch and his team were invaluable during this whole operation, from beginning to end. They not only provided tactical support, as you saw, they also provided intelligence, including names and locations and details we needed."

"Why did Collin get involved in this whole thing?" asked Crabtree.

"Bad luck, really," said Lukas. "Penh approached Torres about two years ago, knowing of his anti-American sentiments and his secret desire to radicalize the Mexican government and 'reestablish the Aztec empire.' Penh enlarged his vision and emboldened him, feeding him cash and technological expertise to help him toward his goal."

"But Collin had nothing to do with any of that," Rob said.

"Yes, that's true," said Lukas. "But you know I've kept an eye on Penh ever since I met him at MIT. I knew he was up to no good from the time I first heard him talk in closed, invitation-only meetings. He had a subsurface hatred that, combined with his genius and power of persuasion, was volatile. He was like a powder keg with a fuse that had been lit. It was only a matter of time before he blew. Collin entered the scene as Penh was amassing wealth and building his infrastructure. One of his more or less legitimate companies was the insurance company that had to pay out after the accident.

"After settling with Collin's lawyer, who wound up dead, by the way, Penh felt the need to 'put Collin in his place' after he disappeared in order to show his team and Torres that he couldn't be bested. In the Asian culture, you lose face when you can't overcome obstacles that should be easy to overcome. See, that thirty million represents the largest settlement ever won against Pacific Casualty Insurance. And it didn't sit well with Penh, not while he was trying to pay for all of this collaboration," Lukas said, waving a hand. "Also, I think that since the RBS thing in May, he has not had access to working capital like he did previously. He needed Collin's money to pay Torres and his mercenaries. Add to that the fact that Collin was this ordinary guy that kept getting away was like a burr under his saddle."

"I never thought I could produce that kind of hatred," Collin said, shaking his head. "I didn't even do anything wrong. At least, not at first."

"I didn't think so either, my friend. How could anyone guess it would have come to this? Like I told Penh up there, it was just bad luck. Your wife's accident started this whole chain reaction. I just wanted to protect you from Penh, not get you involved this deeply in his scheme."

"Not your fault, Lukas. This whole thing is Penh's fault. Penh and fate, I guess." Collin nodded his head slowly. He looked at each of the faces that surrounded him. "It's been a wild ride, that's for sure. One I never expected and never wished for, but I'm glad I was able to help stop that son of a bitch. And I'm glad I had all you guys to help make it happen." Collin made eye contact with each of the men in the circle.

Nic gave an apologetic nod, Crabtree looked sheepish, and McCoy let a wry smile form on his lips.

"A wild ride? That's a bit of an understatement, isn't it?" blurted Rob.

A muted chuckle rose from the group.

A Mexican soldier, dressed in his camouflage battle fatigues, approached them deferentially but urgently. "Sirs, your transport is ready," he said, sweeping his arm toward the front doors. Two armed soldiers met them at the steps that descended to the reception desk and stayed with them as the group moved methodically for Collin's and Rob's sakes until they reached the limousine parked at the curb. It was idling. White smoking drifted up from its tailpipe.

Collin couldn't help but look to his left as they approached the car. Yellow tape marked the area where Penh's mangled body and a pool of his blood still lay, being photographed for the record.

A crescent moon hung in the sky overhead, casting its gentle light over the towering structure. In turn, the glass panes reflected that light, creating a peaceful glow. Rob, Lukas, and Collin piled into the black Cadillac, taking up the whole back seat, while the three agents took the bench facing them. The six of them continued their conversation, each discussing his role and his take on the story as they drove to the airfield.

A Lear Jet awaited them on the tarmac. Four minutes after they boarded the plane, it was taxiing into position at the head of the runway, spinning up its engines in the last preflight check. Collin felt his body being pushed back into the soft leather recliner as the plane picked up speed. A million thoughts and two million emotions ran through his head and his heart. He was going home to Huntington Beach to see his parents for the first time in eight months. Not since the funeral for his wife and three children last July had he seen his siblings. It would be strange, but sweet. A lot had happened since then. His life had been turned upside down and he had been called upon to do things he never thought he would or could do. He was, after all, just an ordinary guy.

Lukas sat next to him and Rob sat in the seat facing him. Memories of their years together in middle school and high school flooded through his mind. He closed his eyes, but all he could see was that open window and the ledge. It caused him to relive those moments where he was slipping off toward oblivion. That was followed closely by the vision of Rob's face as he and his wheelchair hung suspended eight hundred feet in the air. Every detail coming back with vivid clarity. His heart skipped and his body shot forward, eyes wide open.

Rob raised an eyebrow at him. "You OK?"

"Fine. Nightmares, is all," he said.

"Me, too. No way I can sleep right now," said Rob, diverting his gaze out the window.

"You should try. We both need some rest after what we've been through the past few days."

"Yeah." Rob shrugged. "Good luck with that."

When Collin finally settled back down and closed his eyes the second time, he tried harder to block out the terror of recent events. He tried not to think about the man he'd suffocated and caused to drown on the boat, nor the one he had speared in the chest. As he worked those thoughts out of his consciousness, Amy's beautiful, smiling face appeared. She looked happy and content and Collin felt it was time for him to let go of his guilt and pain regarding her death. It was like she was giving him permission to move on. He patted the computer sitting on his lap and told himself he would write this story for her. She would enjoy it.

His eyes fluttered open again at this thought. There was too much energy and excitement and nervousness bottled up to sleep right now, so he gave up trying. Even though sleep was what his body craved most, his mind just wouldn't let it happen. Not yet, anyway.

So he stayed awake, and his friends with him, the new ones and the old ones. They talked about everything. Past, present, and future. He told them about his escape from London, then Germany, then France. He told them about his ordeal at sea and his ordeal in the Cessna and his ordeal in the mountains. He shared the moments of terror when he thought he would die and how he thought Penh would certainly kill him. He told them how he felt he might never get over the fact that he had taken two lives and played a part in Penh's gruesome demise. Most of all, he expressed his heartache about Rob's missing finger.

Rob and Lukas listened attentively and tried to comfort Collin. Rob expressed his confidence that either the reattachment surgery would be successful or he would learn to live without it. "It might screw up my golf game for a while, so be prepared to cover my bets, buddy," Rob said with a grin.

Flummoxed, Collin shot him a look of incredulity. "Who would bet on a golf game when he's missing a finger?"

The three agents onboard, unfamiliar with the type of friendship Rob and Collin shared, looked at each other wide eyed.

Then, almost in unison, Lukas said, "He would," while Rob said, "I would." The three friends burst out laughing while the three agents chuckled tentatively.

After the laughter subsided, Collin turned his face toward the window. America, his home, the land of the brave, was still free and he was about to restart his life there as a normal American citizen.

Thank you

Thank you for reading "Off Guard," the third installment in Collin Cook's saga. I hope you enjoyed the adventure.

If you like the type of fun, clean fiction like "Off Guard" that I write, please take a moment to share your thoughts with other readers by writing a review on Amazon. There's no prescribed way to write a review—just tell people what you thought about the book. Your input helps other readers as they make their decisions about what to read and it helps authors like me connect with new readers.

Your reviews and comments would be greatly appreciated. Self-published authors like me rely on word-of-mouth, among other things, to attract new readers. My goal is to bring you—and other readers like you—action-packed stories that you can share with your friends and family. So, I hope you'll take a moment and help spread the word.

Please connect with me at my website, www.glenrobinsbooks.com. You can download the epilogue for "Off Guard" and sign up for my newsletter. I promise to not clog your inbox. I'll only keep you informed of my next releases and the occasional special offer for deals and freebies and what-not.

You can like me on Facebook https://wwacebook.com/glenrobinsbooks.

I'm also on BookBub if you'd like to to stay informed of promotions and giveaways. https://www.bookbub.com/authors/glen-robins

Continue to the next page for a preliminary look at "Chosen Path," my next novel, scheduled for release in early 2018.

Chosen Path

Chapter 1

Los Angeles International Airport
June 22, 3:44 a.m.

It didn't look right. It didn't feel right. Something was off, compelling him to take a closer look.

No one around. Very few people in this gigantic airport at this time of morning. Granted, he was sitting in the international terminal, which was probably busier than the rest of the airport because of all of the odd arrival times from across the globe. But still, the place was practically empty. Most people congregated in the waiting area where he sat were half-asleep either waiting for a departure or a connection or got here early to avoid traffic and get through security faster. That's what he had done and that's why he was sitting there in the International terminal sipping coffee before 4 a.m.

The two guys lurking about for the last twenty minutes had something going on. No one is that alert, that edgy this early. As far as he could tell, neither one had touched any coffee or Red Bull or tea or anything caffeinated. They were just being weird.

Their heads never stopped turning. Their eyes never stopped darting about. They never relaxed or chatted or checked departure or arrival times on the giant screens hanging down from the ceiling. They never sat down.

Their behavior was strange. Something seemed not right with them, like they were anticipating something, something big. It demanded someone's attention, but no one else paid any mind.

Sure, they looked to be Korean. Nothing odd about that. He, himself, was Korean and there were dozens of other Koreans awaiting KAL's 6:35 departure for Seoul. But these two looked and acted suspicious, so he decided to be vigilant despite the detached non-interest from every other person in the vicinity.

Vigilance is an interesting concept, he thought. People talk about it. Authorities ask for it. The public is warned that it is necessary for their own protection and security. But what is it? What does it entail?

In this case, vigilance meant that Noh Jeong Tae had to stand up when he felt like sitting. It meant that he had to walk when he felt like resting. It meant he had to pay attention when he felt like rethinking his chosen path in life and his destiny and his future by examining his past. He wanted to gain some perspective, but here he was thinking about vigilance instead.

He had a choice to make: follow the two odd dudes or stay with his sixteen Tae Kwon Do students and the five chaperones, all of whom were in various stages of zombie-hood. The two oddly dressed dudes had ducked through a doorway behind the little bake shop. Before they did, he watched them pull the hoods of their sweatshirts over their heads and don black leather gloves. That, too, was strange. Waiting until they thought no one was watching was even stranger.

The door they pulled open, entered, then pulled shut, did not appear to be a doorway for use by the general public. There were no markings or placards on it. No signs anywhere explained the use of that door. It was even painted the same greyish-blue as the walls of the terminal, probably so that it would blend in and not be mistaken for an available exit. But these two dudes peered in all directions before opening it and quickly disappearing inside.

Apparently no one else noticed. No one else was doing anything. No one else was being vigilant when they saw this blatant and obviously suspicious behavior.

He looked at his students, the select group that had qualified to participate in the World Tae Kwon Do championship in Seoul, his hometown. Two from each of his eight classes. One winner and one runner-up. The youngest two, seven and eight years old, were cute, smart, and sassy. The two oldest were seventeen and all teenager. Long hair, hoods over their heads, slumped in their chairs, earbuds in, eyes closed. That was the façade a Korean kid living in America had to put on to fit in. Inside, they were diligent students, respectful of their parents, aware of their culture and history, and proud of it. They had mastered not only the skills of Tae Kwon Do, but also the principles. Discipline. Respect. Self-Mastery. The other students ranged through the intervening age categories. All were good kids from good families, trying to bridge the gap between keeping the values of the old country while assimilating to the new.

The stirrings within him grew stronger the more ticks the clock on the wall registered and the more he stared at the group of kids he was training and teaching and molding to be responsible adults and good citizens. To be strong. To be vigilant.

Jeong Tae, or JT as his American friends called him, couldn't sit still. He sat up abruptly, briefly catching the attention of a handful of his students. He waved off their concern and looked for any sign of vigilance from someone else. Nothing. No one else in the terminal seemed awake enough to notice what was happening. He glanced up and down the two rows of chairs, the airport ones that are stuck together and kind of hard and uncomfortable and that are arranged to face each other. The kids and the chaperones that filled those two rows were either asleep, playing on their gaming devices, enthralled with something on their phones or, in the case of the adults, drinking coffee and speaking in low tones about whatever the latest gossip is amongst the Korean housewives of Orange County. Certainly, none of them were prone to vigilance at 3:45 a.m. It was left to him, willing or not, to check it out, to be vigilant.

JT stood, stretched, and faked nonchalance as he walked toward the bakery. His head swiveled in all directions. No one was watching. No one was being vigilant.

When he reached the unmarked door, he checked the handles. They were locked. He checked again and although the handles didn't turn, the door opened. A quick glance revealed clear packing tape across the latch.

The corridor was long and curved slightly to his left. Dull yellow paint on the walls. Tubular fluorescent lighting, two per can, spaced every six feet running parallel to the hallway. Matted gray carpeting, the low pile kind they put in high traffic areas and lasts forever, stretched out in front of him to eternity, it seemed.

JT moved slowly, side-stepping the first ten yards in case someone caught him. He could run back toward the door if necessary. No sign of the two dudes. Maybe he was just being paranoid. Maybe they belonged there. But vigilance called and he had already decided to respond. If he ignored it, his conscience would never let him rest. His three-year, obligatory stint and his additional seven years as an officer in the Korean army had taught him that. You always do your duty, do it well, then your conscience lets you sleep at night. A lesson reinforced, sometimes forcefully, by his father. His quick rise through the ranks and the several medals that adorned his uniform were testaments to his diligence. Sense of duty. Pride. Vigilance. Whatever you want to call it.

That was a lifetime ago, it seemed, but the lessons were still ingrained, still pushing him.

Maybe it was the army's fault he wasn't still sitting, enjoying his coffee, and contemplating his life. Maybe it was his father's. He'd think about that on the plane ride. Eleven hours in a tin can with wings gave you plenty of opportunity for self-reflection.

The hallway kept going, following the contour of the impossibly large building. As it bent, he could see only twenty feet in front of him. Each time, he told himself, just go to that point, then turn around. Once, twice, three times he went to the predetermined spot and kept going. He knew he wouldn't stop, not until he figured out what odd thing the two odd dudes were doing.

Windows replaced yellow paint on the right-hand wall. They looked out over LAX's northern-most runways. It was mostly dark out on the tarmac. All light, from whatever source, was diffused in a thick, early morning fog typical for the Southern California coastline in June. Only one plane, with its flashing wing lights and bright forward beams, was in motion on the outer fringes. Its hulking mass indistinct as it lurched through the pea soup-like morning. JT figured it had just landed and was taxiing toward one of the many gates at one of the many terminals in this world-famous transportation hub.

JT kept his back against the left-hand wall as he continued his stealthy approach. Another twenty feet to the next decision point. He stopped and looked back. There were noises coming from somewhere. They echoed, making it hard to pinpoint their origin. He checked ahead of him and behind him. No one was coming. This deserted hallway was full of mysteries.

Looking out the window, he saw them in the mottled light, moving quickly, heads ducked. He knew it was them, even though he couldn't see their faces. They were running toward a plane, toward its landing gear. Why was no one doing anything about it? They were splitting up. One went to the right, the other to the left. Each dug into a pocket of his coat as he approached the plane's tires. They were attaching something.

This wasn't right. Someone had to have seen this. Someone had to do something.

The two men turned and ran back toward the hallway. JT ducked down. That's when he saw it. Another indistinct door. This one seemed to lead out into the blackness. It had a window about halfway up its length to match the other windows in the hallway. He scrambled toward it, hoping to hide beyond it before they came through it. But they were too quick. Their feet were pounding up the metal staircase and he still had twenty-five feet to go.

The door burst open. JT was ten feet away. The two odd dudes charged in at full speed, ducking down and checking their watches and smiling. They were talking and he recognized the words and the dialect. North Koreans.

JT froze. The two dudes startled at the sight of another human and stopped cold, eyes as big as saucers as they took in the unexpected. Instincts kicked in. Army training. Special forces combat training. Defensive maneuvers, offensive tactics. It all came back like a steam train through a tunnel. JT instantly pivoted his right leg slightly behind him, shoulder width apart. His fingers curled into compact hammers, raised to chin level, cocked and loaded.

The first dude was the leader. He was bigger and looked older, more in charge. First rule: disable the leader. The leader hesitated only a fraction of a second as he realized the threat and analyzed it. It must not have seemed like much of a threat. A five-foot nine Asian guy, obviously Americanized, wearing torn and faded jeans, the kind with "bling" on them, a trendy T-shirt under a lightweight Dodger's jacket, and comfortable Nikes. Just standing there looking stunned. He's no threat, the guy must have thought. Just a lost tourist. But then he changed his mind. JT saw it flash behind his eyes. Any threat must be eliminated.

The guy closed the gap between them in a flash, expecting to flatten JT. His plan seemed to transmit from his dark, calculating eyes. Knock him to the ground, beat the crap out of him, and run. By the time this little threat awoke, there'd be nothing to wake up to. The deed would be done.

JT bounced his weight to the balls of his feet and brought his hands up in front of him in half a blink, balanced and ready. The guy recognized it too late. He was too close to change course. JT side-stepped the oncoming body and jacked his knee upward, catching the guy in the ribs with such force it threw his upper body high and backwards, landing him on his back. JT felt the crunch of the ribs against his patella, so he knew the guy would be in pain. As soon as he landed, JT dropped to one knee and smashed the edge of his hand sharply into the solar plexus, raised the hand and jabbed again with a full-force blow to the throat, crushing his larynx.

The dude gasped and sputtered, rolling on to his side, struggling for air as he clutched his throat and curled into a ball. Leader disabled, main threat removed.

JT bounced back to the ready position, facing the second guy, the smaller of the two. This guy was scared. Eyes wide, frozen in place, he didn't know how to process what had just happened and certainly didn't know what to do next. Without his leader to give orders, he seemed lost. Then survival instinct must have kicked in. He put up his fists and showed that he had at least some training. The smaller guy stepped forward purposefully, eying JT like a tiger eyes a rival. Taking the aggressive approach, the guy led with his right fist. JT swatted it with his left hand as he bounced slight to his right, coiled up, and swung his right leg out and around so fast the guy barely moved his eyes toward the blur coming in from his left. JT's foot smashed the back of the guy's head like a soccer player doing a mid-air strike to the net. The guy dropped like a stone. A second later, he pushed up against his elbows as if he would rise and continue the fight. Without hesitation, JT drove the sole of his Nike into the side of the guy's face and temple, pivoting on the ball of his left foot as he focused all of his energy in an all-body side kick. The force of the blow launched the guy two feet to the side, inert.

Now JT had a problem. A pile of bodies and a security camera above the door. He looked up at the black orb stuck to the ceiling and knew it had all been captured on a high-resolution digital feed to the airport's main security server.

He waited. It was the only honorable thing to do. Wait and explain.

But then he remembered the devices the two odd dudes had stuck to the legs of the plane.

Without thinking, JT jumped to the door, bolted down the metal staircase and sprinted to the plane. Now that it was him, the grounds crew had reappeared. There were figures moving toward him in the eerie, diffused light, like swamp creatures shouting and waving their arms.

He made it to the left-side landing gear first and went straight to the silver disc with the red flashing light cleverly hidden on the underbelly of the device. He pulled it off and hurled it like a discus thrower, as far as he could toward the empty runway and hoped it would bounce and slide and roll as far as possible. He made it to the second one and chucked it just in time. Then he dropped and covered his ears, waiting for the explosion. It never came, but the baggage guys did. They were closing in on him. He realized the things were not going to blow, so he regained his feet and took off running through the gloom, ducking and dodging behind lugging moving equipment and an half-filled trailer. Sirens blared in the background, growing closer.

As he sprinted toward the stairway, he calculated the odds in his head. There had to be more than just the two guys he'd just taken down and they, too, had to be stopped.

JT made it to the stairs amid clamorous confusion in the foggy darkness. He paused a beat to listen for his pursuers. Voices behind him asked where he had gone and orders were barked out to find him and stop him. With Ninja-like stealth, JT climbed the steps by threes and swung the door open. He pulled it shut and twisted the lock.

As he entered the mysterious hallway, JT saw two more North Korean guys crouched near the bodies, pulling on their arms like they were ready to drag them away. JT bounced to the balls of his feet, whipping an attack plan together in his head in a fraction of a second. As the two new guys dropped their payloads, JT bounded forward with lightning speed, hopped in the air and kicked out with his right foot, catching the closest guy on the chin with a powerful blow. The guy's head snapped back and banged into the yellow wall with a thud. His body went limp and he collapsed on top of the guy he was supposed to drag away.

The second guy got lucky. As JT landed, the guy kicked out at him, connecting with his side, throwing JT against the window. He lunged at JT with his hands going for the neck. JT grabbed both wrists and wrenched them upward, keeping the guy's momentum moving toward him. The knee is a great weapon in hand-to-hand combat. So is momentum when you know how to use it against your opponent. JT lifted his knee and smashed it forcefully into the guy's groin as his momentum carried him forward. JT kept hold of the wrists and the guy dropped to his knees. His eyes were rolling to the back of his head and he groaned, breathlessly. JT jabbed the knee into the guy's face for good measure.

As the second guy from the second team dropped to the floor, he noticed the hallway was full of noises. Shouts, stamping feet, slamming doors. Rushing, excitement, panic.

JT stood perfectly still with his hands in the air.

Nothing else to do.

He had answered the call to vigilance. Now he would answer to the local authorities for it.

Made in the USA
Monee, IL
30 March 2021